A CENTURY
OF STORIES
NEW HANOVER COUNTY PUBLIC LIBRARY
1906-2006

FULL BLOOM

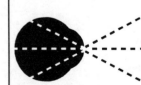

This Large Print Book carries the
Seal of Approval of N.A.V.H.

FULL BLOOM

JANET EVANOVICH AND CHARLOTTE HUGHES

THORNDIKE PRESS

An imprint of Thomson Gale, a part of The Thomson Corporation

Detroit • New York • San Francisco • New Haven, Conn. • Waterville, Maine • London

THOMSON

GALE

LIBRARY OF CONGRESS CATALOGING-IN-PUBLICATION DATA

Evanovich, Janet.
    Full bloom / by Janet Evanovich and Charlotte Hughes.
      p. cm. — (Full series ; #5) (Thorndike Press large print Americana)
    ISBN 0-7862-8710-1 (alk. paper)
    1. Holt, Max (Fictitious character) — Fiction. 2. Bed and breakfast accom-
modations — Fiction. 3. South Carolina — Fiction. 4. Large type books. I.
Hughes, Charlotte, 1954– II. Title. III. Series: Evanovich, Janet. Full series ;
#5. IV. Series: Thorndike Press large print Americana series.
PS3555.V2126F835 2006
813'.54—dc22

    2006016053

U.S. Hardcover:
ISBN 13: 978-0-7862-8710-9
ISBN 10: 0-7862-8710-1

Published in 2006 by arrangement with St. Martin's Press, LLC.

Printed in the United States of America on permanent paper
10 9 8 7 6 5 4 3 2 1

FULL BLOOM

CHAPTER ONE

Destiny Moultrie's long black hair hung like a silk curtain on either side of her face as she gazed down at the dainty palm she held, studying each line and crease carefully. "You're going to meet a tall, dark, and handsome man —"

Annie Fortenberry snatched her hand away. "Oh no, you don't. You're not saddling me with a . . . a man!"

Destiny arched one brow. "You don't like men? They come in handy on cold winter mornings."

The petite woman sitting across the antique Pennsylvania farm table, which seated twelve, nodded, and a thick strand of copper hair fell across her forehead. She raked it back, and it disappeared into the tousled mop that barely grazed her shoulders and gave her a girlish look, even at thirty. "You're right," she said. "On cold winter mornings when you don't want to leave your warm bed and haul the trash to the street. That's the only thing a man is good for."

"Then I probably shouldn't tell you the rest. The really *good* stuff."

"Good stuff?" Annie's green eyes registered interest. She could use some really good stuff in her life. She offered her hand once again.

"It says the sex will be dy-nuh-mite!"

Annie reclaimed her palm and looked at it. "Where does it say that? You made that up."

"The Divine Love Goddess never makes up stuff."

Annie glanced up and noted the serious expression on Destiny's face. Despite the early hour, the woman's makeup had been artfully applied, emphasizing deep-set indigo eyes and high cheekbones. Annie wondered how long it took Destiny to achieve that look. Her own makeup regimen took all of three minutes, beginning with a light foundation to tone down her freckles and ending with a quick swipe of her mascara wand. "Hmm," she said, taking care to hide the doubt in her voice, even though her friend Jamie Swift had claimed Destiny was the real thing. "Very interesting."

Destiny suddenly sneezed. "Uh-oh. I can tell I'm close. I always start sneezing when I'm on to something."

"Good sex, huh?" Annie said. "Jeez, I might have to reconsider. As long as I'm not stuck with him for the rest of my life," she added, wishing she were really more sophisticated and open to casual sex. Instead she followed Dear Abby's advice that couples should be in love before crawling between the sheets together. Abby obviously didn't have this hormonal thing going on that made Annie think about sex a lot.

Destiny sneezed again. "Wow, that was a big one. Either I'm right on-target or I've got a cold. There was a draft in my bedroom last night."

Annie stood and hurried to the kitchen counter, where she kept a box of tissues. She plucked several and handed them to Destiny, who dabbed her nose. "I'm sorry you became chilled last night," Annie said. "It has been so warm this winter that I haven't bothered to turn on the heat."

Which was true. Beaumont was experiencing record-high temperatures for February, and it wouldn't be long before everything was in full bloom. New shoots had already begun pushing their way up through the dirt, and Annie had spied teeny buds on the large peach tree out front. But the old antebellum mansion-turned-bed and breakfast nestled between massive, centuries-old live oaks permitted little sunlight. That, combined with the West Indian coral stones from which the house had been built, kept it a good ten degrees cooler inside than out.

Destiny propped her elbows on the table. In the next chair, an aging overweight tabby cat named Peaches uncurled and stretched before dropping to the floor with a thud. She walked over to her empty food dish, stared for a moment, and then turned to Annie as if to say, *What's with it?*

"The, um, draft in my room last night had nothing to do with the temperature," Destiny said. "There's a spirit in this house."

"Oh yeah?" Annie cocked one eyebrow.

"A ghost," Destiny said. "A dead person, in this case a woman, who for some reason is still hanging around."

Annie didn't know how to respond, so she said nothing.

Destiny shrugged. "It happens to me all the time. Dead people latch on to me like flies to molasses."

Peaches made a guttural sound deep in her throat and gave Annie what she referred to as the evil eye. The cat raised her paw and whacked the plastic dish hard. It skidded across the floor and hit the wall.

"Your cat is hungry," Destiny said.

"She has already eaten," Annie replied. "Just ignore her."

"You've never seen the spirit?" Destiny asked.

"I don't believe in ghosts."

"I'll bet you've felt her presence. A sudden drop in temperature or a feeling of being watched?"

Annie's look was noncommittal, but she remembered instances, a brush of cool air against her arms or the back of her neck, guests complaining of missing items that usually showed up in unexpected places at a later date, plus sounds in the night. "I think you have to be open to that sort of thing," she said. "I'm not."

Destiny didn't look convinced, but she didn't push. "So, do you want me to finish your reading? Find out if you're going to enjoy the Big O anytime soon? Or multiples thereof," she added.

"Multiples?"

"I don't like to brag, but my own personal record is five."

"Holy crap!"

"He was young and good-looking, and we had this chemical thing going. Not to mention the fact he was slow handed, and

11

pushed all the right buttons, if you get my drift."

"Sounds like a keeper to me." Annie hadn't had her buttons pushed in a long time.

"Which is why I married him." Destiny sighed. "It didn't work out."

Annie knew Destiny had been married five times but was currently single. Until a couple of months ago, the woman had enjoyed a hot-and-heavy romance with a hunk named Sam, but she'd pulled back when he began using the *M* word. Destiny had no desire to marry anytime soon.

"So why did you divorce this guy if he was so good in the sack?"

"You still have to be able to talk to a man at the breakfast table, and he wasn't very bright. As time went on, my passion dwindled."

Annie hadn't felt passionate about anything since Jiffy Peanut Butter came out with a reduced-fat variety. "That's too bad," she said.

Peaches began swatting the cabinet door where her food was stored. "That's it," Annie said, getting up from the table. She picked up the cat and lugged all twenty-two pounds of feline and fur to the back door. Peaches hissed. "Go catch a mouse," Annie said, and put her out. "That cat has one goal in her life, and it's to drive me crazy."

"She's uneasy because of the spirit. Cats sense these things."

Annie shook her head. "She's always been snooty and difficult, but my grandmother adored her. Unfortunately, the cat has never liked me."

"She needs to meet a nice tomcat."

"Too late. She's been spayed."

"That explains her sour moods. A good roll in the hay works wonders."

"Well, the only male I'm looking for at the moment is my worthless handyman, Erdle Thorney," Annie said, "but I don't have to be psychic to know that he's laid up drunk somewhere. Wait till I get my hands on him. I'm going to hog-tie him and kick butt."

"Some people like being tied up," Destiny said, studying her nails, "or so I've heard."

Annie grinned. "I don't think we're talking about the same thing." She couldn't help but like the quick-witted, free-spirited woman who had become something of a celebrity since starting her column in the *Beaumont Gazette* less than a year ago. Destiny used her psychic powers to give people, mostly the lonely-hearted, guidance and direction. She stood out in a crowd in

13

her outrageous clothes, which included leather, fake fur in an assortment of colors, and plunging necklines that emphasized perfect oversize breasts. Annie would have given her grandmother's sterling silver to know if they were the product of good genes or a boob job.

"If this Erdle person isn't doing his work, why do you keep him?"

"I sort of inherited him, as well as that crazy cat, after my grandmother died. He lives upstairs in the carriage house out back. He's supposed to do the yard work and repairs around here in exchange for free room and board. I hate to fire him, because he's worked here since I was a kid. He knows there is going to be a big wedding here in two weeks, and that I want everything to be perfect."

"I wouldn't worry about it," Destiny said. "Jamie says your parties and weddings are beautiful. I think it's amazing you're able to provide all that *and* run a bed-and-breakfast."

Annie smiled at the compliment. "I do a lot of juggling, but I enjoy it. This wedding will be special to me since I've known Jamie for so long. We met shortly after she took over the *Gazette*. After her father died," Annie added, remembering how Jamie had struggled for years to keep it afloat before taking on a silent partner. That partner had been none other than multimillionaire investor, technological genius, and philanthropist Max Holt. In less than a year they had turned the *Beaumont Gazette* into a top-notch newspaper and watched subscriptions triple.

In their spare time they had cleaned up town corruption, avoided being killed by hit men and a crazed swamp dweller, and brought down two top Mafiosi.

Despite it all, Max and Jamie had fallen in love and had chosen Annie's home in which to be married. Max and Jamie preferred small and simple to the pomp and fuss of a celebrity wedding that would create a media circus. Which was why the wedding was so hush-hush; even the guests had been sworn to secrecy. Annie hoped they were able to pull it off. She was determined to give Max and Jamie a wedding they would remember for the rest of their lives.

Only . . .

A storm had passed through several nights before, littering the yard with leaves and branches, and Erdle was AWOL.

The rain had seeped through the ballroom windows where Max and Jamie's wedding dinner was to be held, damaging the wood floors and drawing attention to the fact that the floors desperately needed sanding.

And Annie had little spare time on her hands, what with cleaning and cooking three meals a day for her full-time tenants and preparing for a luncheon, a baby shower, and a dinner party all scheduled for that week. Not that she was complaining; that's what kept her bills paid.

Annie's tenant, Theenie Gaither, came down the back stairs. She wore a simple blue housedress, ankle socks, and white sneakers. Her short blue-gray hair, which she had washed and styled once a week at Susie Q's Cut and Curl, had been sprayed so heavily that tornado winds would have snatched her head off her shoulders before mussing her hairdo. "Good morning," she said in a light, fruity-textured voice. She glanced at Destiny, and Theenie's smile faltered briefly as she took in her breasts. "Do we have a new guest?"

Annie introduced the women. "Destiny will be staying with us for a while," she said. "There was a fire in her apartment building late last night, and the residents were forced to evacuate until a building inspector checks it out."

"They think it was faulty wiring," Destiny said. "My landlord is so cheap he won't do

16

anything to the building unless he's forced."

"Oh my," Theenie said, looking at Annie. "Is the wiring okay here?"

"Yes, Theenie," Annie said, knowing the woman tended to fret over every little thing. "Guess what?" she said, hoping to redirect Theenie's thoughts before she found something else to worry about. "Destiny works for the *Beaumont Gazette*. She's the Divine Love Goddess Adviser."

Theenie looked impressed. "I thought I recognized your name. I read your column every day." She headed toward the automatic coffeemaker, where Annie had already set out her favorite mug. "I assume Destiny knows about you-know-what," she said, glancing at Annie, who nodded in response.

"I think it's very romantic that Max and Jamie are going to be married on Valentine's Day," Destiny said.

Theenie gave a shiver of delight. "We're all so excited! I can't wait until I'm allowed to tell my friends at the beauty parlor. They will be so envious. And Jamie is going to be a beautiful bride."

"Jamie's the one who told me about this place," Destiny said, "and I'm glad she did. It's so . . ." Destiny paused as if trying to come up with the right word. "Unique," she finally said.

Annie laughed. "*Outlandish* would better describe it," she said, "but it was my grandmother's dying wish that I not sell it or make cosmetic changes." She gave an eye roll.

"I wouldn't change it, either," Destiny said. "I think it's quaint."

"It grows on you after a while," Theenie said. She carried her mug to the table and sat next to Destiny. "No offense, but are you really psychic? I mean, there are a lot of phonies out there."

"I'm the real enchilada," Destiny proudly stated.

"Oh my! Wait until Lovelle finds out. She lives here, too, but she's in New York City visiting her daughter." Theenie leaned closer. "But then you probably already know that," she said in a hushed voice. "I'll bet you even know what street her daughter lives on." She didn't give Destiny a chance to reply. "Tell me, do you sense anything strange going on in this house?"

Destiny opened her mouth to respond but was cut off when Annie bolted from her chair. "I just heard a car pull into the driveway," she said. "I'll bet it's Erdle." She raced to the window. "Yep! Boy, is he in trouble!" She opened a drawer and pulled out a large rolling pin.

"Uh-oh," Theenie said.

Annie threw open the door. "Wait till I get my hands on that man!"

Theenie jumped from her chair with the agility of a woman half her age. "Now, hold on, Annie," she said. "Let's not do anything rash."

But Annie was already gone.

Wes Bridges parked his Harley in front of the massive three-story antebellum mansion and stared at it for a full minute before he thought to cut his engine. "Damn!" he said, climbing from his bike. "Now that's something you don't see every day."

He took in the four-column portico, each fluted column adorned with plump gold cherubs. Lavishly carved dentil molding ran beneath the eaves, and wrought-iron balconies sprouted from every window, designed in curlicues and rosettes. The look was repeated in the fanlight of what appeared to be an extra room or attic gable that made up a partial fourth floor. Gray moss clung to the live oaks and shuddered in the breeze, and a large tree, currently bare, stood to one side. An elaborate fountain dominated the front yard, spilling water onto yet more cherubs, all naked, some performing what appeared to be sexual acts.

"Interesting," he said, noting a sign out front that read: *The Peachtree Bed-and-Breakfast. Vacancy.*

"Perfect," he said. Wes pulled off his helmet and took the walkway toward the house, admiring the expansive piazza, which looked as if it could accommodate at least one hundred guests. Antique wicker settees and rockers with fat floral cushions offered seating and a great view of the marsh and the bay beyond. Pots of pink and white geraniums softened the look of the coral stone exterior.

Wes paused at an ornate door and studied the solid brass knocker of a naked man and woman embracing. One side of Wes's mouth turned up. Beside the door, an iron plaque dated the house back to 1850. Instead of using the knocker, he rapped on the door and waited. He was about to knock again when he suddenly heard a man cry out several times. It seemed to be coming from the back of the house.

Wes cleared the front steps, rounded the house, and raced up the driveway, following the sounds of loud, anxious voices. He paused at a waist-high wrought-iron gate and stared as an attractive redhead in jeans and a long cotton shirt chased a disheveled middle-aged man across the yard, a rolling pin poised in her hand.

"Run, you lazy good-for-nothing drunk!" the woman yelled.

The man ducked behind one of several oaks shading the backyard. "Put that thing down, Miss Annie!" he cried. "You're liable to hurt somebody."

"Damn right!" she said.

"Please don't hit him," a gray-haired woman pleaded from the back steps of the house. Beside her, a woman with long black hair and large breasts cheered Miss Annie on.

"Give him what for, Annie," she said laughingly.

The redhead chased the frightened man around the tree several times. She slammed the rolling pin against the bark twice, missing the man by a good twelve inches. Nevertheless, he continued to duck and run. "Help!" he cried. "Somebody save me!"

"Oh, for the love of —" Wes leaped the fence and ran toward the two. "Lady, stop!" he shouted.

Annie darted around the tree once more as Erdle tried to maintain a safe distance, all the while crying out for help. He ran pretty fast for someone who'd just come home from a three-day drunk, she thought. She could see the fear in his eyes as she smacked the tree again with her rolling pin. She had no intention of actually hitting Erdle, but she wasn't about to let him know that. She was so intent on her chase that she paid no heed to the chorus of voices behind her.

She was only vaguely aware of movement beside her as she raised the rolling pin high in the air and aimed once more for the tree. A disembodied hand shot into her line of vision, and her aim faltered. There was a loud, resounding *thwack,* and Theenie screamed. Annie heard a dull thud, spun around, and froze when she spied a brown-haired man sprawled across the ground. She gasped and dropped the rolling pin, then let out a squeal when it fell and bounced off the man's forehead.

"Now look what you've gone and done!" Erdle said, pointing.

Annie's eyes flew open in horror as she stared down at the handsome unshaved man in worn jeans, T-shirt, black denim jacket, and biker boots. "Where on earth did he come from?" she cried.

Theenie and Destiny raced down the steps and across the backyard as the stranger lay there unmoving.

Theenie gaped in horror. "You killed him!"

"Dang right she killed him," Erdle said. "If the first blow didn't do it, the second one surely did."

The man groaned and pushed himself into a sitting position. He rubbed the back of his head and winced. "What the hell?"

Annie knelt beside him. His hair was the color of Brazil nuts, thick and slightly wavy, falling just past his collar. He wasn't a local; she would have remembered him. "I'm so sorry," she said. "Are you hurt? Here, let me help you up."

Menacing brown eyes locked with hers. "Don't touch me, lady. What are you, crazy?"

"That's *exactly* what she is," Erdle said. "Mean *and* crazy."

Annie glared at Erdle. "Don't give me any lip, mister. I'm not finished with you."

"If you come near me I'm calling the cops," Erdle said. "I'm going to get me some of that hot pepper spray or maybe one of those stun guns. Or maybe I'll get me a big Doberman or a pit bull —"

"Shut up, Erdle, or I'll snatch you bald-headed!" Theenie shouted, causing the group to pause in surprise. She sniffed, folded her hands properly, and gave the stranger a saccharine sweet smile. "Excuse me, sir," she said ever so politely, "but I used to be a nurse's aide, and I think I'd better have a look at your head. Would you mind very much?"

Wes looked at her. "Are you armed?"

"I don't believe in keeping weapons. You're safe with me."

After a moment, he shrugged.

While the others watched, Theenie carefully parted his hair. "Oh my," she said. "You've already got a nasty lump. I need to put ice on it."

"What about my forehead?" Wes said, wincing when he touched it.

"It's not so bad. Erdle, help this gentleman to his feet. We need to get him inside."

"I can manage," Wes answered gruffly. He stood, towering over the rest of the group. He jabbed a finger toward Annie. "Stay away from me; you got that?"

Annie drew herself up to her full height, but at five foot two she was a good twelve inches shorter than the man. His shoulders were wide, at least twice the width of hers. "I didn't mean to hurt you. I said I was sorry."

"Sorry doesn't get it," he said. "The only thing I need from you is the name of your lawyer."

Annie gawked at him. Lawyer! He planned to sue her! She would lose everything, her home and the business she'd worked night and day for the past three years to build. She would have to try to get her old book-keeping job back at Bates's Furniture.

"Oh dear," Theenie said. "You can't sue Annie. She doesn't have any money."

"That's right," Erdle said. "Her grandma invested all her money in one of them Viagra-like drugs, but it was yanked off the market when men started having embarrassing and prolonged erections."

Annie closed her eyes and wished she could crawl beneath something and never come out. She could feel the man's eyes on her, but she was determined to remain cool. She would deal with Erdle later. Right now she needed to try to dissuade this angry stranger from taking legal action. "Excuse me, but you were trespassing on my property, and I didn't even see you come up behind me."

Wes opened his mouth to reply, but Theenie interrupted.

"Now, now, let's not fuss," she said. "We need to see to this young man's head. Come this way, Mr. . . ."

"Bridges," he said. "Wes."

"And I'm Theenie," she replied, motioning for him to follow her to the house.

Wes glanced in Annie's direction once

more before doing as he was told. The others fell into line behind him. Annie tried not to notice how nicely the man's jeans molded to his backside, but Wes Bridges was a definite ten in the rear-end department. Oh, Lord, what was she thinking? The poor man could be seriously hurt, he would probably sue her from here to Timbuktu, and she was staring at his behind. She shouldn't have spent the morning hearing about Destiny's sex life. Annie could almost smell the testosterone oozing from his pores. And she wasn't the only one looking; Destiny was eyeballing him as well.

Once inside, Theenie pointed to one of the ladder-back chairs. "Have a seat, Wes, and I'll get an ice pack."

He did as he was told, but the dark scowl on his face told Annie he was not a happy man.

"That could be *me* sitting there," Erdle said, standing just inside the door, holding the screen open as though preparing to bolt. "You could have knocked my brains out, Miss Annie!"

She turned to him. "I've never so much as laid a hand on you, Erdle Thorney. I was just trying to scare some sense into you. Some handyman you are. The yard is a mess! Have you forgotten we have an important wedding here in two weeks?"

"Somebody is actually going to marry you?" Wes asked in disbelief.

"She's already married," Theenie said, "but her husband left her three years ago."

"You're looking at one dangerous woman," Erdle said.

Annie pointed. "Out!" she ordered him. "Go pack your bags. I'm evicting you."

Erdle gaped. "But Miss Annie, you can't just throw me out. Your dear grandmother, God rest her soul, was perfectly happy with my work."

"That's before you began spending all your time in the bars."

"I'll get started on the yard work right away," Erdle said. "You just make me a list of what you want done." He hurried out the door before she could reply.

"This is a crazy house," Wes told Theenie as she placed the ice pack on his head.

Destiny gave a snort. "You don't know the half of it."

Annie noticed Wes giving Destiny the once-over, which was no surprise. Any woman who had breasts *out to there* was bound to draw attention, and the come-hither look Destiny returned obviously did not go unnoticed, because one side of his lip turned up slightly. Annie wished she'd hit him harder. "This is *not* a crazy house," she said. "You just happened to show up at a bad time."

"Annie's under a lot of stress," Theenie said, "and with good reason."

Annie clenched her teeth. "I am *not* stressed."

"You look stressed to me," Destiny said. "It doesn't take a psychic to figure that out."

"We have a famous person getting married here in two weeks," Theenie told Wes. "We're not allowed to say who because we don't want the media to find out, but he's more famous than Donald Trump. That's why our Annie is pulled tighter than a rubber band."

"I am not stressed," Annie repeated loudly.

Theenie lifted the ice pack and checked Wes's head. "Oh my, this doesn't look good. Not good at all."

"Let me see," Annie said.

Wes held up one hand as though to stop her. "Look, but don't touch."

Annie sighed and stepped closer, grimacing at the nasty-looking lump. The one on his forehead was beginning to swell as well. "I should probably take him to the emergency room."

"Good idea," Wes said. "I'll be able to file a police report for assault and battery."

"I don't think she really meant to hit you," Destiny said.

Annie felt herself nod in agreement, although she suspected it wouldn't hold much water with the man. He might be the best-looking thing she'd seen in a long time, but he was bound and determined to make her pay. Instead of trying to offer him another apology, which she knew he wouldn't accept, she hitched her chin high. "Perhaps you'll think twice before getting involved in other people's business."

He frowned but didn't reply.

"I think we should call Doc Holden," Theenie said. "He'll know what to do. He's just next door," she told Wes. "Won't take but a jiffy."

Annie made the call despite Wes's objections that he didn't need a doctor.

Five minutes later the back door was thrown open by an elderly white-haired man carrying a black doctor's bag. He glanced about the room until his gaze fell on Wes. "You must be the patient."

"I prefer to use the word *victim,*" Wes said, darting a look in Annie's direction.

"What'd you say?"

"Doc, you might want to turn up your hearing aid," Annie said.

He shot her a disgruntled look as he

fiddled with the flesh-colored object in one ear. "You're going to be old one day, young lady." He adjusted his glasses and lifted the ice pack from Wes's head. "Oh boy, that's a nasty-looking lump. What happened?"

"Some deranged woman hit me over the head with a rolling pin."

"That would be Annie," Doc replied.

"It was an accident, Doc," Annie said.

Theenie nodded. "She meant to clobber Erdle."

"What's this bump on your forehead?"

"Another accident," Annie said.

Doc sighed and looked at Annie. "How many times have I warned you about that temper of yours?"

"I wasn't trying to clobber *anyone*."

Doc suddenly noticed Destiny. "Don't I know you?"

She introduced herself: "I write a column for the newspaper. You've probably seen my picture."

"She's the Divine Love Goddess Adviser," Theenie said. "She's psychic."

Wes sighed. "Now I *know* I'm in a crazy house."

Destiny folded her arms across her chest, which was no easy task. "Excuse me, but that was a very rude thing to say."

Doc patted Wes's shoulder. "I know it

looks a little kooky around here, son, but Annie can be quite pleasant when she isn't trying to do a person bodily harm."

Annie threw up her hands. "Jeez Louise! I give up."

"Now then," Doc began, "you *do* have quite a knot back there, but that's good." When Wes arched a brow in question, the old doctor went on. "It means the swelling is probably confined to the outside, and that lessens the risk of brain injury." He pulled a penlike gadget from his bag, flicked on a light, and shined it in Wes's eyes. "How's your vision? Any blurring?"

Wes looked about the cheery kitchen with its tall white cabinets, partially wainscoted walls, and green-and-white-checkered wallpaper. "I'm fine."

"How bad is the pain?"

Wes grunted. "Feels like I've been hit over the head by a two-by-four. A couple of aspirin might help."

"You don't think I should take him to the ER?" Annie asked Doc.

"Not unless you plan on hitting him again." He reached into his bag and pulled out a small white envelope. "These tablets will help with the pain. You can take one every four to six hours."

Wes shook one of the large white tablets

into his palm as Theenie went for water. "I need to escape this madhouse while I'm still able," he said.

Doc shook his head. "I don't recommend that you drive right now. Not with a head injury," he added. "And don't go to sleep, either. You don't appear to have a concussion, but we don't want to take any chances."

"What the hell am I supposed to do in the meantime?" Wes asked.

Doc shrugged. "Make Annie cook you breakfast. It's the least she can do after trying to kill you."

Annie gaped. "Hellooo," she said, waving her hands in the air. "Has anybody heard a word I've said? I was *not* trying to kill him!" She flung her hands to her sides when nobody paid attention.

Theenie handed Wes a glass of water. He gave a huge sigh and popped the pill into his mouth, but it was so large he had to swallow several times to get it down. He reached into his back pocket for his wallet. "What do I owe you, Doctor?"

Doc chuckled as he snapped his black bag closed. "Not a thing," he said. "I stopped practicing veterinary medicine a long time ago."

Wes looked up in disbelief. "You're a

veterinarian?" He turned to Annie. "You called an *animal* doctor to treat me?"

"He was close by," she said defensively.

A clatter sounded from the top of the stairs leading into the kitchen. Wes looked up. "What was that?" he asked.

"I didn't hear anything," Annie said quickly.

"This house is haunted," Destiny said, drawing a gasp from Theenie.

Wes just looked at her.

Doc shook his head. "Well, I'd better get back to what I was doing," he said. He started for the door with Annie on his heels. He paused suddenly. "Wish I could remember what I was doing." He shrugged. "Oh well, it'll come to me eventually."

"Don't forget your bag," Theenie said.

"Ooopsie-daisy, can't leave that behind." Doc took the bag. "It's tough getting old," he told Wes. "My mind isn't as sharp as it used to be. Take care of that head now. I don't want to have to put you down." He chuckled as he walked out.

Annie watched him go. In the backyard, Erdle was picking up branches. She gave a hopeful sigh.

"I hope I'm not as forgetful as Doc when I get old," Theenie said.

"You *are* old," Destiny blurted, and then

covered her mouth when the woman looked hurt. "I'm sorry; I didn't mean to say that. I didn't sleep well last night, what with that spirit on the loose."

"You're beginning to scare me," Theenie said.

Wes turned to Annie. "You let a crazy, senile veterinarian treat me?"

"He's not really senile," she said. "He's, um, forgetful. I don't think he's crazy, either. He was just kidding about putting you to sleep."

"That's good to know."

She offered him a tight smile. "Well now, it looks like you're stuck with us for a while. At least until we're sure you're going to be okay. How about I cook you something to eat like Doc suggested?"

Wes shook his head. "No thanks."

"Then I'll make a fresh pot of coffee," Annie offered. "Like Doc said, you don't want to go to sleep."

He gave a grunt. "Lady, I wouldn't think of closing my eyes in this house."

CHAPTER TWO

Annie had just put on the coffee when the doorbell rang. She hurried to answer it and was surprised to find Jamie Swift standing on the other side, her dog, Fleas, beside her. "Oh, crap." Annie had forgotten they were supposed to meet that morning.

"Nice to see you, too, Annie."

"Sorry. It's been a bad morning." She stepped aside so Jamie could enter, and then closed the door behind her. She suddenly noticed that her friend didn't look so good. "What's wrong? Are you ill? Are you having second thoughts about getting married? That's perfectly normal, you know. A lot of brides and grooms get cold feet. Getting married is one of the most stressful events in our lives, even if you love that person deeply." She had to pause to catch her breath. It was the spiel she often gave brides.

"Do I really look that bad?" Jamie asked.

The last thing Annie wanted to do was

hurt her friend's feelings. Again. "Oh no, it's just —"

"I'm on a diet," Jamie said. "I'm so hungry I could eat dirt."

"Let me make you something," Annie offered, then wished she hadn't. She did not want Jamie to meet Wes Bridges and have him recount the morning's events to her, and his belief that Annie was a threat to society.

Jamie shook her head. "I *can't* eat. I have to lose seven pounds before the wedding." She groaned. "I've never really been on a serious diet," she confessed. "Fleas and I live on double cheeseburgers, butter pecan ice cream, and my first true love: doughnuts."

"Uh-oh," Annie said. "Having trouble fitting into your wedding dress?" Annie knew Dee Dee Fontana, Max's sister and Jamie's soon-to-be sister-in-law, had insisted on flying Jamie to New York to meet her designer, a Frenchman who created gowns for the rich, the famous, and the royals.

"I fear facing that dress," Jamie confessed. "Although it is absolutely gorgeous, the material clings to every curve and is unforgiving of the slightest weight gain. And I've been so anxious about the wedding and leaving the newspaper for my honeymoon

36

that I wasn't paying attention to how many doughnuts I was eating."

"Would you like to go over the menus at another time?" Annie asked, hoping they could reschedule.

"I'll be okay." Jamie glanced about. "Um, should I have left Fleas in the car?"

"He's safe," Annie said. "I put Attila-the-cat out earlier." Annie couldn't help but smile at the homely bloodhound Jamie had inherited when she'd purchased an old pickup truck. The dog had been part of the deal. Annie patted his bony head. "How are you this morning, handsome? You look a little sad."

"That's his woe-is-me look," Jamie said. "Since I've been on my diet we haven't had any *i-c-e c-r-e-a-m* in the house."

"Poor baby," Annie said to Fleas.

"Then yesterday he caught me sneaking my *s-u-i-t-c-a-s-e-s* from the attic. You know how he gets when I *l-e-a-v-e* him."

Annie nodded. "Okay, let's go into the dining room. Would you like something to drink? Or maybe some carrot sticks?"

Fleas slid to the floor, covered his eyes with his paws, and gave a mournful sigh.

Jamie shook her head. "No thanks. Vera has been force-feeding me carrot and celery sticks for two days. She won't even let me have cream or sugar in my coffee."

Annie chuckled. Sixty-year-old Vera Bankhead was Jamie's secretary and assistant editor. The fact that she was a strict Southern Baptist did not stop her from carrying a loaded Smith & Wesson .38 in her purse, which she had been known to use. "Well, you certainly don't want to cross Vera."

"I almost prefer her shooting me point-blank to eating another raw vegetable," Jamie said.

Annie led Jamie into the large dining room, and they took a seat at the long table, a custom-built replica of an 1820 Imperial Extending Table, only this one was adorned with bronze and gilt, as was most of the furniture in the house, with the exception of the kitchen, which had been added on long after the house was built. Numerous leaves could be added to the table so that it could accommodate thirty people. A massive Regency gilt-wood mirror almost covered one wall, reflecting light from the chandelier. On the opposite wall, a large bowfront sideboard held Annie's grandmother's fine silver and china. As a young girl, Annie had thought the dining room one of the most spectacular rooms in the house.

Until she realized that the deep red walls, black and red velvet draperies, and naked cherubs painted on the ceiling were not exactly tasteful. Not to mention the silk tapestry of women in highly suggestive poses. Unlike her mother, who considered it tasteless and downright disgraceful, Annie had learned to take it in stride.

Except for the large marble, phalliclike sculpture that had been placed beside the graceful free-floating staircase in the foyer. Annie had been twelve years old when she'd asked her grandmother why anyone would want a carving of a man's *thing* in the entryway.

The elderly woman had chuckled. "It's art, dear. And it's been in this family for many years."

Annie had broken a cardinal rule when, after her grandmother's death, she'd packed the sculpture and had it carried to the attic.

Annie noted the amused look on Jamie's face as she took it all in. "Are you sure you still want to get married *here?*" Annie said.

Jamie looked surprised. "Why wouldn't I? You have a reputation for putting on the finest weddings money can buy."

"Yes, but the guest list doesn't usually include senators, heads of state, and tycoons. Some people might find the house, um, offensive."

"If that were the case, you wouldn't have

so many people wanting to marry here." She sighed. "I just hope none of the guests talk," she said. "I have never seen a man more determined to avoid the press than Max."

"People have a right to their privacy," Annie said. "Even celebrities. And Max shouldn't have to deal with TV cameras and newspaper reporters on one of the most important days of his life." She reached for a manila folder that was simply labeled: *H. Wedding.* Thankfully, it was quiet in the kitchen. "By the way, how is Max?"

"He's working hard to tie up loose ends before we leave for the honeymoon, which he still insists on keeping a surprise."

"Everyone is talking about the new polymer plant he's building," Annie said. "It's going to create a lot of well-needed jobs in this town."

Jamie nodded. "And hopefully save the lives of a few motorists. It's the same material that was used to build Max's car. He and a NASA employee experimented for a couple of years to make the product more durable, and I can tell you it's stronger than steel. A leading car manufacturer is anxiously awaiting the first sheets to come off the production line."

"You must be very proud of Max," Annie said, and then grinned. "I know it's a little soon to ask, but have you talked about starting a family?"

Jamie's smile suddenly drooped.

"Uh-oh, wrong thing to ask," Annie said, wishing she could take it back.

"I'm scared, Annie. Terrified. I don't know anything about being a wife; what on earth would I do with a child? I don't even know how to raise this dog. I mean, look at him," she said, pointing to Fleas. "He has no self-esteem."

As if trying to prove her point, Fleas managed to look even more pathetic.

"Take a deep breath, Jamie," Annie said. "It'll be okay."

Jamie sucked in air.

"Like I said, you're just having pre-wedding jitters and that's perfectly normal. And nobody says you have to have a baby. Oprah Winfrey doesn't plan on having kids, and everybody *adores* her."

"Yeah, but I sort of want a family," Jamie said.

Annie suspected as much. Jamie's mother had left while Jamie was still in diapers, and her father had not been able to fill the gap. "So take your time and stop stressing over it," Annie said. "You'll know when you're ready." She laughed. "I mean, good grief,

Dee Dee's going to have a baby in how long?"

"Three weeks. But she doesn't count, because Frankie has hired three nannies."

Annie chuckled. Frankie and Dee Dee were well liked in the community because of their eccentricities and fun-loving nature. A retired wrestler, Frankie had turned his attention to politics the previous year when he suspected the local government was corrupt. He'd called on brother-in-law Max Holt to help him look into it, and they'd found more than they'd bargained for. In the end, Frankie had emerged a hero and won the mayoral election hands-down.

Annie suddenly remembered the injured man in the kitchen; she needed to get down to business. "Let's concentrate on one thing at a time," she said. "You're marrying a great guy who's madly in love with you. The fact that he's drop-dead gorgeous and filthy rich is only the icing on the cake. And speaking of cakes —" Annie pulled out a picture of the wedding cake Jamie had selected, a French pound cake with Grand Marnier buttercream frosting. It was simple yet exquisite. "I've been thinking," she said. "Since you're planning on white tea roses for the wedding, how about I tint the frosting on the cake off-white and place some of the rosebuds on top for decoration? That sort of thing is real popular now."

"Sounds beautiful."

"Great." Annie hurried on. "As for the menu, I typed up everything we agreed on so you and Max can look it over in case you want to make any changes."

Jamie reached into her oversize handbag and pulled out several envelopes. "I've received the last of the responses to the wedding invitations, so we're looking at about fifty guests. I hope you know that Max and I cut the list to the bone," she added.

"I can easily accommodate that number of people," Annie said, having hired someone to knock down the wall separating the den and oversize study when she needed the space for various businesses that held monthly meetings there. It also served well for small weddings. "I'll situate the tables near the walls in the ballroom so there will be room for dancing," she added. Annie hoped she could do something about the water damage before the wedding. "Okay, what's next?"

"Oh, wait; I forgot to mention that Max's parents can't make it. His mother had a mild heart attack several days ago. She's getting out of the hospital tomorrow, but her doctor wants her to stay close to home. So you can scratch their names from the list."

Annie made a note to herself. "I know Max will be disappointed."

"He is. But he wasn't that close to them while growing up. His cousin Nick and his wife, Billie, practically raised him."

"Moving right along," Annie said, hoping they could wrap things up, "the minister will be here early in case you or Max would like a private moment with him. The photographer is all taken care of, and the flutist and harpist will play before, during, and after the ceremony, at least until the band starts. Well, it's not really a band, just a three-piece ensemble."

"I have no idea what I'm supposed to do when I get here," Jamie said anxiously.

"That's what the rehearsal is for. No change in number of people for that?"

"Nope."

"The florist will arrive a couple of hours early, so we'll have plenty of time to decorate."

"I just hope I fit into my dress," Jamie said grimly.

"You will. Any questions?"

"I think that covers it."

Annie checked her wristwatch. "Oh, look at the time!" She stood, hoping she didn't appear rude but knowing she needed to check on Wes Bridges, who was probably on the telephone with his lawyer that very moment.

Jamie stood as well. "I need to get back to the office anyway. By the way, how is Destiny settling in?"

"Theenie and I really like her. She's hilarious. Perhaps *outrageous* is a better word."

Jamie laughed. "Most of what she says is in fun, so don't take her too seriously." They had turned for the living room when the swinging door leading to the kitchen was suddenly thrown open and a frantic-looking Theenie poked her head through. "Trouble in the kitchen," she said. "Big trouble."

Annie darted a look at Jamie. "Gotta run." She raced into the next room, where she found Wes slumped at the table. "Oh no!" she cried. "What happened?"

"He passed out," Destiny said.

A frowning Jamie stood in the doorway, trying to make sense of what was going on. "Who is *that?*"

Annie glanced her way. Damn. She hadn't even heard Jamie follow her. "Long story."

"You wouldn't believe it anyway," Destiny told Jamie.

Annie tried to shake the man awake. There was no movement. He began to snore

45

lightly. "Oh, great!" she muttered. "Wes, you have to wake up!" she said loudly. She shook him harder, so hard he slipped from the chair and hit the floor with a resounding thud. His head bounced once, and he groaned.

Theenie cried out in alarm and then covered her mouth, but her eyes slid side-to-side, clearly panicked. "We're going to kill the poor man yet."

"Would somebody *puh-leese* tell me what's going on!" Jamie insisted.

"We should try to sit him up," Annie said as Theenie gave Jamie a rapid-fire rundown of events. "Maybe that'll wake him."

Jamie blinked several times as though trying to digest the explanation. "I'll help."

Working together, Annie, Jamie, and Destiny managed to get Wes into a sitting position, but his head lolled to one side. Annie stood over him, bracing her feet on either side as she slipped her arms beneath his and pulled. He was too heavy, despite Destiny and Jamie trying to pull him up from behind. Annie paused to catch her breath and Wes fell back once more, dragging her with him. Fortunately, Jamie prevented his head from hitting the floor again.

Annie suddenly found herself lying flat

against the man, chest-to-chest, thigh-to-thigh. Before she could make a move, Wes smiled in his sleep and enveloped her in his arms. Her jaw dropped. Whoa, mama! She couldn't remember when she'd last been this close to the opposite sex, but danged it if didn't feel good. *Too* good, she thought, his tight muscles pressed against all her body parts.

Her stomach fluttered.

Her nipples hardened.

Her gizzard quivered.

"Oh my," Theenie said, one hand at her breast as though she feared her heart would fly right out. "This won't do. This simply won't do."

Annie sighed.

Destiny and Jamie gawked.

Theenie stepped closer. "Annie, this is not proper behavior. You must get up this instant!"

Destiny laughed out loud. "You really do need to get off of him, honey. The man needs medical attention. You can lie on top of him once he's better."

Jamie grinned openly.

Annie tried to pull free, but it was useless. "He has me in a death grip." She craned her head so that she could see Theenie. "You might want to call Doc."

Theenie hurried to the telephone and dialed while Destiny and Jamie looked on in amusement.

"This is not funny, you guys," Annie told them. "He could be badly hurt. Not only that; he has already threatened to sue me."

"Doc's on his way," Theenie said, hanging up the phone. She gave Annie a funny look. "What's wrong? Why are you squirming?"

"She's copping a feel," Destiny said. She bit her fist.

"I am not!" Annie said. "I'm just, um, trying to get comfortable."

Jamie looked at Destiny. "I'm sure it's not as easy as it looks, just lying on him like that."

"I should *not* be listening to this," Theenie said, eyeballing each of them. "I know three young ladies who are going to feel terribly guilty if something happens to that poor man."

The back door swung open a few minutes later and Doc stepped in, once again carrying his black bag. "Now what?" He came to a dead halt when he spied Annie lying across Wes. "Oh boy," he mumbled. "I'm almost afraid to ask."

"He's out cold," Annie said, "and he won't let go of me."

Doc suddenly looked sheepish. "I was

afraid of this."

"Afraid of what?" Theenie said.

Doc sighed. "I'm not positive, but I'm pretty sure I gave him the wrong medication."

"What did you give him?" Annie almost shrieked.

"I, well, accidentally gave him a tranquilizer. It's mostly used for large animals." He swallowed, and his Adam's apple bobbed. "Livestock."

"Oh, shit!" Annie cried. "He's going to be mad as hell when he wakes up. Wait! Maybe we shouldn't *let* him wake up. How many more of those pills do you have?"

Theenie planted her hands on her hips. "I'm going to pretend you didn't say that." She turned to Doc. "Is he in danger?"

"No, but he's probably going to be out for a while. That's not good considering he has a head injury. That and the fact he won't let go of Annie."

"Life can be hard like that," Destiny said.

Annie felt a sense of dread. "We have to get him to the hospital."

Theenie shook her head and began to pick at her fingernails. "If we do, they'll ask questions. Doc could get into a lot of trouble for dispensing medication, seeing as how he's not practicing anymore."

"Oh boy," Doc muttered under his breath.

Annie gave a huge sigh. "I'm going to lose my house. I'll have to sleep in the bus station and keep my stuff in a grocery cart."

"We'll be homeless," Theenie said. "I'll have to sleep in a cardboard box. Everybody will find out. I won't be able to show my face in Susie Q's Cut and Curl." She pulled a lace handkerchief from her pocket, put it to her nose, and sniffed. "My hair will be a mess."

Destiny and Jamie exchanged glances.

Annie looked at Doc. "Think of something fast."

"Be nice if we could wake him. Maybe we could get him into the shower and douse him with cold water."

"Okay," Annie said calmly. "Theenie, call Erdle. We'll need all the help we can get. Doc, don't you think you should check his pulse or something?"

"Good idea." Doc got down on his knees and pulled a worn stethoscope and penlight from his bag. He listened to Wes's heart, shone the light in his eyes, and took his pulse. "Everything seems normal."

Erdle came through the door and almost stumbled over his own feet. "Miss Annie!"

"Don't just stand there, Erdle, help me!" she said. "See if you can pry the man's hands loose."

Erdle hurried around behind her and tried to pull her free. "Golly, he's strong as a bull!" He pulled with all his might.

Wes opened his eyes and stared into Annie's face. His words were slurred when he spoke. "You got, um, a nice, um . . ." He frowned as if trying to come up with the word. Finally, he closed his eyes.

Annie shook him. "What?"

His eyes remained closed. "A nice ass," he said. Once again, he began to snore.

"Oh, I shouldn't be listening to this," Theenie said, covering her ears.

Everyone in the room was silent for a moment. Annie stared openmouthed at the man beneath her. So he'd noticed her after all. Her ego moved up a notch. Not that he was her type, mind you. Not that she had a type. But Wes looked, well, he looked a little dangerous, a little rough around the edges. Besides, she'd sworn off men.

Still . . . Wes made her feel sort of feminine, like she should go upstairs and put on a pair of panty hose.

Not a good sign.

Erdle managed to lift Wes's arms, and Annie shimmied out, her cheek rubbing every bone and muscle along the way, although she did her best to lift her head and not touch his crotch.

"Wow," Destiny said. "I hope it was as good for him as it was for you."

Annie shot her a look as she took a deep breath. "Okay," she said, trying to pull her muddled thoughts together. "I think it'll be easier if we drag him into the bathroom. Theenie, you hold his head off the floor so it doesn't bounce. Erdle, you grab the other arm. The rest of you, get his legs and try to shove him in the direction of the bathroom while Erdle and I pull." She waited until everyone was in place. "Okay, let's do it!"

The six of them went to work, pulling Wes across the kitchen, the hall, and finally into the bathroom. They paused in the cramped space to catch their breath. Annie pushed the shower curtain aside. "Okay," she said, "I think it would be better if we got his legs in first."

"Are we going to put him in with all his clothes on?" Theenie asked.

They exchanged looks. "Maybe we should at least strip him down to his underwear," Annie said.

"What if he doesn't wear underwear?" Theenie asked. "He doesn't exactly look the type."

"I'll check," Doc said. The women turned their backs. "Yep, he's wearing them."

"Okay," Annie said to Erdle, trying to sound businesslike and matter-of-fact, even though her pulse was going wacko. "Let's strip him down." The others, including a disgruntled Destiny, stepped from the room. Erdle and Annie managed to free Wes from his clothes, with the exception of a pair of boxer shorts adorned with red hearts.

"Get a load of that," Erdle said.

"Huh?" Annie tried not to stare at the lean, muscular body, but it would have been impossible not to look. She knew Erdle was referring to Wes's boxer shorts. "I'm sure he didn't purchase them for himself. Probably his wife or girlfriend."

"Awesome," Destiny said, peeking around the door. "It's almost worth it just to see that. Cool boxers, huh?"

Annie tore her gaze from his body. "Okay, everybody back in here. Let's get him in the bathtub."

It was not an easy task, but once they'd settled Wes into the tub, Theenie stuffed a towel beneath his head to protect it from further harm. Annie pulled the curtain closed and turned on the cold water full force. She reached in and adjusted the spray so it would hit his face. The man remained immobile. After several minutes, Annie turned off the water and looked at Doc.

"He's not responding."

"Let's give it time. He should come around eventually. I hope I'm not here when he does."

Annie didn't bother to hide her annoyance. "What should we do with him in the meantime?"

"Be best to dry him off and cover him with a blanket," Doc told her.

Annie gaped. "You mean *leave* him in the bathtub?"

"I don't think we're going to be able to get him out."

Annie shook her head sadly as she moved to the linen cabinet. "This day can't get any worse."

"Unless he dies," Theenie said fretfully. "I don't know what we'll do then. Probably we'll go to jail. Which is probably a whole lot better than being homeless when you think about it," she added, only to frown. "Unless, well, you know what happens behind prison walls. We could end up in a cell with a big woman who decides to make us her *b-i-t-c-h*." She shuddered.

Destiny just looked at her. "Have you ever considered taking Xanax?"

Theenie ignored her. "I'll grab a blanket," she said, hurrying from the room.

Annie dried Wes from head to toe, all the

while trying to ignore how good he looked. "His underwear is soaked," she said as Theenie returned with the blanket.

"Best to get him out of them," Doc replied.

Annie took a step back. "I'm not doing it."

"Let me do it," Destiny said.

Theenie squared her shoulders. "No, *I'll* do it," she said, surprising everyone in the room. "It's not like I haven't seen my share of naked bodies, what with being a nurse's aide and all." She looked at Destiny. "Besides, this should be done in a professional manner."

Destiny gave a grunt. "Yeah, right. You want to get a look at Mr. Big as bad as the rest of us."

"I'm not listening to that kind of talk," Theenie said, covering her ears. "La la la la la."

Destiny looked at Jamie. "Is it me or what?"

Theenie glanced at Annie. "Is she done talking dirty yet?"

Annie nodded and Theenie dropped her hands to her sides. "Okay, everybody out," the older woman said. "I have a job to do. And no peeking," she added, looking right at Destiny.

Annie followed the others out of the bathroom. She skidded to a halt. Standing on the other side of the door was her friend Danny Gilbert. She feigned a smile as her cohorts in crime scattered.

"I rang the doorbell," he said. He glanced about the room. "Why does everybody look so serious? Is something wrong?"

Annie pulled the bathroom door closed. "Wrong?" She tried to think fast. "Oh well —" She jumped as a moan sounded from the bathroom.

"What was that?" Danny asked.

Annie shot a frantic look at the others. "Um, Theenie isn't feeling well."

"Digestive problems," Doc said authoritatively. "It happens to the best of us."

Another moan. Danny looked concerned. "Is it serious?"

"Not sure." Doc chuckled. "Might have to put her down."

Annie rolled her eyes. "She'll be fine."

The bathroom door opened and Theenie stepped out, holding Wes's boxer shorts. "I'm glad to have that behind me," she said. "It wasn't as easy as I thought it would be." Her eyes widened when she spied Danny. "Oh, I didn't know we had company." She wadded the boxers in her hands.

"Are you okay?" he asked.

"I'm a little sore from all the strenuous activity, but —" She stopped abruptly as though realizing she'd said more than she should. "I think I'll just put these in the dryer," she told Annie, hurrying away.

"I really need to head back to the office," Jamie said, already backing away. "I'll see myself out." Fleas, who'd managed to sleep through the whole thing, got up, shook himself, and followed.

Annie managed to say a quick good-bye before she turned to Danny. "What are you doing here?"

He looked surprised. "Just thought I'd drop by for a cup of coffee."

"Oh." It wasn't unusual for Danny to stop by if he was in the neighborhood; he was like family. He and Annie started hanging out together years before, during the summers she spent with her grandmother. Some people mistook them for brother and sister, since they both had red hair and green eyes. "Um, gee, I wish I could visit with you," she said, slipping her arm through his and prodding him toward the living room, "but we're up to our ears in work, what with the wedding and all." She hadn't even told Danny who was getting married.

He looked amused. "Are you throwing me out?"

"No, of course not," she said, opening the door and shoving him onto the piazza. "I'm just, um, really busy right now. Bye." She started to close the door.

"Wait! I'd also hoped you might want to take in a movie this week."

"Movie? Oh, right," she said quickly. She and Danny usually grabbed a quick dinner and saw a movie every week. "May I get back to you on that?" she asked.

"Well, sure. Hey, are you okay? You seem awfully nervous."

"Nervous?" She thought she was acting pretty calm considering there was an unconscious butt-naked man in her bathtub. "I just need to go through my to-do list for the wedding; after that I'll have a better idea how long it's going to take. I'll call you."

"That's fine," he said. He turned. "By the way, whose Harley is that? It's one mean-looking machine."

Annie wondered how she'd missed the massive chrome and black motorcycle. "It must belong to one of Erdle's friends. See you later." She closed the door and leaned against it. She gave an enormous sigh of relief when Danny pulled away in his car. She knew darn well who the motorcycle belonged to; it had Wes Bridges written all over it. That would explain his biker clothes.

What she didn't know and couldn't figure out was why Wes had shown up in her backyard in the first place.

Several hours later, Wes was still out cold, and Destiny was in her room taking a nap. Annie prepared a meat loaf for dinner and iced a pan of brownies while Theenie peeled potatoes. They worked in silence, but every so often Theenie would look at Annie and shake her head.

"I know," Annie finally said. "I can't believe we have a naked man lying in the bathtub, either."

"I'll set the table," Theenie said once she'd put the potatoes on to boil.

"Thanks." Annie was grateful that both of her full-time tenants were only too eager to help around the place; it made her job a lot easier. She was only forced to hire help when her bed-and-breakfast was full. She checked on Wes, shook him lightly, but there was no movement.

Destiny came downstairs looking rested. She wore tight jeans and a low-cut royal blue blouse with gold moons and stars that did not detract from her cleavage.

"Something smells good," Destiny said. "What can I do to help?"

As Annie put the finishing touches on dinner she assigned Destiny a small task.

Erdle showed up as the women carried the food to the table. He had showered, changed his clothes, and scrubbed the dirt from beneath his fingernails, a rule Annie had put into place long ago. He took his usual chair, tucked his napkin inside his collar, and waited for the women to sit, but his eyes were fixed on Destiny.

"Please say grace, Erdle," Annie said, not because he was particularly good at it but because she thought it might put him on the path of the straight and narrow. So far it hadn't worked.

He bowed his head. "Rub-a-dub-dub, thanks for the grub."

Theenie pursed her lips. "I wish you'd learn a new prayer. That is not at all proper. One of these days the ground is going to split right open and swallow you whole."

He shrugged and looked at Annie. "I picked up all the branches, raked the leaves, and trimmed the weeds," he said proudly as they passed the food around. "We've got some leftover pine straw in the carriage house, so I'll put it out tomorrow."

Annie knew Erdle was just sucking up so she wouldn't evict him. "You'll have to stay on top of it so it stays nice. In the meantime you can start tilling that patch of ground behind the carriage house."

Erdle shifted in his chair. "That tiller is pretty old, been sitting around for years. I'm pretty sure it don't work."

"It works. I've already checked."

Erdle paused and fixed a weary gaze on her. "Tell me again why you want that land tilled?"

"I've already told you I want to plant a vegetable garden back there. It's more than large enough." Annie hoped by planting her own vegetables she would save on the grocery bills. "I need to get started right away, with the weather being so warm."

"You can't grow nothing back there. Not enough sun."

"You're wrong. It gets the morning sun."

"You're just not up early enough to notice," Theenie said.

Erdle didn't respond. Instead, he concentrated on his food.

Annie kept her gaze fixed on him. The man would stall as long as he could to keep from doing any work. "Erdle?"

"Okay," he said. "I'll get on it."

Annie was about to pin him down as to *when* he would get on it, but a sound from the bathroom startled her. She jumped from the table and hurried in that direction with Destiny and Theenie right behind. Wes was still lying in the tub, his eyes open. "Oh, thank goodness!" Annie said. "You're awake."

He didn't look happy to see her. "Would you care to explain why in the hell I'm lying naked in this effin' bathtub?"

CHAPTER THREE

Annie opened her mouth to speak, but nothing came out.

Theenie peered around her. "How nice to see you awake. You're just in time for dinner."

Wes ignored her, his gaze fixed on Annie. "I asked you a question."

"Okay, but you're not going to like the answer."

"Somehow I managed to figure that much out for myself."

"It's not Annie's fault," Theenie said, beginning to fidget with her hands. "As hard as it must be for you to believe, she's had nothing but your best interests at heart since she accidentally hit you, uh, twice."

"The medication Doc gave you was stronger than we thought," Annie said, deliberately being vague. She didn't want Doc listed in Wes's lawsuit.

He stared back at her for a full minute.

Finally, he sat up and rubbed the back of his head, wincing when he touched the knot. "How long have I been out?"

"All day," Annie said.

"What the hell did the man give me, a horse tranquilizer?"

Annie and Theenie exchanged looks. "It was an accident," Annie said.

Wes scowled. "*Another* accident? There seems to be a lot of that going around." His gaze narrowed on Annie. "Are you the one who undressed me?"

"I did that," Theenie cut in quickly. "I'm accustomed to seeing naked men. It used to be part of my job."

Wes seemed to ponder that before turning back to Annie. "I want my clothes, and I want them now."

Annie pointed. "They're hanging on the back of the door here. While you get dressed, I'll prepare you a plate. We're having meat loaf." She and Theenie hurried from the room.

The group was silent when Wes entered the kitchen a few minutes later, fully dressed, with the exception of his denim jacket, hooked over one finger. He leaned close to Annie. "Mind telling me what happened to my boxer shorts?"

"Oh, I left them on top of the dryer,"

Theenie said. She stood and hurried into the laundry room, but when she reappeared she looked confused. "They're gone." She looked at Destiny.

"What? You think I took them?"

"Well, they didn't just walk away."

The three women looked at one another, then at Erdle.

He shook his head. "I don't wear boxer shorts with hearts on them."

All eyes landed on Wes. "I got behind on my laundry, and they were my last pair. Besides, I didn't know they would be on display in a house full of strangers."

"I'm sure they'll turn up," Annie said. "Won't you join us for dinner? I know you have to be hungry."

Wes hesitated. Finally, he draped his jacket over the back of the chair and sat as everyone began passing food to him. Annie had prepared him a glass of iced tea and set it beside his plate. He stared at it for a moment.

"I didn't poison it," she said.

He took a tentative sip.

They ate in silence. Destiny finally broke it when she asked how Max and Jamie's wedding plans were going.

Theenie gasped and slapped her hand over her mouth. "We're not supposed to mention names," came her muffled reply. She cut her eyes to Erdle.

"What do I care who's getting married here?" he said with a shrug.

"Please don't discuss it with anyone," Annie told him. As she gave Destiny an update she could feel Wes's eyes on her. She looked at him, and their gazes locked for several seconds before she looked away.

A clatter from above made them pause and stare at the ceiling.

Wes glanced around the table at the anxious faces. "Are there other guests here?"

"It's just the wind rattling the window-panes," Annie said.

"Yeah, right," Destiny muttered.

Theenie looked at Wes. "You know, our Annie puts on the most beautiful weddings," she blurted, obviously trying to change the subject. "Her clientele is growing by leaps and bounds."

"Is that so?"

"Her parties are just grand."

"I don't think Wes is interested in all that," Annie said, her face growing warm.

Theenie went on. "Annie usually does all the cooking, but Lovelle and I help. We're full-time tenants. Lovelle is away at the moment. We used to have another tenant named Dora, but she died."

66

Wes arched one brow and turned to Annie.

"It wasn't my fault. She was elderly and died of natural causes."

"How long have you had this place?" he asked.

Annie was surprised he was being civil to her. "The house has been in my family for generations, but I only opened the bed-and-breakfast a few years ago. This is my slow season."

He sat back in his chair and regarded her. "I might be interested in renting a room."

Everybody gaped. Erdle, in the process of swallowing, almost choked. "You'd actually rent a room from her after what happened? Man, you must be desperate."

"I only need a place for a week or two, and I hate motel rooms."

"Well, I . . ." Annie tried to pull her thoughts together. She glanced at Theenie, whose face seemed to have drained of color. Destiny looked amused.

"I can provide references," he said. "Except for that short stint in prison."

Theenie dropped her fork, and it clattered in her plate.

"Just kidding," Wes said.

"You should rent him the master bedroom," Erdle said. He looked at Wes. "It's huge. Has cable TV, a fireplace, one of those claw-foot tubs in the bathroom, and a big mirror on the ceiling."

"Wow, that sounds like my kind of room," Destiny said.

Annie managed a tight smile. "I don't normally rent it out. Only if I'm booked and have no other choice."

"Why aren't you using it?" Wes asked.

Erdle answered for her. "She moved out of it when her husband ran off with another woman."

"Thank you for sharing, Erdle," Annie said.

Wes seemed to be doing his best to swallow a smile. "How long has your husband been gone?"

Annie avoided eye contact. "Three years."

"Does he live around here?" Wes asked.

"If I knew where he lived I would serve him with divorce papers." She gave a dismissive wave. "I'd rather not talk about it."

"I'd like to see the room after dinner if that's okay."

"I have other rooms."

"Yes, but I'm willing to pay twice what you would normally charge for the master."

"Why on earth would you do that?" she asked.

"Because it offers a lot more than a motel

room and because the food is good here." He almost smiled. "And I have a thing for overhead mirrors."

"Amen to that," Destiny said, drawing a frown from Theenie.

"I'd jump on that, Miss Annie," Erdle said, "seeing as how you could use the money."

Annie finally shrugged, trying to appear indifferent. "Sure." She would show Wes the room, but that didn't mean she was going to rent it to him. Annie didn't have to look at Theenie to know the woman was probably gnawing her bottom lip ninety-to-nothing.

Thirty minutes later, Annie led Wes to the second floor and into the master suite. The bronze and gilt furniture had been hand-carved along the lines of French provincial, only fancier — or ostentatious, as her mother had often remarked — adorned with hearts, curlicues, and rosettes. As in the dining room, the red walls and red velvet draperies were in keeping with the original decor. Annie had left the nineteen-inch color TV that her husband Charles had purchased for the room.

"What a shame," Wes said, looking at it.

Annie gave him a puzzled look.

He shrugged. "I don't think television sets belong in a husband and wife's bedroom, but that's just me." His gaze wandered to an overstuffed chair and ottoman near the fireplace.

"I converted all the fireplaces to gas," Annie said. "It's really nice falling asleep with a fire burning."

He turned to her. "Oh yeah?"

The look he gave her made her think of snuggling between crisp sheets and thick blankets on a cold night, hair-roughened legs entwined with smooth ones, a warm fire painting shadows on the walls. Annie crossed her arms. It felt weird standing alone with Wes in the bedroom she'd shared with her husband for two years. "The bathroom is through that door," she said, nodding toward it.

Wes turned his attention to the lavishly carved mirror over the bed. "Nice," he said. "Did you decorate this room?"

"Oh no," she said quickly. "It was done by an ancestor. The family insisted on keeping the house as close to the original design and decor as they could. With the exception of the kitchen," she added. "The original kitchen was detached from the house, as kitchens were in most homes of that era. It burned."

70

"Your ancestors had unusual tastes."

"Yes."

"Where do you sleep?"

Annie tried not to let herself gaze too long into those liquid brown eyes. "Next door. And Theenie is just across the hall," she added, and then wondered why she'd felt it necessary to let him know they wouldn't be the only ones sleeping on that floor. "There are five bedrooms on the third floor, although some are small. My grandmother had an elevator installed once she began having trouble getting around, but it's slow and cantankerous." She couldn't help noticing the odd way he looked at her. Was he sizing her up? Trying to decide if she was really as crazy as he thought? She probably *was* crazy to even think of renting to him.

"I can't believe you moved out of here. Bad memories?"

He asked a lot of questions. "It just felt too big for one person."

He cocked his head to one side, studied her lazily. "Your husband obviously wasn't a smart man. I can't imagine why he would cheat on you."

"It's quite possible he was a jerk," she said matter-of-factly.

"Well, you're still young. You'll meet your prince charming one day."

71

"I like my life just fine the way it is."

"Is that why you wear those big shirts? So guys won't notice you?"

He suddenly smiled, and Annie felt her toes curl. Jeez! "Yeah. I'm one of those women who have to dress down in order to keep the men at bay."

"You still look pretty damn good."

"I might have to resort to sackcloth."

He reached into his back pocket and pulled out his wallet. "You'll probably want references so the blue-haired lady doesn't jump ship the minute I move in." He fished through several business cards, handed one to Annie. "This guy will vouch for me."

"Was he your warden?"

"My banker." He gave her another card. "And this is my lawyer. I just pay him a flat fee to keep me out of the big house."

"That's always helpful. What kind of business are you in?"

"I'm a professional photographer."

She couldn't hide her surprise. It sounded so tame, and the man before her looked anything but. "How interesting. Maybe you'll show me some of your work."

"I don't think you'd approve."

Both brows arched high on her head. "Oh yeah? What kind of pictures do you take?"

"Mostly women."

72

"Um." She opened her mouth, closed it, and then opened it again. "Are they, uh, you know?"

"Some of them wear clothes."

Annie gulped.

"You'd make a perfect model." He reached for a stray lock of hair and twirled it around his finger. "The rich texture of your hair, slightly mussed, as though you just climbed from your bed after making love. The rosy flush I just brought to your cheeks by mentioning it."

Her scalp tingled at his touch, sending tiny ripples of pleasure down her back. Theenie was probably wondering what was taking them so long. "I don't think so," Annie said, thinking how much she sounded like Theenie. She stepped back and tucked her hair behind her ears.

"Doesn't matter. I've branched out. I like traveling to different parts of the country taking pictures of quaint little towns. 'Course, it's not as much fun as what I used to do, and it doesn't offer the fringe benefits." He winked.

Annie stared dumbly. "Do you have any questions about the room?"

"How soon can I move in?"

It was not yet nine o'clock the next morning when Annie called a meeting of sorts with Theenie and Destiny. "I've decided to go ahead and rent a room to Wes Bridges."

Destiny shrugged. "Hey, it's your house."

"Oh my," Theenie said. "Are you sure?"

"I know he looks, well —"

"He looks like one of those biker dudes," Theenie said.

"Just because he rides a Harley doesn't make him a biker," Annie said. "He's a photographer, and he has excellent references."

Destiny took a sip of her coffee. "A photographer, huh?"

Annie nodded. "He wants to take pictures of Beaumont. Because of its historic value," she added.

"What does he plan to do with the pictures?" Theenie asked.

"I don't know. Maybe he sells to travel magazines."

Annie noticed Destiny frowning. "What?"

"Something doesn't feel right."

Annie and Theenie exchanged glances.

"You think he might be lying?" Theenie said, gripping her coffee cup. "Do you sense we're in danger?"

Annie rolled her eyes. "Of course we're not in danger," she said, wishing Destiny would keep her concerns to herself instead of giving Theenie something else to worry about. "I wouldn't have rented to him unless I felt he was safe."

"He's not likely to kill us in our sleep or anything like that," Destiny said as though trying to reassure Theenie, which only caused the woman to start her lip-nibbling routine.

Annie felt the beginnings of a headache. "I've already told him he could have the room." She'd barely gotten the words out of her mouth when a door slammed upstairs. Annie and Theenie jumped.

"What in blazes was that?" Theenie said.

"It's just the wind," Annie said dismissively, refusing to meet Destiny's gaze.

"How can it be the wind when all the windows are closed?" Theenie asked. "I'm telling you, something isn't right in this house, and it seems to be getting worse. And now we've got a man moving in who could be a cold-blooded killer for all we know."

"He is *not* a killer," Annie said.

Theenie didn't look convinced. "You don't know that. You don't know that his references are valid. He could have paid somebody to lie for him. Killers do that sort of thing for each other. And remember, he even mentioned he was in prison. What if he wasn't joking? What if —"

"He's not dangerous," Annie interrupted, "and I don't think he's trying to hide anything. He told me stuff about himself that he didn't have to tell me."

"What stuff?" Destiny asked.

Annie gave a big sigh. "I wasn't going to mention it, but, well, he admitted that he used to take pictures of women. I sort of got the impression they weren't wearing much."

Theenie looked shocked. "You mean they were nude?"

Annie nodded.

"That's probably where they got that old saying: less is more," Destiny said.

"Oh my," Theenie said. "You know what that means."

Both Destiny and Annie looked at her questioningly.

"It means he probably wonders what we all look like naked."

Destiny chuckled. "Then he and I are even, because I've been wondering the same thing about him."

Annie didn't respond, but for some insane reason she wasn't crazy about the idea of Destiny thinking about Wes in the buff.

"Especially after seeing him in his under-wear," Destiny added. She leaned closer to Theenie. "Why don't you enlighten us?"

Annie looked at Theenie, almost ashamed that she was as eager as Destiny for information.

Theenie blushed profusely. "I most certainly will not discuss such private matters. I was acting as a professional when I, um, undressed him, so it's not something I would have noticed."

"Oh, give me a break," Destiny said. "You may have a little age on you, but you're not blind."

"May we change the subject?" Theenie asked.

Annie nodded. "Good idea. I have more pressing matters. Has anyone seen Erdle? His car isn't in the driveway."

"I heard him go out last night," Theenie said. "Probably passed out somewhere. But if you think you're going to chase him with that rolling pin again, you're wrong. I hid it."

"I don't need a rolling pin," Annie said. "I've got my bare hands."

Annie stormed into the kitchen shortly before lunch, almost bumping into Theenie, who was watering houseplants. "Erdle is still not home," she said.

"That's it! I'm throwing him out the minute he shows up." Annie spied Danny

Gilbert sitting at the kitchen table and blushed. "Oh, hi, Danny."

"Bad day?" he asked.

She shrugged. "I'm just irritated with Erdle, but that's nothing new."

"I hear you got problems with the house."

Annie glanced at Theenie.

"Well, Danny *is* a carpenter," the woman said. "I showed him the damage in the ballroom."

"You should have come to me sooner, Annie," he said. "I can take care of the floor. I even have my own sander."

"Oh, I couldn't possibly impose —"

"Don't be silly. Of course, this means you're going to have to go see that new western with me."

Annie moaned. "A western? I'd rather sit through *The Mummy* again than watch a western."

He grinned. "That's part of the deal, Anniekins. Take it or leave it."

Annie hated to ask for help, hated to put people to any trouble, but she was desperate. "Oh, all right," she said, pretending to be put out. "I suppose you'll expect me to spring for the popcorn, too."

The doorbell rang. "I'll get it," Theenie said. She hurried into the living room.

Danny was discussing what color stain he

wanted to put on the floor when Theenie returned with Wes beside her. "Look who's here," she said, eyes darting about the room nervously. "He even brought his clothes."

Annie did not miss the fact that Theenie had her arms crossed as though Wes might somehow be able to see through her prim white cotton blouse. She also didn't miss Danny's raised brows. Not that she blamed him. Wes looked like the worst kind of ruffian standing there in his faded jeans, a black T-shirt, and his denim jacket. He carried a large backpack.

"You were expecting me, right?" he said.

It took a few seconds for Annie to find her tongue. "Yes, of course." She turned to Danny, who was still staring. "This is Wes Bridges," she said. "He's renting a room for a couple of weeks. Wes, this is my good friend Danny Gilbert."

Neither man made a move to shake hands. Finally, Danny nodded. "Nice to meet you."

"Same here," Wes said. He turned for the stairs and, without another word, hurried up.

Annie felt Danny's eyes on her even before she looked his way. His look was incredulous. "What?" she asked.

"You actually agreed to let that guy move in?" he whispered.

79

"I wasn't crazy about the idea myself," Theenie said. "Not that Annie bothered to ask my opinion, mind you, and I'm pretty sure he has a checkered past."

"It's only for two weeks," Annie said, wishing Danny wouldn't worry about her so much. Theenie said it was because he was sweet on her, even though Annie always insisted that Danny was only acting out of friendship. "Besides, he has excellent references."

"He's here to take pictures," Theenie said, giving a massive eye roll. "But I'm not going to expand on that topic in mixed company."

Danny's eyes softened. "Annie, if this is about money . . ."

She didn't miss the tender look, the genuine concern in his voice, and Annie was certain it didn't go unnoticed by Theenie. It was times like this that she wondered if the woman might be right about his feelings toward her. "You're beginning to fret as much as Theenie," she said lightly.

The front door opened and closed, followed by the sound of light footsteps. Annie looked up to find her other tenant, Lovelle Hamilton, standing in the doorway.

"I'm baaack," she announced with a flourish.

Annie smiled. "Welcome home." Lovelle was an ex-ballerina who'd never made it big, although to hear her tell it, one would have thought otherwise. One of her claims to fame was having met Mikhail Baryshnikov at a cocktail party. She was string bean thin due to a daily dance regimen she practiced in Annie's ballroom.

"How was your trip?" Theenie asked.

"Fabulous. You know how much I love New York, having lived there most of my life. My daughter and I shopped at all the best stores, of course. I bought everybody gifts." She glanced about the room. "What's wrong? Why does everyone look so tense?"

"We have a new guest," Theenie said.

Lovelle smiled. Even at seventy-something, the woman was still striking, her makeup perfect and her platinum blond hair cut in the latest style. No blue rinse for Lovelle. "That's nice. I hope she's easy to get along with."

"It's a *he*," Theenie replied.

"Oh, goody. Is he handsome?"

All eyes fell on Annie.

"I suppose some women would consider him handsome in a rugged sort of way. I prefer a more conservative look." She punctuated her remark with what she hoped was a high-handed sniff, but the truth was she'd been thinking about Wes Bridges more than she should. Her thoughts had run amok the minute she caught sight of him in those boxer shorts.

The back door opened and Doc stepped inside. "I just stopped by to see if our patient fully recovered yesterday."

"What patient?" Danny asked.

Annie waved off the remark. "It's a long story." She turned to Doc. "He's fine. In fact, he just moved in."

"You let him move in?" Doc asked, his brow furrowing. "What about the lawsuit?"

"What lawsuit?" Danny asked. "Wait; let me guess. Another long story."

Annie nodded. "Something like that."

"Would you like a cup of coffee or iced tea?" Theenie asked Doc.

"No, I can't stay. I just learned my daughter in Tampa is having gallbladder surgery, so I'm flying down to help out with the grandkids, although they're old enough to do for themselves. Don't know how long I'll be gone."

"I hope the surgery goes well," Annie said. "Do you want me to grab your mail and newspapers while you're away?"

"The Martins already offered. It's less complicated for me to travel now that Leo is gone," he added sadly.

Annie nodded. Leo had been a stray dog eating from bags at the garbage dump when Doc had found him. Doc had brought him home, cleaned him up, and the two had lived in harmony for fifteen years before Leo died in his sleep of old age some eight or nine months ago. Annie had looked after the animal when Doc traveled; in turn, he had taken care of Peaches the few times Annie went away. "Well, you have my number," she said. "Call me if you think of something."

"Thank you." Doc started to leave and then turned. "Oh, I almost forgot. Do you need to borrow my gardener? I paid him for the whole day, but he finished up early. Man works hard and fast, unlike Erdle."

"Is he good with a tiller?" Theenie asked. "Annie wants the ground tilled behind the carriage house so she can plant a vegetable garden."

"He can do anything that pertains to yard work." Doc looked at Annie. "You want me to send him over?"

"I would love to borrow him," Annie said, delighted. Things were definitely beginning to look up. "Thank you, Doc, and have a safe trip."

He nodded and disappeared out the door. Danny stood. "I need to run home and get my sander. Maybe by the time I get back I won't be so confused." He shook his head as he let himself out.

"I think Danny is jealous of Wes," Theenie said.

Annie arched one brow. "You're not serious."

"I've noticed the way he looks at you."

"No way," Annie said firmly. "Danny and I have known each other since we were kids. He's like a brother to me." They didn't look convinced.

Lovelle said, "You have to admit he comes around a lot."

Annie grabbed her jacket from a hook by the back door. "Have the two of you forgotten that I'm still legally married? Now, if you'll excuse me, I need to talk to Doc's gardener."

Wes unpacked the few clothes he'd brought with him. He opened the closet door to hang his jacket and found several men's suits pushed to one side. Annie obviously hadn't gotten rid of all her husband's clothes. He checked the pockets. Nothing. He moved to the window, pulled the curtain aside, and saw Annie talking to a man in denim overalls. Wes left his room and listened near the top of the stairs for a moment. The others seemed to be deep in conversation. Very quietly he made his way to the door next to his, opened it, and stepped inside.

The bedroom held Annie's scent, clean and fresh but not flowery or overbearing like some perfumes. Wes closed the door, taking care not to make a sound. The simple four-poster bed was covered with a bright quilt. Beside it, a night table held a telephone and several books. He checked the window again; Annie was still talking to the man. Wes turned and began to search the room.

Annie finished her conversation with Doc's gardener and started for the house. She heard the sound of Wes's motorcycle engine as she climbed the back steps and entered the kitchen. He obviously wasn't hanging around for lunch. She opened the refrigerator, pulled out several packages of luncheon meat and cheese and the potato and cheese soup she'd made two nights before that was popular with her tenants. She heard a noise in the dining room and decided to check it out. She pushed open the swinging door and found Theenie and Lovelle standing before an open drawer in the buffet. They jumped when they saw her.

"What are you two up to?" she asked.

Theenie looked flustered. "Oh, um, we thought we'd check the silver and see if it needs polishing."

"You polished it three days ago," Annie said.

"Yes, but we want to make sure it sparkles for the wedding."

Annie looked from one to the other. Lovelle glanced away; Theenie began fidgeting. "You know I don't use my grandmother's silver for business functions. I have special flatware that I bought in bulk," she added, although she knew Theenie was perfectly aware of that fact. Annie noted a cardboard box on the table and looked inside. Her grandmother's serving pieces, each in its individual velvet pouch, had been placed inside. "Okay, what's *really* going on?"

"It wasn't my idea," Lovelle said.

Theenie's face reddened. "Now, Annie, I know you're not going to like this —"

"You're hiding the silver," Annie said in disbelief.

"I thought it best under the circumstances," Theenie whispered. "One can never be too careful."

"She thinks the new guest might steal it," Lovelle said.

Theenie shot her a dark look. "Traitor."

Annie crossed her arms over her chest. "Put it back."

Theenie hesitated. "If you say so, dear."

Annie was still shaking her head when the doorbell rang. She found Jamie and Max standing on the other side. "Well, hello," she said, delighted to see them.

"Hello to you, good-looking," Max said, dropping a kiss on her cheek. "If you get any prettier I'm going to have to change brides."

"See that?" Jamie said. "We're not even married yet, and he's already looking at other women."

Annie grinned at Max. She had liked him the minute they met. "He can't help himself. I'm hot stuff." She stepped back. "Come in."

"We just stopped by to drop off Destiny's mail for her column," Jamie said.

"You're in time for lunch. I'm about to heat up a big pot of my famous potato and cheese soup." She noted the sudden pained expression on Jamie's face. "Ooops, I forgot about the diet."

"I'm not on a diet," Max said, "and I love potato soup. Jamie can wait in the car with Fleas."

Jamie nudged him hard.

"You can't leave poor Fleas in the car," Annie protested.

Jamie chuckled. "He refused to get out and risk running into Peaches."

"I can put her out."

"Don't worry," Max said. "Muffin is singing Celine Dion songs to him."

Annie shook her head. Muffin was Max's talking computer, and she possessed the technology to do everything except bear children. In fact, she was more like a real-life assistant than a piece of machinery.

"I insist you stay for lunch," Annie told Jamie. "I'll make you a nice salad with fat-free dressing."

Jamie sighed. "I was afraid of that."

Destiny looked happy to see Jamie and Max. "Sit down," she said, pulling out the chair beside her, unaware that Peaches had already claimed it. The cat snarled and hissed. "Uh-oh, the cat from hell is using that chair. Perhaps you should choose another."

"I've never known Peaches to be in such a foul mood," Theenie said.

"It's because of the ghost," Destiny told her.

Max looked interested. "Ghost?"

Destiny nodded. "I'm surprised Jamie didn't mention it. You wouldn't believe what all goes on in this house." She leaned closer to Max and started to say something.

"What can I offer you to drink?" Annie interrupted before Destiny had a chance to regale Max with stories. Annie had no desire for Destiny to share with Max Holt all the craziness that went on in the house.

"I'm fine for now," Jamie said.

Max nodded. "I'm okay."

"It's like this," Destiny began.

"Are you sure?" Annie almost shouted, making them jump. "I have coffee, tea, orange juice, apple juice, diet root beer —"

They shook their heads and turned their attention back to Destiny.

". . . Two percent milk, soy. You know, I'll bet a glass of wine would be nice. I can —"

"Annie, what's wrong with you?" Jamie asked. "Why are you so jumpy?"

"It's the new tenant," Destiny said with a big grin. "You know, that half-naked guy you helped us stuff in the bathtub yesterday? He just moved in."

Max looked at Jamie. "Huh?"

Wes turned into the driveway of a modest ranch-style house, parked, and cut his engine. He removed his motorcycle helmet, climbed from the bike, and made his way toward the front door. The woman who opened it had hair the color of black shoe polish, wore a bright red caftan with matching lipstick and lime green bedroom slippers. A long, skinny cigarette dangled from her mouth.

"Wes Bridges?" she asked, talking around the cigarette. "I expected you yesterday." She had a three-pack-a-day smoker's voice; sounded like she'd been sucking on them since first grade.

"Life isn't always predictable, Mrs. Fortenberry. May I come in?"

"Yes." She stepped back and waited for him to enter before closing the door behind him. "You can call me Eve." She motioned to a lumpy chair that was the same avocado green as the dated shag carpet. Wes sat.

Garlic hung heavy in the air. Wes blinked and rubbed his eyes. The ash on Eve's cigarette was an inch long. He eyed it closely.

"I'm making spaghetti for a sick neighbor," Eve said. "Do you like garlic?"

"In reasonable doses."

"It cures all sorts of ailments, you know. May I offer you something to drink?" When Wes declined, she sat on the worn sofa across from him. She took a deep draw from her cigarette, and the ash grew longer. Finally, it fell unnoticed by her on her dress.

"Now then," she said. "What have you got for me?"

"I've rented a room from your daughter-in-law."

She gave a dry hacking cough. "You work fast."

"I don't believe in wasting a client's time or money," he said.

"What do you think of Annie? Is she a kook or what? Her grandmother was a kook. Like they say, the apple doesn't fall far from the tree."

Wes looked thoughtful. "It's too soon to tell."

Puff, puff, cough. "And how 'bout that house? I ask you, have you *ever?*"

"Nope, never."

"You know it's an old bordello or, as my daddy would say, God rest his soul, whore-house."

Wes arched both brows. "Oh yeah?"

"Before the Civil War. I read up on it a long time ago." She paused. "Did Annie mention my son?"

"I was told he left her for another woman."

"That's the cock-and-bull story she gave the police, and the reason they did such a piss-poor job of investigating. That Lamar Tevis, he's the police chief, is an idiot. He bought this fancy-schmancy deep-sea fishing boat three years ago. He's going to retire as soon as he pays it off and start a deep-sea fishing charter service. He's just biding his time until then."

"You don't believe your son left Annie?" Wes asked.

"Hell no. I wouldn't have hired you otherwise."

Wes glanced around the living room. "Perhaps we should go over my fees again."

"My check for your retainer cleared the bank, didn't it?" she said stiffly. When he nodded, she went on. "I can cover your expenses, Mr. Bridges. As I told you over the phone, my husband died three months ago. Fortunately, he had a sizable insurance policy, so I was *finally* able to do something about my son's disappearance. I'll spend every dime of it if I have to in order to find out what really happened to Charles."

Wes gave her a kind smile. "Eve, your son's car was found at the Savannah airport. No luggage. He cleaned out the savings account he shared with his wife. He had enough money to fly anywhere in the world."

She looked embarrassed. "My son worked hard for that money. Do you have any idea how much it costs to keep up a place the size of Annie's? The electric bill alone would break me." She took a long drag from her cigarette. "There was no record of him getting on a plane, no paper trail, nothing. We've already been over that. The bottom line is Charles would never have stayed gone this long without contacting me. No matter what the circumstances," she added. "I spent twice the going rate to hire you because you're supposed to be the best in the business. I want my son found."

Annie and Theenie were in the process of cleaning up after lunch when Danny Gilbert arrived back with his sander. Annie insisted that he eat something before going to work. As he waited for Annie to prepare him a sandwich and heat a bowl of soup, Lovelle recounted her days as a professional ballerina.

At the other end of the table, Destiny, Jamie, and Max discussed newspaper business and chuckled over a couple of letters that had been addressed to the Divine Love Goddess Adviser.

"Some people are so loopy," Destiny said. "Listen to this one: 'Dear Love Goddess Adviser: Some months ago I discovered my husband was a cross-dresser. After the shock had passed, I decided to make the best of it, and now we share our clothes. What has

93

me so frustrated is the fact that he doesn't *ask* if he can borrow my clothes; he just grabs what he needs out of my closet. When he returns an outfit I often find food stains on it, but he never offers to take anything to the dry cleaners. I have complained, but he doesn't listen. Could you please settle this dispute? I fear our marriage may be in deep trouble unless we can work this out.' "

Max and Jamie laughed.

"Oh, and listen to this one," Destiny said. " 'Dear Love Goddess Adviser: I am probably overreacting, but I suspect my husband is cheating on me. He doesn't return home some nights until almost midnight, and he reeks of Chanel Number Five. I have found lipstick on his shirt collar, long scratches on his back, and the other night when he undressed, his underwear was on backward. Do you think I'm just being one of those suspicious wives?' "

Jamie laughed until her sides hurt as Destiny continued to read several more. Annie was happy to see her friend looking more relaxed, and the private smiles Jamie and Max shared when they thought nobody was looking would have made most women envious.

Danny finished his lunch and carried his dishes to the sink, where he rinsed them.

Wes entered the kitchen, a camera hanging from his neck. All eyes turned to him, and the chatter stopped. "You must be the other new guest," Lovelle said, and introduced herself. She had met Destiny earlier.

"Nice to meet you," he said politely.

Max stood and made introductions as well. If Wes recognized Jamie, he didn't say anything. "Nice camera," Max said. "Are you a photographer?"

Wes nodded. "I've been able to get some great shots this morning. Beaumont is a beautiful town."

"It grows on you fast," Max said.

"Wes, would you care for a sandwich?" Annie asked, wishing just once she could round up everybody at the same time for meals. Seemed like she was always offering somebody something to eat; felt like she was working at the Huddle House.

"I grabbed something earlier," he said. "Nice to meet you," he told Max and Jamie as he headed upstairs, stepping aside for Theenie, who was on her way down.

"Good grief!" Lovelle said when Wes was out of hearing distance. "Where did you find *him?*"

"He sort of found us," Annie said.

"Annie almost killed him," Theenie said. "Then Doc almost killed him."

"Perhaps I should explain," Annie said. She had opened her mouth to do just that when she heard a man's voice out back shouting her name. He sounded frantic. "What in the world!" She threw open the back door and found Doc's gardener racing across the backyard, calling out to her loudly.

Footsteps sounded on the stairs and Wes hurried into the kitchen. "What's going on? Is somebody hurt?"

Annie was already on the back porch, the others behind her. The gardener stopped at the back stairs, staggered once, grabbed the porch rail. His face was ashen. He tried to speak.

Annie hurried down and touched his arm. "What's wrong?" she said. "Are you injured?" She looked for blood, didn't see any.

"It's terrible," the man managed. "Worst thing I ever seen."

"What is it?" she demanded.

"Back yonder. Behind the, um, that carriage house."

Wes pushed through the group and cleared the back steps in one jump. He was the first to arrive at the gaping hole, with Max and Danny right behind him. Wes knelt beside it, and his eyes froze at what he saw. "Holy shit!"

Max joined him. "Holy shit is right."

Wes looked at Danny. "Keep the women back."

Danny turned. "Don't come any closer, okay?" he told them.

Theenie and Lovelle came to an abrupt halt, but the others rushed forward.

"What is it?" Annie said.

Jamie blinked several times, trying to make sense of what she was looking at. "Bones?" she asked.

"It's a skeleton," Max said.

Annie gave an eye roll. "Oh, Jeez, it's my grandmother's dog. She had Erdle bury him somewhere back here after he died. I'd forgotten about it."

Wes shook his head. "Sorry, Annie, but this is no dog. It's a human skeleton."

"Oh, I can't see this," Theenie said, backing away. She turned and hurried toward the house. Lovelle followed.

Annie stared back at Wes in disbelief. "That's ridiculous!"

"He's right, Annie," Max said.

"It looks human to me, too," Jamie said, and Destiny agreed.

Annie stepped closer and looked. "Oh, shit, I have a dead person in my backyard! Oh, shit. Oh, shit."

"There's some kind of cloth there," Max said.

Wes nodded and glanced over his shoulder. "Look, this is obviously a crime scene, and I'd rather not jeopardize any trace evidence." He didn't see the look Max gave him. "So I'd appreciate it if everybody would please move back."

Danny convinced the women to step away.

"It's not like I've never seen dead people before," Destiny told him. "They follow me everywhere I go."

Max and Wes were quiet as they studied the site. "Looks like the cloth was yellow at some point," Max said, "although it's hard to tell."

"There's some kind of insignia on the material," Wes said.

Max grabbed a stick. "Only one way to find out."

Destiny stood there, a knowing look in her eyes.

"Be careful," Wes whispered. "There could be hairs or fibers."

"You sound like you know what you're talking about," Max said, very gently lifting a portion of the material.

"I watch a lot of TV. Enough to know we shouldn't be doing this. Okay, hold it right there, and I'll see if I can read it." Taking great care not to disturb anything, Wes leaned forward. "Looks like a *C* and an *F.*"

"Have you found anything?" Jamie called out.

"Some kind of yellow material," Max said. "Could be a shirt or a jacket. Initials *CF* on it."

Annie and Jamie looked at each other, their eyes wide and disbelieving. "No!" Annie said. "That's impossible!" She shook her head. "It can't be. It just can't be."

"Annie . . ." Jamie stepped closer, reached out.

"No!" Annie cried, and pushed her away.

"What the hell?" Wes leaped to his feet and raced toward Annie as she screamed. He shook her hard. "Annie, what is it?"

She opened her mouth, tried to speak, couldn't. Her eyes were glazed.

Wes looked confused but did as he was told.

Jamie looked at him. "It's a jacket. I was with Annie when she purchased it. *CF* stands for *Charles Fortenberry.*"

"My husband," Annie choked. Her eyes rolled back in her head before everything went black.

Wes was there to catch her.

CHAPTER FOUR

Police Chief Lamar Tevis studied the shallow grave closely, turning his head this way and that as if to get a better look, as one officer snapped pictures and another surrounded the area with yellow crime scene tape. Finally, Lamar stood and brushed the dirt from the knees of his khaki uniform. "It's a body, all right," he said. "I'm not an expert on this sort of thing, so I can't tell how long it has been there. Takes one of those forensic whatchamacallits for that. They may have someone at the Medical University in Charleston, but there's no telling how long it'll take them to get around to it."

Wes, who'd already introduced himself, shook his head. "I don't think you'll need a forensic anthropologist," he said, earning raised eyebrows from Lamar. "At least for the time being," he added. "Mrs. Fortenberry is certain the body is that of her husband."

Lamar glanced at Max as if seeking verification. Max told him about the jacket and initials. "Jamie was present when Annie purchased it."

Danny Gilbert crossed the yard and joined the men. "Afternoon, Lamar," he said. They shook hands.

"What are you up to these days?" Lamar asked. "Done any fishing lately?"

Danny shook his head. "Work has been keeping me busy. I'm sanding Annie Fortenberry's wood floors today."

Lamar frowned. "Uh-oh. That sounds pretty suspicious if you ask me."

"Why is that?" Wes asked.

"A woman finds a body in her backyard and claims it's her missing husband, and all she can think of is having her floors sanded?" Lamar reached into his shirt pocket and pulled out a small notebook. "I'd better write that down. Might prove helpful in the investigation."

Max and Wes exchanged looks. There was a hint of a smile on Max's lips.

"Actually, Annie is taking it pretty hard," Danny said. "She's lying down."

"I've known Annie since she was a book-keeper at Bates's Furniture," Lamar said. "I bought several rooms of furniture there. Used to go in once a month to pay on my bill. You know Herman Bates sells good-quality furniture at reasonable prices, and he offers discounts if you buy multiple rooms."

"So what do you think?" Max asked, nodding toward the grave.

"Well, I questioned Annie when Mr. Fortenberry first turned up missing and his mother started making all kinds of wild accusations. I'll tell you, that Eve is a piece of work. But I saw no reason to suspect foul play. 'Course this changes everything. By the way, who found the body?"

"Doc Holden's gardener." Wes pointed to the man, who was sitting on a tree stump, shaking his head and muttering to himself.

"Who's he talking to?" Lamar whispered.

"He's still pretty upset," Max said.

Lamar motioned for the officer who'd finished taking pictures. "I need for you to question that fellow over there," he said, nodding toward the gardener. "And go easy on him; he looks just shy of a straitjacket."

A car pulled into the driveway. Editor Mike Henderson from the *Gazette* hurried toward them, accompanied by Vera Bankhead, Jamie's secretary and assistant editor. She held a camera.

"Oh, cripes," Lamar said. "Just what I need. Let me do all the talking."

"We heard the news on the police scanner," Mike said. "Somebody found a body in Annie Fortenberry's backyard," he added. "What can you tell us?"

Despite the grave expression he wore, it was hard for most people to take Mike seriously, not only because he was young and still had that fresh-out-of-college look, but also because he was so noticeably unorganized. He seldom ironed his shirts, and scraps of paper fluttered from his pockets when he reached for his stash of pens, which often leaked and had stained most of his clothes. He was known to chase women, and he'd had his eye on Destiny Moultrie for months. Jamie often claimed she was trying to raise him to be a *real* editor.

"No comment," Lamar said.

Mike just stared back as if unsure what to do.

Sixty-year-old Vera Bankhead planted her hands on her hips. She looked younger than her age thanks to a complete makeover the year before, which included a Susan Sarandon hairstyle, and a new wardrobe that had put Vera on the top ten best-dressed list for the women at Mount Zion Baptist Church. The fact that Vera never missed a Sunday and could quote Scripture word-for-word did not deter her when it came to getting what she wanted. She could be quite formidable.

"Cut the bull, Lamar," she said. "It's our job to report the news. You know how hard it is to come up with a decent headline in this town."

"Are you armed?" Lamar asked.

"Not at the moment."

Lamar looked relieved. "All I can say right now is yes, we do have a body, but we don't know anything yet."

"Do you suspect foul play?" Mike asked.

Vera looked at him. "That has to be the dumbest question I've ever heard. *Of course* there was foul play. Dead people don't bury themselves."

Mike's face turned a bright red.

Vera looked at Lamar. "Do you have a suspect?"

"If I did I certainly wouldn't spill my guts to the newspaper."

Vera gave a menacing frown. "Are you smart-mouthing me? Because if you are I'll tell your mama and she'll slap you from here to Texas. She didn't raise you to talk back to your elders."

This time when Wes looked at Max he was having just as much difficulty keeping a straight face.

Lamar glanced their way. As if sensing their amusement, he hitched his chin high and squared his shoulders. "This is police business, Vera," he said, "and I'd appreciate it if you'd keep my mama out of it." He gave them a stern look. "And I don't want either of you going near the crime scene, you hear? The medical examiner will raise holy hell if he gets here and finds anything disturbed."

Vera tapped her foot impatiently. "How am I supposed to get a picture?"

Lamar pondered it. "Tell you what. You can take a picture of me *pointing* to the crime scene."

Vera sighed and shook her head. "It's shameful what you'll do to get your picture in the paper, but I guess that'll have to do for now." She raised the camera to her eyes and focused.

Lamar threw back his shoulders, sucked in his paunch, and gave a big smile, one arm outstretched, his index finger pointing to a small mound of dirt beside the open grave.

Vera lowered her camera. "What do you think you're doing? I'm not taking this picture for your high school yearbook. You need to look serious."

"Oh yeah." Lamar frowned at the camera and waited for Vera to snap his picture.

"Now, if you will excuse me," he said, "I have work to do." He glanced at one of his deputies. "Nobody goes near the scene," Lamar said, cutting his eyes at Vera. The officer nodded and crossed his arms over his chest as Lamar headed toward the house.

Vera pursed her lips and looked at Mike. "If I weren't a good Southern Baptist I'd give Lamar Tevis the finger."

Annie blew her nose again and tossed the tissue into the wastebasket beside her bed. Jamie and Theenie sat on either side; Destiny and Lovelle stood at the foot. "I feel so guilty," Annie said. "All this time I've been telling people Charles left me for another woman. I never once suspected he was dead."

"Don't feel guilty, sweetie," Theenie said. "Charles probably would have left you anyway had he lived."

There was a knock at the door. Lovelle opened it. Lamar walked into the room. His gaze immediately fell on Jamie. "Your, um, editors are outside looking at the crime scene. I'd appreciate it if you'd make sure they don't mess with anything. You know how ornery Vera can be."

"Mike and Vera are professionals," Jamie said, although she knew Vera would stop at nothing to get a story, even if it meant breaking the law. And since she intimidated Mike, he would pretty much follow along. Jamie looked at Annie. "I'd like to touch base with them before they head back to the office. Will you be okay?"

Annie nodded.

Lamar waited until Jamie was gone. "Mrs. Fortenberry, I was hoping I could ask you a few questions if you think you're up to it."

"There's no need to be formal, Lamar," Annie said, offering him the closest thing she had to a smile. "Is it okay if my friends stay?"

"Whatever makes you comfortable."

"Why don't you grab that chair?" she said.

"Thanks." He picked up the ladder-back chair and placed it closer to the bed. "Okay then," he said before pulling out his note-pad once more. "I understand you have reason to believe the body out back is your husband's."

"I'm positive."

Lamar looked regretful. "Well then, let me offer my sincere condolences. I know this can't be easy for you." He paused a moment. "I'm thinking maybe we could go over what happened the day Mr. Fortenberry disappeared if you don't mind."

"I don't know what more I can tell you,"

she said. "We covered everything when my mother-in-law filed a missing person's report on Charles three years ago."

"Sometimes people think of things later that might help," Lamar said. "I haven't had a chance to look at the file, and I want to make sure I have everything. Could you tell me again when you saw him last?"

Annie gave Lamar the exact date. "It was around six AM," she said. "Our conversation was brief because I was getting ready to drive to my mother's house in Atlanta. She'd been sick with the flu, and it turned into pneumonia. I was with her for a week."

"Did your husband appear to act differently in any way? Like maybe he was worried about something?"

"Not that I remember, but then, I was really concerned about my mom at the time, so I wasn't paying close attention."

Lamar nodded as he took notes. "Do you know of anyone who disliked your husband enough to kill him?"

A tear slid down Annie's cheek as she shook her head. "I don't know *anyone* who would actually commit murder."

"In most cases, the killer knows the victim." Lamar paused. "I think I need to be up-front with you, Annie. The spouse is usually the first person we look at."

Annie couldn't believe what she was hearing. "Are you saying I'm a suspect?"

"Hold it right there, Lamar!" Destiny said, stepping closer, her jeweled hand on one out-thrust hip. "I happen to know a little about the law, and if you're charging Annie with murder . . ." She paused and looked at Annie. "You need to keep your mouth shut and call an attorney."

"I'm not charging Annie with anything," Lamar said defensively, his eyes flitting to Destiny's low-cut blouse, "but if it comes to that I'll certainly notify her of her rights. I happen to know a little bit about the law myself."

"I'll answer your questions," Annie said. "Only I'd appreciate it if you'd take down that crime scene tape as soon as you possibly can. I'm having a big wedding here."

"Uh-oh." Lamar arched one brow and started to make a notation in his book. "That's going to look bad for you."

"It's not *my* wedding!" Annie said, wondering how Lamar could be so dense at times. She saw Destiny shake her head.

"Annie doesn't even like men," Theenie said. "She almost killed the last one who showed up at her door."

"Uh-oh," Lamar said.

"It was an accident," Annie said, giving

109

Theenie a would-you-kindly-shut-your-mouth? look. Theenie offered a sheepish smile. Annie explained what had happened the morning of Wes's arrival. "Now the whole world knows," she said.

Lamar looked thoughtful. "I know about Erdle's drinking," he said. "Have you ever seen him get violent?"

Annie shook her head. "Never. Besides, he wasn't here at the time. An old army buddy from Mississippi rented a condo in Hilton Head that week and invited Erdle to join him. The guy even wrote out an affidavit on Erdle's behalf."

"Was anyone else in the house? Any guests?" Lamar added.

"All this happened before I turned the place into a bed-and-breakfast. Doc checked on Peaches several times while I was away, made sure she had plenty of food and water. I knew Charles wouldn't bother; he hated that cat. But Doc said he didn't bother stopping over until the day after I left because he knew I always put out extra."

"Yes, I questioned Doc at the time," Lamar said. "He claimed he didn't see anything out of the ordinary. He's so senile; if he *had* seen anything, I don't think he would remember."

Annie nodded. "His memory comes and

goes, but he's ninety years old, so I'm not surprised. Now, about that crime scene tape."

Lamar looked apologetic. "I can't take it down till we're done. My men will be going over the area during the next couple of days, sifting through dirt looking for evidence. I can't have folks traipsing about, disturbing the crime scene."

"Come on, Lamar, cut me some slack here. It's going to be bad for business."

"I'll see what I can do," he mumbled, although he seemed more concerned with finishing up. "I only have a couple more questions. I'll probably find the answers in Mr. Fortenberry's file, but I want to make sure I have the name of his dentist, and if he had any broken bones that would prove without a doubt that the, um, remains are his."

"He saw Dr. Hensley. As for broken bones, I know he fractured his left wrist in high school playing football."

"I assume we'll find a wallet on him, unless he was robbed, of course. Did he carry a lot of cash on him?"

"I don't know."

"Any jewelry? A watch or wedding ring?"

"He claimed he couldn't wear his wedding ring because it caused his finger to swell," she said. Lamar didn't see her roll her eyes at the others as he jotted the information on his notepad. "He wore a Seiko watch with a gold band that I bought for his birthday, but I don't remember what kind of wallet he carried."

"Anything engraved on the watch?"

"No."

"Anything else you can think of that might help?"

"The yellow jacket with his initials, of course."

"This is a good start," Lamar said, closing his notepad. "If you think of something else, give me a call."

"Do you know how long they'll keep him?"

"I can't say for sure, since it's a murder case." Lamar stood and put the chair back in its place. He continued to stand there for a moment as though he had something on his mind. "Do you have plans to travel anytime soon?"

"Are you telling her not to leave town?" Destiny asked. She didn't wait for his reply. "See, Annie, I told you to hire a lawyer."

"I can't afford a lawyer," Annie said.

Lamar tossed Destiny a dark look. "I never said she couldn't leave town." He looked at Annie. "You haven't been charged with anything; I just wanted to know if you'd be around in case I need to ask you some more questions. And don't worry about the cost of a lawyer. If it comes to that and you can't afford representation, the court will appoint someone."

Annie felt a sense of dread wash over her. She tried to keep the sarcasm from her voice. "Well, that certainly eases my mind."

Wes knocked on Annie's door an hour later. When he didn't get an answer, he opened the door quietly and peeked in. She was alone, lying in bed, staring at the ceiling. "Is it okay if I come in?" he asked.

"Sure."

He approached the bed. "I thought I should tell you, they've taken the body away."

"Thank God."

"I'm sorry, Annie. I know this can't be easy."

She nodded. "Charles was only thirty years old at the time of his death. I may not have liked him very much, but I never wanted him dead." She suddenly gasped. "Oh, I forgot. Somebody is going to have to break the news to his mother. I don't want her to find out on the six o'clock news."

"I'll make sure it's taken care of," Wes

said. "You've got enough on your mind right now."

"Lamar said they always look at the spouse first, which means I'm the main suspect."

"Don't take it personally; it's normal procedure."

"How do you know that?"

He shrugged. "That's always been the case."

"Do you think I killed him?"

"No."

"How can you be so sure?"

"I can't see you killing *anyone*, much less dragging a body across the backyard and burying it." He smiled as if to ease the tension. "You're a bit of a runt."

"I'm stronger than I look."

"Remind me not to arm wrestle you. I'd hate to lose to a girl, especially a half pint like you."

Annie knew he was teasing her in hopes of cheering her up. "My mother-in-law thinks I'm responsible for his disappearance. She'll probably hound Lamar to arrest me."

"Did the two of you get along?"

"Not because I didn't try. But I think she was jealous. If Charles didn't call her every day she'd pout. Later, she became as resentful as Charles when I refused to sell this place."

The door squeaked. Annie looked up and found Danny peeking in. He glanced at Wes, then back at Annie. "How're you doing, sport?"

She smiled. "I'm hanging in there."

Wes seemed to take that as his cue to leave. "If there's anything I can do, please let me know."

"Thank you."

Danny stepped aside so Wes could exit. Annie swung her legs over the side of the bed. "I need to get up and start dinner."

"Don't worry about it. I've already placed an order for several large pizzas. They'll arrive by suppertime."

Annie couldn't hide her relief. "What would I do without you?"

"That's what I keep telling you. Now wash your face and come downstairs. Everybody is worried about you."

"What's wrong with my face?"

"Your eyes are swollen, and you've got black gunk under them. Matter of fact, you look like hell."

Annie winced. Lord, Wes Bridges had seen her looking that way and hadn't mentioned it. "Gee, thanks," she muttered.

"At least I'm honest."

Annie nodded. That much was true. Danny had been the only friend to tell her the truth when she'd first suspected Charles of cheating. Most people didn't want to become involved in a couple's marital problems, but Danny felt as though she should know. "I'll be down in a few minutes," she said.

He started to leave and then turned. "Annie, I don't like to interfere in your business, but . . ." He paused. When she looked up in question, he went on. "It's Wes. I don't completely trust him. Be careful, okay?"

The light was fading when Wes parked his motorcycle in front of Eve Fortenberry's. She met him at the door wearing a frumpy dress, bedroom slippers, and holding a cigarette. She took one look at his face and stepped back as though she knew something terrible was coming. "What is it?"

"We've found your son."

"And?" Her eyes were cold and hard, daring him to give her bad news.

"Eve, I'm sorry."

Her face crumpled. "No," she said, shaking her head. She covered her mouth. Wes stepped inside and closed the door behind him.

Erdle arrived home the following morning. Annie stepped outside the minute his car pulled into the driveway. "I need to talk to you."

"You're throwing me out."

She thought he sounded surprisingly sober. "Not at the moment. Something bad has happened." She gave him the news, then said, "Lamar Tevis suspects me."

Erdle sighed. "Then I'm probably on the list, too," he said. "Everybody knows I wouldn't have given two cents for him."

"You weren't even here at the time. You have an airtight alibi."

"I forgot. Damn, it seems like it all happened about ten years ago. But you had an alibi, too. You were in Atlanta with your mother, remember?"

Annie didn't respond.

"This place is very strange," Destiny announced two days later as she joined Annie, Theenie, and Lovelle in the kitchen.

"You got that right," Lovelle said. "There aren't many places where you can find a dead body in your backyard."

"Must we discuss this at breakfast?" Theenie asked. "And in front of Annie to boot?"

"I'm okay," Annie said, staring into her

coffee cup. But she didn't look okay. Dark circles made half moons beneath her eyes, and she'd barely eaten since Charles's remains had been discovered. "I guess everybody in town knows by now," she said, nodding toward the folded newspaper beside her cup, where the morning headlines had drawn attention to the discovery. Jamie had called to apologize in advance, but Annie didn't blame her for printing it; reporting the news was Jamie's job.

Annie shoved the thought from her mind and looked at Destiny. "What's the problem?"

"Some of my lingerie is missing."

"Oh boy," Theenie said.

"I'm not accusing any of you," Destiny said hurriedly. "I already know who took them."

"Oh boy," Theenie repeated.

"Would you please stop saying that?" Lovelle insisted. "You sound like a broken record." She leaned closer to Destiny. "Who do you think took your things?"

"The spirit, to get my attention. That's the way it is with dead people."

Annie noted the fear in Theenie's eyes. "I'm sure there's a perfectly reasonable explanation," she said.

Destiny studied Annie closely. "You're in

denial. This place is haunted, and the ghost has latched on to me, and you just don't want to hear about it."

Lovelle leaned closer to Destiny. "We don't really talk about it."

"Oh, I get it," Destiny said to Annie. "You're afraid it will hurt business, so you try to sweep it under the rug. There are other things about the house you're not proud of as well. Do you think people don't already know? Or *feel* it? The air is thick with . . ." She paused. "It's like a sexual undertow."

Three pairs of eyes looked at her, but nobody said anything.

"I know damn good and well I'm not the only one who feels it," Destiny said.

Lovelle leaned closer. "I've never told anybody this, but since I moved into this house I have had a lot of sexy dreams."

Theenie gnawed her bottom lip. "Well, I'll have to admit I've dreamed about Clark Gable a lot."

"Was he naked?" Lovelle asked.

"Absolutely not! Mr. Gable is a gentleman. All we've done is share a few kisses."

Annie was thoughtful as she took a sip of her coffee. She wasn't about to admit that her sex drive was in overdrive. And she'd certainly had her share of illicit dreams. She looked up and found the others watching her. She shrugged. "I hate to disillusion you guys, but I'm so tired by the time I drag myself to bed that it's all I can do to brush my teeth before climbing in."

Destiny merely gave Annie a smile that told her she knew better.

"I'm sorry your things are missing," Annie told her, "but I'm sure they'll turn up." She gave a weary sigh.

"Annie, honey, what's wrong?" Theenie said. "I can always tell when something is bothering you."

"I'm just annoyed, that's all. Two guys from the local TV station knocked on my door this morning and shoved a microphone in my face while I was still in my bathrobe."

"And you weren't wearing makeup, I'll bet," Destiny said.

Annie shook her head. "And yesterday I caught a couple of women sneaking around the backyard, no doubt looking for the grave, and the traffic has suddenly picked up because people want to see the woman who supposedly murdered her husband and buried his body in the backyard."

Theenie reached over and covered Annie's hand. "I shouldn't have hidden your rolling pin."

"On top of that, I got a call late last night

from a member of the Red Hat Society. She canceled today's luncheon."

"But you've already prepared most of the food," Lovelle said.

"I can freeze some of it," Annie said.

"Did she say *why* she was canceling?" Theenie asked.

"She didn't have to. I knew this was going to happen. It's bad enough people have to read about it in the newspaper and see it on the news; that idiot Lamar still has crime scene tape stretched from one end of the neighborhood to the other. I don't blame them for canceling."

"I'm sorry I complained," Destiny said. "I didn't get much sleep last night, and I get grumpy when I'm tired." She gave a laugh. "It's not like I don't have a ton of lingerie."

Theenie suddenly brightened. "You don't have to freeze the food, Annie. You can use it tomorrow evening for the Ladies Night Out group."

Annie gave a rueful smile. "They won't be coming, either." Only she hadn't found out until after she'd spent more than one hundred dollars on two large standing rib roasts, not to mention all the other items she'd purchased. She noted the concern on the women's faces and felt guilty for burdening them with her problems. "It's okay," she said. "I'm sure this is temporary." They didn't look any more convinced than she was.

Footsteps sounded on the stairs and Wes entered the kitchen. His hair was still wet from his shower, but he hadn't bothered to shave. He looked from one woman to the other. "What's wrong?"

Theenie didn't hesitate. "Somebody is stealing Destiny's underwear, and Annie has had two cancellations." She covered her mouth and shot an apologetic look at Destiny. "I'm sorry I brought up your unmentionables. Sometimes things just pop right out of my mouth before I think."

Destiny shrugged, propped her elbows on the table, and leaned forward slightly, the cameo attached to her gold necklace sinking between her breasts. "It's okay," Destiny told Theenie. "I'm not easily embarrassed."

Wes turned to Annie. "Who canceled what?"

"It's not important," Annie said. The absolute last thing she wanted to do was tell Wes her problems.

Theenie suddenly brightened. "There's still the baby shower on Saturday."

Annie smiled and nodded. She wasn't one to let things drag her down for long. "You're right. You and Lovelle need to start thinking about the decorations." Annie knew both women got a kick out of sifting through her large cardboard boxes where she kept all sorts of decorations neatly packed and labeled; they would choose just the right items and spend hours putting them up.

Wes turned his attention back to Destiny. "You're missing lingerie?" he asked. "There's a bunch of, uh, female stuff hanging over the shower rod in my bathroom. I was wondering what they were doing there."

"See, I told you they'd show up," Annie said.

"Yes, but I didn't put them there," Destiny replied. "The ghost did it."

Wes looked at her. "What ghost?"

A sudden clatter overhead made them jump. Peaches, napping in a pool of sunlight at the window, leaped to her feet, arched her back, and hissed.

"That one," Destiny said.

Annie chuckled and waved it off. "It's just the wind."

"That's what she always says," Theenie told Wes.

"Destiny is pulling your leg about the ghost," Annie went on. "We obviously have a prankster in the house, don't we, ladies?" Even as she said it she felt a brush of cool air on the back of her neck, making her hair

123

stand on end and sending shivers down her spine.

Dusk had settled in as Destiny stepped over the crime scene tape surrounding the still-gaping hole. The deputies had worked for two days, combing the area for evidence, before deciding they'd probably found all there was. Yet the garish yellow tape remained. Standing before the grave, Destiny closed her eyes and remained perfectly still. A cold wind whipped through the branches of the tall oaks, rustling the leaves and causing the gray moss to wave and shudder. Finally, Destiny knelt beside the hole and ran her fingers through the black dirt that would have made a perfect vegetable garden had Charles Fortenberry not been found buried there. Destiny let the dirt sift through her fingers.

"What are you doing?" a male voice asked.

Destiny turned and found a baffled-looking Erdle standing there. "You wouldn't understand."

"Nobody's supposed to go on that side of the tape."

"You plan on turning me in?" She sounded indifferent.

"You could be destroying evidence."

Destiny laughed. "If those local yokels

haven't found anything by now they're not going to."

"What makes you think you will?"

"Because my methods are different."

Erdle cocked his head to the side, studying her closely. "Chief Tevis says you're as crazy as a bedbug."

"That's because I always steal his thunder each time he hits a dead end and is forced to call on me. And because I won't sleep with him. Imagine that."

"So, were you able to get any messages from the *beyond?*" Erdle asked in such a way that made it obvious he didn't believe in her abilities.

She shook her head. "Too many people have been over it, which lessens my chances of picking up on anything. Lamar should have let me have at it first." She regarded Erdle. "You got any idea who might have killed Charles Fortenberry?"

"If I did know I wouldn't tell. Way I see it, he got exactly what he deserved."

CHAPTER FIVE

It was late when Wes stepped out onto the piazza, slipping into his denim jacket to ward off the night chill. Moonlight peeked through the overhead branches, offering just enough light that he could make out the silhouette of someone sitting on the wicker swing. "Annie?"

"I couldn't sleep." She huddled deeper into her terry-cloth bathrobe and pulled the afghan around her shoulders.

"Me, neither." Wes crossed the piazza. "May I join you?"

Annie scooted to one side, and he sat down. "Would you like for me to make you a cup of hot chocolate?" she asked. "It sometimes helps me fall asleep."

"Aren't you off duty?"

She was able to make out his rugged face in the moonlight, the certain way he held his head that gave him an air of confidence. She liked that about him. That and the probing, alert eyes that not only convinced her of his intelligence but also made her feel he was always on top of things. "I like to see to the comfort of my guests," she said.

"Oh yeah?"

She didn't have to look at him to know he was smiling. "There are limits, of course," she said, unable to resist smiling back at him.

"I don't think I've seen you relax more than ten minutes since I moved in. You're always moving."

"There's a lot involved in running this place."

"So what do you do for fun?"

"Sometimes Danny and I see a movie."

"Is he your boyfriend?"

"Danny?" Annie chuckled. "No, we're just friends. I've known him for years."

"He seems protective of you."

"Yes." She wouldn't tell him that Danny sometimes carried it to extremes, that he often offered more advice than she needed. "He was there for me when my marriage hit the skids. I don't know what I would have done without his support."

"Maybe he'd *like* to be your boyfriend," Wes said.

Annie caught the teasing lilt in his voice. She laughed. "Danny would be the first to tell you I'm not looking for a boyfriend."

Wes nodded thoughtfully. "So why'd you marry this Charles in the first place? Sorry to say it, but he sounds like he was a jerk."

Annie looked at him. "You ask a lot of questions; you know that?"

"I've always been curious. You can tell me to mind my own business."

She shrugged. "Charles could be charming when he wanted, which is why he did so well in real estate." She wouldn't tell Wes how lonely and vulnerable she'd been when she met Charles, shortly after her grandmother's death. She wouldn't mention her dreams of a big family, how she'd yearned for it growing up. Those things she kept close to her heart. "It just didn't work out," she finally said, knowing she sounded like it had been no big deal when it really *had* been a big deal.

"You weren't married long."

"Two years."

"You got any idea who could have killed him?"

"No. And Lamar Tevis probably won't look too hard, since he thinks I did it. I guess he suspects the truth: that inside I'm a dangerous, cold-blooded killer."

"He's probably seen you with your rolling pin." Wes slid his arm along the back of the swing, reached for a thick strand of her hair, and rubbed it between his fingers as though testing its texture. "I think you're dangerous."

"Oh yeah?"

"Those big green eyes of yours, those cute freckles. A deadly combination, if you ask me."

"Makes it easier to snare my victims," she said lightly, although she was uncomfortable with his fingers in her hair, stroking downward, his knuckles grazing the back of her neck. She shifted on the swing. "Um, Wes?"

"You don't like that?" He pulled his hand away.

On the contrary, she liked it too much. But she had no business sitting in the dark with him and letting him touch her in a way that made her think of what it had felt like lying against him. The swing moved, and when she looked up, she found he'd slipped closer. She could feel the heat from his body. A light breeze ruffled his hair. His brown eyes looked black.

"I have to go in," she said. She gathered the afghan more tightly around her shoulders and made to get up.

"That's too bad," he said, "because I like looking at you in the moonlight."

His voice was as smooth as the velvet spread that covered her bed, and his lazy-as-a-river smile tugged at her innards. The man knew what he was doing.

"Okay, Wes, listen up," she said, still trying to keep things light between them so he wouldn't know he was getting to her. "I believe in saying it like it is."

"I like that about you."

"Um, thank you," she said.

"You're welcome."

He was trying to sweet-talk her; that's what he was doing. He'd probably sweet-talked his way into more than one woman's heart and bed, but not this one. No sirree. She had his number, could see right through him. Wes Bridges had definitely met his match.

"Now then," she said firmly. "I think I know what's on your mind, so maybe I should remind you that the absolute last thing I want or need in my life is a man."

He nodded emphatically. "That's for sure."

He was agreeing with her? "*Especially* a man who only plans on hanging around a couple of weeks and is just looking for a good time."

"Especially that."

"I don't like being tied down or having

somebody tell me what to do all the time."

"Can't blame you for that."

"I like my life just the way it is, except the part about finding my husband's remains in the backyard and being the number one murder suspect." She added quickly, "But I plan to clear my name and —"

"Annie?"

"Yeah?"

"Could you just shut up for maybe one minute?"

She blinked, and without warning he dipped his head and pressed his lips against hers. Holy cow, she hadn't even seen it coming, and her mouth dropped open in surprise. Wes obviously took that as an invitation, because before she could unscramble her brain, he'd pulled her closer and slipped his tongue past her gaping lips. Jeez Louise, but the man knew his way around a woman's mouth! The kiss deepened, and she grasped his jacket with both hands, feeling as though she were riding on one of those wild carnival rides that turned her inside out and upside down and made the world around her spin all topsy-turvy as though everything was out of control.

She thought of pulling away and then decided one more minute wouldn't hurt. His lips were gentle but persuasive, and before she knew it, Annie found her tongue mingling with his. He enveloped her in his arms, and the next thing she knew, her own arms had slipped around his neck. The afghan slid from her shoulders, and she could feel his heat seeping through her bathrobe and gown, and she was straining against him wanting more. She was sorry when he raised his head.

For a moment they just looked at each other, and Annie mentally tried to pick up the pieces of her scattered brain and put them in order and find the part labeled *logical thinking*.

"Annie?"

She grappled for an intelligible word. "Huh?"

"That was dynamite."

Dynamite? Dy-nuh-mite. Eeek! "Destiny!" she almost hissed. "It's all her fault!"

"I have no clue what you're talking about, but I haven't enjoyed kissing a woman that much in a long, long time. I think we should do it some more."

Annie swayed against him. "I don't think —" But it was too late because there they were, those warm lips, stealing her self-control and turning her brain to mush again. And there *she* was, kissing him right back and thinking no man had ever tasted so good. And then her body went wacko: her nipples hardened and strained against her flannel gown and her stomach began flip-flopping like a fish out of water and way low in her belly she felt the flicker of something warm and sweet. That *something* conjured up thoughts that she had no business thinking: Wes warm and naked between her scented sheets, his big hands on her body.

Time to stop.

Annie pulled away quickly and sucked in a deep, shuddering breath. She would give her heart a few seconds to settle down, and then she would admonish him for his actions. Yep, as soon as her pulse steadied she was going to let him have it and have it good.

She sank against him.

Wes pressed his lips against her forehead. "I've half a mind to sweep you up in my arms and carry you upstairs."

She had half a mind to let him do it.

"But I know that the absolute last thing you need or want is a man in your life."

Annie's face burned as he tossed her words right back at her. Worse, she could hear the amusement in his voice, which could only mean he hadn't lost one ounce of control while kissing her and somehow she was going to have to save face.

"Thank you, Wes," she said evenly.

"Thank you?"

"For proving to me that I was right about us," she said, trying to sound sorrowful even as her heart felt as though it were beating in each ear. "Please try not to take it personally, you're a fine kisser and all, but there's just no chemistry."

"At least you gave it a chance."

She stood on legs that felt like overcooked noodles. "We can be friends."

He nodded. "Yeah, we still have that."

She turned and started for the door.

And ran right smack into a wicker rocker, stubbing her big toe. Damn! She lost her balance, fell over the arm, and her face hit the seat. Shit!

Wes was at her side in an instant, pulling her up. "Are you okay? Did you hurt yourself?"

Annie bit back the loud yowl and four-letter words that threatened to spew from her mouth as pain roiled in her toe, shot through her foot, and shimmied up her calf. Tears burned her eyes. "I'm fine," she said, managing a small chuckle. "I always bump into that chair."

"You might want to move it," he said.

Damned if he didn't sound like he was

having a good time. What she really wanted to do was chew the effin' chair into a million pieces and spit it into an open sewer.

"Do you need help getting upstairs?"

Her toe throbbed inside her bedroom slipper. It would be just her luck to have broken the damn thing. She'd probably smushed it to smithereens. "No, no," she said, forcing herself to walk on it and not hobble to the door. Only later, when the surgeon was forced to amputate, would she admit to Wes that it had been a painful experience.

He opened the door for her and she stepped inside. "Good night," she said.

"Sweet dreams, Annie."

She thought she heard him laugh softly as he closed the door behind her.

Theenie was the first to join Annie in the kitchen the next morning. "Boy, don't you look nice," she said, pausing at the sight of Annie in her newest jeans and a starched pale pink oxford shirt. "And you're wearing makeup."

"I always wear makeup," Annie said, trying to sound perky despite having slept very little during the night. She had finally climbed from the bed in the wee morning hours and dragged her throbbing toe to the bathroom, where she'd found a nighttime

135

pain reliever that had allowed her to get a couple of hours' sleep before the alarm clock blared her awake at 5:00 AM. She was still fighting grogginess and a hurting toe, but she was determined to keep it to herself. She checked the oven, where she had already put in an egg, sausage, and cheese casserole.

"You don't do your eyes up like that except on special occasions," Theenie said. "Like when you and Danny go to a show in Charleston."

Annie entertained the thought of grabbing the sponge from the sink and stuffing it into Theenie's mouth. "It's no big deal, okay?" The casserole was beginning to bubble around the edges. Annie slid in a pan of homemade biscuits before reclaiming her chair at the kitchen table, where she'd begun making up her to-do list for the day.

Theenie joined her a moment later, coffee cup in hand. "I thought I'd never fall asleep last night," she said, batting a dainty hand against her mouth as she yawned. "Peaches kept me awake walking up and down the hall making those weird sounds in her throat that she does when she's not happy."

"Gee, I don't recall Peaches ever being happy," Annie said. As if acting on cue, the cat plopped from her chair, walked over to her now-empty food dish, and stared into it. She nudged it with her nose several times and then paused long enough as though waiting for Annie to get up and put more food in it. When Annie didn't make a move to do so, Peaches raised one paw and whacked the dish. As usual, it skidded across the kitchen floor.

"Did you remember to feed Peaches?" Theenie asked.

Annie looked amused. "Does it look like she has ever missed a meal?"

"As I was saying," Theenie began, "after about two hours of listening to Peaches growl like she sometimes does, I finally got up and carried her to your room, which was no easy task, mind you, considering how much she weighs, but I was hoping you could get her to calm down. Only you weren't in your bed. I got worried."

Annie pretended to be very interested in making her list. "That must've been when I stepped outside for some fresh air," she said in an offhand manner.

"Yes, I saw you," Theenie said.

With pen poised in midair, Annie held her breath and waited.

"With Wes."

Peaches walked over to the cabinet door.

Bam, bam, bam.

"Kissing," Theenie said.

Annie looked at her. "You were *spying* on us?" Like they said, the best defense was a good offense.

Theenie sniffed as though she had just been insulted. "Of course not. I simply pulled the curtain aside to see if you were on the piazza, and there the two of you were, plastered together like Velcro. I don't mind telling you I was shocked." She gave another sniff.

Bam, bam, bam.

"Good morning," Lovelle said from the bottom of the stairs.

Annie jumped. She hadn't heard the woman come down. "Oh, you startled me."

"Everybody in this house is as nervous as a long-tailed cat in a room full of rocking chairs," Lovelle said. "Theenie, you don't look happy. What's wrong?"

"Oh, nothing," she said in a voice that suggested otherwise.

"That's good," Lovelle said, going to the coffeepot.

"Except I didn't get a wink of sleep last night," Theenie said.

Lovelle glanced at her. "That's too bad."

"I'm just too old to have to lie in bed and worry."

Lovelle carried her cup to the table and sat down. "Why were you worried?"

"No reason."

Lovelle turned to Annie. "I see you're already making your list."

"It's not like I don't have enough on my mind, what with Destiny talking about a spirit and Doc's gardener finding human remains in the backyard. Not to mention Annie renting a room to some biker stud who —"

"Oh, for Pete's sake!" Annie said, tossing her pen aside. She looked at Lovelle. "Theenie saw Wes and me kissing last night."

Lovelle looked pleased. "Oh, yummy, is he a good kisser? He looks like he knows a few things."

Destiny came downstairs in a flowing satin flamingo pink bathrobe and matching slippers. "Good morning," she mumbled, staggering toward the coffeepot.

"You sound tired, dear," Theenie said.

Destiny filled a cup and joined them. "Yeah, well, it's hard to rest when you've got a ghost hanging around you twenty-four/seven."

Theenie nodded sympathetically. "If it makes you feel any better, almost nobody slept well last night."

"Theenie saw Wes kissing Annie on the piazza last night," Lovelle said.

Destiny shrugged. "I'm not surprised. I saw a hot romance in Annie's future when I read her palm." She looked at Annie. "Is he as good in bed as I told you he'd be?"

Theenie's mouth fell open. "You went to bed with him?" she asked Annie.

Annie felt her face burn clear to the tips of her ears. "Of course not!"

"What are you waiting for?" Lovelle said. "I can tell by the way he looks at you that he's hot for you."

"He looks at her like she's naked," Theenie said, rolling her eyes. "I knew Annie shouldn't have rented to him."

"I'll tell you what he's thinking," Lovelle said. "He's thinking he'd like to dunk his doughnut you-know-where."

"I shouldn't be hearing this," Theenie said, stuffing her fingers in her ears.

"It would do you good to get laid," Destiny said, giving Annie a hearty wink.

"La la la la la —," Theenie began loudly.

Annie was relieved when the telephone rang. She answered before it could ring a second time.

The woman on the other end of the line wasted no time. Annie just listened. "I see," she said after a moment. "Of course I understand. Please call me in the future if I can be of service." She hung up, slipped her hands into an oven mitt, and pulled out the casserole and biscuits.

Theenie pulled her fingers from her ears and looked at Annie. "I can tell by the look on your face that you just got bad news."

Annie began putting the biscuits in a cloth-lined basket. "The baby shower is off."

"That's not fair!" Lovelle said. "How can people be so rude? You've lived in this town practically half of your life. I can't believe *anyone* would think you killed your husband."

"It'll pass," Annie said, hoping she was right.

Someone tapped on the back door. Annie unlocked it and found Danny on the other side. He tousled her hair as he entered the kitchen. "Good morning, ladies." He glanced around the table at the serious faces. "Or is it?"

"It's a wonderful morning," Annie said. "The coffee is hot, and I just pulled breakfast from the oven." She poured Danny a cup of coffee, and he carried it to the table. As though following Annie's lead, all three women gave him a bright smile.

"I'll set the table," Destiny said, and went for dishes and flatware while Theenie and

Lovelle continued to smile in such a way that one would have thought they'd just been handed a gift certificate to the local Family Dollar Store.

Danny smiled back and took a sip of his coffee.

"When will you be finished staining the ballroom floor?" Lovelle asked. "I need to get back to my exercise routine."

"I plan to put a couple of coats of polyurethane on top of the stain," Danny told her. "It'll be a few more days."

Annie glanced his way. "I took a peek at the floors last night. They're gorgeous."

Erdle came through the back door looking haggard. He sat at his usual place. Danny passed him the basket of biscuits. Erdle took one and bit into it.

"What time did *you* get in last night?" Theenie asked.

"I wasn't keeping track," he said.

Lovelle sniffed. "You smell like a beer can."

"It's my new aftershave."

"Aftershave, my foot," Lovelle said.

Wes came downstairs. Everybody but Erdle looked up. "Mornin'," Wes said. He glanced at Annie, and their gazes locked. "How are you?"

"Great. You?"

"Same."

"Coffee?"

He nodded. "I can get it."

"No, I'll do it."

They both reached for the cabinet door at the same time, but Annie was quicker. The door swung open and banged Wes's head. He winced and stepped back.

"I'm so sorry," Annie said. "Are you okay?"

"I'll know when my vision clears."

Annie carefully reached inside the cabinet for a mug, filled it with coffee, and offered it to him.

Their fingers brushed.

Annie felt something quicken in her stomach and let go.

Just missing her big toe, the cup fell to the floor. It shattered and splashed coffee on the floor and cabinet doors. "Oh, look what I've done!" Annie said.

"Did you burn yourself?" Danny asked as Wes and Annie began picking up the broken pieces.

She shook her head, too embarrassed to look up. Theenie and Lovelle got up and hurried to the broom closet.

"She didn't get much sleep last night," Destiny said.

"Oh yeah?"

"It's a long story," Annie said.

Theenie and Lovelle stepped up with the broom and mop. "Annie, sit down before somebody gets hurt," Theenie said. "You, too, Wes," she added. "I'll get your coffee."

Annie and Wes did as they were told.

A door slammed upstairs. "That crazy woman is at it again," Destiny muttered. "I'd kill her if she weren't already dead."

"Like we don't have enough problems," Lovelle said, sweeping the last of the glass into a dustpan as Theenie followed with the mop. "Dead body in the backyard, dead person roaming the house, it's no wonder everybody is canceling."

"You've had more cancelations?" Danny asked Annie.

She shrugged. "No big deal. It's not like I don't have enough to do what with planning a wedding."

Something shattered overhead, making everyone jump. "Dammit!" Destiny said, bolting from the table. "She's breaking my stuff." She raced upstairs.

Erdle looked at Wes. "This is why I drink."

Wes propped his elbows on the table and said nothing. Theenie brought him a cup of coffee, and he thanked her.

"I know this is going to sound crazy," Danny said to Annie, "and I can't believe

I'm even suggesting it, but if you *really* suspect there is some kind of entity in this house, you might consider calling a priest."

"We're waiting to see if Destiny can lead her to the light," Lovelle told him. "In the meantime, be careful or she'll steal your underwear."

Danny nodded as though it made complete sense. "I'll be sure to keep them on at all times."

"That's advice we should all follow," Theenie said, tossing a look from Wes to Annie.

Erdle got up from his place, carried his plate to the sink, and rinsed it out. He placed it in the dishwasher and started for the door.

"Where do you think you're going?" Annie said. "I've got a whole list of chores for you."

Erdle sighed and reclaimed his seat.

The doorbell rang. Theenie started from the room. "Don't answer it," Annie said. "It might be another reporter."

Theenie squared her shoulders and grabbed a meat mallet from the drawer. "I'll make him sorry he ever set foot in the yard."

Wes and Danny watched with interest while Erdle rested his head on the table.

Lovelle smiled. "I'm so glad Theenie is

beginning to show assertiveness."

"I just wish Doc hadn't left town," Annie said, "in case she hurts somebody."

Peaches, who'd been quiet for a while, returned to the cabinet. *Bam, bam, bam.*

Annie sighed.

Bam, bam, bam.

Annie shook her head. "I don't know which is worse, having to deal with a cantankerous cat who hates me or having to spend every spare dime I have on the upkeep of a tacky whorehouse."

"Now, Annie, you know you don't mean that," Theenie said from just inside the doorway. Max and Jamie stood beside her.

A door slammed upstairs. "Stop throwing my stuff!" Destiny shouted.

Bam, bam, bam.

"Good morning," Annie said to Max and Jamie without missing a beat. She gave them a big smile. "And good morning to you, handsome," she told Fleas. She'd barely gotten the words out of her mouth before she heard a hiss and a snarl, and a streak of orange fur flew past her. Fleas yelped and took off, and a second later there was a loud crash from the living room.

"Uh-oh," Jamie said, and turned.

"Don't worry," Annie said calmly. "Theenie, would you please make sure Fleas is okay and put Peaches out?"

"Of course, dear. Here, you can have the mallet back."

"Jamie, you and Max sit down," Annie insisted, "and I'll pour you a cup of coffee."

Max grinned. "I sort of get the feeling we dropped by at a bad time."

"We can't stay," Jamie said quickly. "Destiny called and asked if we would drop off her mail again. She sounded awful. Is she sick?"

"She's just tired."

"Annie, you don't look so well yourself," Jamie said. "Are you okay?"

Annie glanced around the room and saw what looked like pity on her friends' faces, and she crossed her arms.

"Okay, everybody listen up," she said, giving them a stern look. "I know things look bad right now, but I've been through tougher times than this." She paused. "Okay, except for my husband being buried in the backyard."

"And the part about you being the murder suspect and all," Lovelle reminded, "which is destroying your business."

Annie wished Lovelle hadn't brought that up. "Yes," she said calmly. "But once my name is cleared everything will be back to normal. The point I'm trying to make —"

"Boy, this cat weighs a ton," Theenie interrupted, coming through the doorway with Peaches in her arms. Wes and Danny both hurried over to help her; Danny took the cat and Wes opened the door for him. "Fleas is okay," Theenie said, "but Peaches jumped on the end table in the living room and broke that statue. You know, the one that looks like a man and woman are *doing it?*" She was breathing heavily, obviously from exertion. "I never liked that statue, and I don't know why anyone would have it sitting around, but then I keep forgetting a bunch of floozies used to live here. Oh, look, Peaches scratched me."

"That cat has lost her mind," Lovelle said as more racket sounded from the second floor, "and all because we have some spirit running amok in this house."

"As I was saying," Annie began, "I expect things to calm down very soon. Certainly before the wedding," she added quickly, looking at Jamie and Max. "But in the meantime, I would appreciate it if you guys would stop with those woe-is-Annie looks, because that's going to piss me off. You really don't want to piss me off right now."

Erdle raised his head and looked around the room. "She's right. You don't want to piss her off on account of she's mean and dangerous. If you don't believe it, just ask *me,* 'cause I know firsthand."

"Erdle, do you mind?" Annie said.

He nodded and slumped over the table once more.

Wes grinned. "Well, if it's any consolation, I don't feel a damn bit sorry for you, Annie. But that doesn't mean some of us can't help. I've got a couple of friends who work for the police force in Columbia. They'll be able to advise me on what we should do, since it doesn't look like Lamar is up to the challenge."

"I'm pretty good at digging up information, if you need it," Max said.

Danny nodded. "And I can start taking Lamar fishing. If I keep him busy he won't have much time to screw up the case."

"I know what I can do," Jamie said. "I can write a huge story about this place. I'll get Vera to take a lot of pictures. Annie will have more business than she can handle."

"Lovelle and I will do whatever Annie needs us to do," Theenie said. "Right, Lovelle?"

Lovelle suddenly looked excited. "Oh, and if Annie needs money I can give a recital in the ballroom. We'll charge fifty dollars a pop."

Erdle lifted his head once more, looked around. "I'll give up drinking."

Chapter Six

"I hate going into this attic," Annie told Wes that evening. "It always gives me a bad case of the heebie-jeebies. I've seen a couple of bats up here." She shuddered.

He followed her up a short landing that led from the third floor to the fourth-floor attic, the only room on that floor. "I'll bet this is where Destiny's spirit spends most of her time."

Annie gulped and missed the next step. She teetered, but Wes immediately reached out and prevented her from toppling and knocking him down the stairs as well. Instead of releasing her once she'd regained her footing, he slipped his arms around her waist and pulled her against him.

Annie was very conscious of her hips pressing into his hard body. "Um, Wes?"

He nuzzled the back of her neck. "Yeah?"

Annie closed her eyes as his lips caressed her nape. Her skin prickled, and tiny shivers ran down her spine. Oh boy, she thought. The man only had to touch her, and her body went ape-shit.

"Excuse me," she said, using the same tone Theenie used when she took Erdle to task over his drinking. Wes kissed his way to one ear and nipped Annie's earlobe gently with his teeth, and she forgot what she had been about to say. Her bones started to melt.

"I want to make love to you," he said.

Instant adrenaline rush, followed by flash of heat low in her belly, followed by shaky noodle legs. Not a good sign.

Wes turned her around, looked into her eyes. "What d'you think?"

"Um." Annie gave herself a mental shake to clear her head. "We should probably think about it carefully. We don't want to rush into anything."

"We don't?"

"Definitely not. I have it on good authority that men and women who fall into bed out of simple lust only end up feeling empty or disappointed because despite meeting their sexual needs, lust does not address emotional needs. They often experience guilt, resentment, and low self-esteem. Even worse, they are at higher risk for sexually transmitted diseases. If you watched Oprah or read 'Dear Abby' you'd know that."

Wes just looked at her. "You're serious?"

"Absolutely. They offer sound advice on just about every subject, ranging from office affairs, ending relationships gracefully, to tips for getting along better with your mother-in-law and the drawbacks of body piercing, to name just a few." Annie paused to draw in breath.

Wes looked confused. Finally, he released her. "So do you want me to go into the attic first?"

"Yes, please. And check for bats."

He opened the attic door, found the light switch, and flipped it on. He stepped inside. Annie waited just outside.

"Wow, there's a lot of stuff in here," Wes said.

"Do you see anything flying around?"

"Nope. Don't worry; I won't let anything get you."

Annie peered inside the open doorway. When she didn't see any ugly black objects darting about, she stepped inside but remained close to her point of exit. "I sorted through a ton of boxes after my grandmother died, and I donated a lot of items to the women's shelter. But that was before the bat flew at my hair. I almost killed myself trying to get out of here."

Wes lifted several sheets and peeked beneath them. "You've got a lot of cool antiques."

"My grandmother refused to part with anything that was handed down through the family. No telling how long they've been up here."

Wes motioned toward several tall file cabinets along one wall. "Is that where you keep your income tax records?"

Annie nodded. "Third cabinet, top drawer," she said. "They're filed by year and marked as backup copies." She remained where she was as Wes crossed the room, opened the file drawer, and pulled out what he needed.

"I'm assuming you and Charles filed jointly?" he said.

"Yeah." She told him what years to look for.

Annie was relieved to leave the attic behind. Returning to the kitchen, Wes set the files on the kitchen table and began flipping through one of them.

"What are you looking for?" Annie asked.

"Charles's Social Security number, credit card receipts, cell phone bills, and anything else that might be helpful."

"He charged all his business expenses on American Express."

Wes found an envelope marked: *Business Receipts*. He opened it, thumbed through them, and pulled one out. "Where is the Hilltop Steakhouse?" he asked.

"It's in Mosely, about twenty-five miles from here, on the way to Charleston."

"The two of you went often?"

"I've never been."

"Obviously he took somebody, because there are eight or ten receipts and the bills are pretty steep."

"Those were probably the nights I stayed home and ate tuna fish sandwiches."

Wes glanced up at her. "He traveled?"

Annie nodded. "His boss, Norm Schaefer, owns several real estate franchises in and out of state, so they often took turns attending monthly sales meetings, and Charles enjoyed going to various seminars, mostly geared toward sales or real estate. And there were golf tournaments and fishing trips with customers. Mostly out of town, of course," she added flatly.

Wes checked his watch and closed the folder. "There's a lot to go through here," he said, "and it's getting late. Why don't we call it a night and I'll look through the files first thing in the morning? In the meantime, I'll keep this in my room, away from the others."

Annie knew Wes would probably spend most of the night studying the files, but he was trying to spare her feelings. "Just so you know, I've gotten over Charles's indiscretions. You don't have to keep secrets from me."

"Good." He smiled. "Tell you what, Red. I'm going to need the latest picture you have of him."

" 'Red'?"

"It seems fitting."

Annie hurried into the formal living room and opened a cabinet along one wall. She pulled out a photo album and flipped through the pages, quickly bypassing her wedding pictures. She found a couple of photos of Charles taken only a few months before his disappearance. She felt a dull sensation in her stomach as she studied them. Finally, she carried them into the kitchen and handed them to Wes.

He gave them a cursory glance. "Not a bad-looking fellow."

Annie shrugged. "I guess I wasn't the only woman in town who thought so." But she didn't want to think about Charles. Her big toe was hurting, and she needed to get off her foot. "I suppose I should get to bed."

"I'll follow you up."

Wes carried the files upstairs. He reached

his room before she did hers. "You might want to have a doctor look at that toe if it doesn't feel better in the morning," he said once she'd arrived at her bedroom door and opened it. She frowned, wondering how he knew the toe was giving her problems when she'd been so careful to hide it.

But she had a feeling Wes Bridges knew or suspected more about her than he was letting on, and that worried her.

It was not yet 6:00 AM when Annie finished frying bacon and stirring blueberries into a large bowl of batter for waffles that she planned to serve for breakfast once her guests began waking. This was her favorite part of the day, the house so quiet she could hear the leaves on the live oaks rustling in the breeze just outside the window over her sink. She had added an extra place setting in case Danny arrived early, and she'd filled a carafe with coffee and put on a fresh pot. She poured a second cup, grabbed her notepad, and carried them to the table, where she started her daily list.

Max and Jamie's rehearsal dinner was only a few days away, and the wedding was drawing nearer. So many things to do in the meantime, she thought, even though she, with the help of Theenie and Lovelle, had managed to tackle several major cleaning projects after the Christmas and New Year's guests had gone and all the decorations had come down. The marbled entryway and pillars had been cleaned, as had what seemed miles of solid mahogany baseboards, elaborate trim, wainscoting, and floor-to-ceiling panels in the study. The porcelain tubs and sinks in all six bathrooms sparkled, and Annie had spent a solid week on her knees scrubbing the tiled floors and walls, oftentimes using old toothbrushes to get the grout clean as well.

Perhaps if she concentrated on what remained to be done she wouldn't spend so much time worrying. Not that worrying had ever solved a thing, her grandmother had told her many times after Annie had moved in and found herself tackling the expenditures and upkeep of the mansion. She wished her grandmother had worried more and spent less money so that Annie hadn't been forced to pinch every dime and nickel of her inheritance to renovate the spacious eight-bedroom mansion and prevent it from falling into total disrepair. Not only had the woman lost a bundle in the stock market; she'd also donated money to every imaginable cause.

Annie's mother, Jenna, who'd married

money and profited greatly when she'd divorced Annie's father, Gunther Worthington III, had little to do with her own mother and wasn't concerned about expenditures, since the woman had always lived frugally when Jenna was growing up. However, when Jenna discovered, after her mother's death, that the family fortune had dwindled to almost nothing, she had been furious.

"So much for your inheritance," she'd told Annie. "I should have my head examined for not taking that *woman*" — as she often referred to her mother — "to court and having her declared incompetent. Not to mention that old geezer who managed her finances. All you have now is a tacky broken-down whorehouse."

There were times Annie wondered what her grandmother had been thinking when she'd made Annie promise not to sell the house, and times Annie wondered what *she* had been thinking when she'd agreed.

Annie glanced up at the sound of boots on the stairs. Wes was dressed in his usual faded jeans and a blue work shirt that emphasized his tan complexion. He paused and glanced around. "Where is everybody?"

"Sleeping. Theenie's light was still on when I got up during the night to see to

Peaches. Theenie sometimes sits up late reading."

"How long have you been up?"

"Since five. I like getting up early so I can spend a few minutes by myself before putting breakfast on. The house is so quiet and peaceful this time of day."

Annie wondered if he had any idea how good he looked in the morning, fresh from his shower. Not that he looked bad in the afternoon and evening as well, she thought. The man was too damn handsome for his own good. "How about a cup of coffee?" She started to get up.

"Sit," he ordered. "I can get it myself." He crossed the kitchen, opened the cabinet, and reached for a coffee mug. He filled it and joined Annie at the kitchen table. "I see you're planning your day," he said, noting her list. "You forgot one thing."

Annie glanced down. "I did?"

"You haven't scheduled any time for R and R. When's the last time you went dancing or enjoyed a nice meal in a restaurant, where it wasn't up to you to clean up afterward?"

"I don't remember."

"Your problem is you spend too much time closed up in this house."

"You're saying I'm boring."

He looked thoughtful as he reached over and stroked her cheek. "You are the least boring person I've ever met. You've surrounded yourself with people who love you, and you obviously enjoy what you do." He pulled his hand away and reached for his mug.

"But?"

"I don't see you taking much time out for yourself. You're always looking after other people. I guess my question is: who takes care of Annie?"

"It works both ways. These people are the closest thing I've ever had to a real family. Not that my grandmother didn't love me dearly," she added quickly, "but I was more like her caretaker."

"What about your parents?"

She smiled. "They are very nice people, but they had no idea what to do with a child. My mother much prefers me as a grown woman who will lunch and shop with her when I visit, sip expensive wine by the pool, and make sympathetic noises while she regales me with horror stories of growing up in this house. That way she doesn't have to feel guilty for staying away all those years."

"Do you see her often?"

"No, she hates this place, and it's hard for

me to visit her in Atlanta with my business and all, but we usually talk on the phone once a week. Only right now she's spending a month with friends in West Palm Beach. Our lifestyles are vastly different."

"Does she know about the recent discovery in your backyard?"

Annie shook her head. "I'll tell her about it when it's all over. No sense worrying her."

"What about your father?"

Annie chuckled. "Like I said, a very nice person who *still* has no idea what to do with a child, especially a grown daughter. He lives in the south of France, sends nice checks for birthdays and Christmas, which I use to make ongoing repairs to this house."

"Brothers and sisters?"

"Nope. You?"

"There are seven of us, three girls and four boys."

"Holy cow!"

"I'm the middle child, who, according to statistics, gets the shaft. Somebody obviously didn't inform my family of that fact, because I pretty much had it okay." He picked up his and Annie's coffee cups, refilled them, and carried them to the table.

A noise from the stairs caused them both to look up. Destiny nodded a weary "good morning" as she cleared the last step and paused, giving a huge yawn and blinking several times as though she was trying to make herself fully awake. "Coffee," she said, stumbling toward the pot.

Annie noted the tired look on her face. "Another sleepless night?"

Destiny nodded. "Dead people don't sleep. I need to check on my apartment, see when I can return." She sank into a chair across from Wes. "Not that it matters. Once a spirit person latches on to me they usually follow me everywhere. Until I convince them to go to the light," she added. She glanced at Wes. "You don't believe a damn word I'm saying. You think I'm crazy."

He shrugged. "I've noticed a few oddities around here that don't seem to have a valid explanation."

"Now you know."

"I wish there was something I could do to help," Annie said.

"Do you believe in spirits?" Wes asked her.

She hesitated. "Okay, I'm going to tell both of you something I've never told anyone, only you'll have to keep quiet about it because I don't want to frighten the others." She spoke quietly. "My grandmother used to talk to herself. At least I thought she was talking to herself, but when I finally asked her about it, she told me there was a woman, a ghost, trying to communicate with her." Annie paused and looked at Destiny. "You were right. There were many times I felt a presence. Some of my guests have reported seeing things, some sort of apparition, and sometimes I would see something out of the corner of my eye."

"I don't know why you're trying to hide it from Theenie and Lovelle. They've suspected for some time. As for your fears that it might hurt your business, I think it could draw people. Do you have this place listed on a Web site?"

Annie shook her head.

"Lucky for you I know someone who might be able to design one for you," Destiny said. "You've met Jamie's editor, Mike Henderson."

She nodded. "What does he charge?"

"He worships me; he'll do it for free. But you have to be willing to give *all* the facts about the house, because that's what is going to draw people."

Annie wondered how much Destiny knew.

"You mean the part about it being a brothel at one time?" Wes asked.

"How did you find out?" Annie asked. "Not that it's a secret. Most people know the history."

Wes avoided a direct answer, but he

grinned. "The house pretty much speaks for itself, Annie."

She nodded. "Supposedly it closely resembles the way it looked back in the eighteen fifties. My grandmother had an old photo album of pictures taken after it was built, but I haven't seen it in years. I suspect it's somewhere in the attic." She gave an eye roll.

"This spirit was one of the women who lived here when it was a bordello," Destiny said. "Unfortunately, I can't get any information from her because she's mute."

Wes cocked a brow, and Destiny went on. "In most cases, spirits who hang around long after they've died have suffered a tragic death. Most of them are still in shock; sometimes they don't even know they're dead. In the case of this particular spirit, she was strangled to death. She has the marks on her neck."

It was the first time Annie had heard about the marks, and she shuddered. "You're right," she said. "If you read the history of this house you'll learn that her name was Lacey and she *was* a prostitute. She was murdered by her lover, who was promptly hanged."

Destiny pondered it. "I think she may have witnessed the hanging," she said. "That, combined with her murder, may have traumatized her so badly that she can't speak. Or," she added, "her vocal cords may have been severely damaged in the strangulation."

Wes shook his head. "This all seems pretty far-fetched. Why are you able to see the spirit so clearly and the rest of us can't?"

"Because I'm psychic and more open to this sort of thing," Destiny said. "She wants to communicate with me, but she can't, which leaves her frustrated and angry. Which is why she sometimes throws things, mostly my stuff," she added, "and that, combined with almost no sleep, pisses *me* off. I'm usually more patient with spirits.

"Anyway, I recently began having visions of what it was like back then. I see women dressed in corsets and gartered black stockings and wearing heavy rouge; I see well-dressed gentlemen following them upstairs." She suddenly sneezed. "Only the wealthy could afford to visit. Does the name Fairchild mean anything to you?" she asked Annie.

"Oh yeah. The Fairchild family settled here before the Revolutionary War. They were wealthy and highly respected. Some became politicians. There are still a few descendants living here, but most of them moved to Charleston."

"For some reason I keep seeing that name in my mind." Destiny shrugged. "By the way, the house *does* look much the same as it did back then." Another sneeze. Annie went for the box of tissues. "Except for the kitchen and some of the furniture," Destiny added, yanking a couple of tissues from the box.

Wes looked intrigued by what Destiny had to say, but it was difficult to tell how much, if any, of it he believed. "How often do you have these, um, visions?"

"I can't predict them," Destiny said. "Sometimes they're very clear; other times they're vague and I spend hours trying to decide their meanings." Destiny sipped her coffee in silence for a moment. "Having this spirit around could work to your advantage," she told Annie.

"How?"

"Spirits are not limited by time or space. I'm willing to bet Lacey knows who murdered your husband. She probably saw the whole thing."

Annie gaped.

"Which is why I wish she would communicate with me," Destiny went on. "I probably shouldn't have yelled at her for getting into my stuff. I'll probably have to start sucking up to her if I hope to get her to cooperate. I hate sucking up to dead people."

Annie laughed. "Could you imagine me marching into Lamar Tevis's office and telling him some ghost had solved the murder?"

Destiny shook her head. "No, but if this spirit could tell us who the killer is we might be able to point Lamar in the right direction."

Annie heard a noise at the top of the stairs. "We need to drop the subject for now. I don't want the others to know." She barely had time to get the words out of her mouth before Lovelle came down, dressed in gray slacks, a silk dove gray blouse, and a cream-colored cashmere sweater.

"Good morning, ladies," she said brightly.

"Boy, you look nice," Annie told her. "What's the occasion?"

Lovelle patted her hair. "I'm having breakfast with a friend, and then we're driving to Savannah for an art show."

Annie smiled. Although Savannah was only forty-five minutes away, she could not remember when she'd last been. "Sounds fun."

Lovelle draped her sweater over one chair. "I wish I could find my fuchsia scarf. I always wear it with this outfit."

Destiny looked up. "It's in my room. I meant to bring it down and ask who it belonged to."

"Well, how in heaven's name did it get there?" Lovelle said.

Destiny shrugged. "Probably the same way my lingerie ended up in Wes's bathroom."

"Hey, you didn't hear me complaining," Wes said. "I like having women's lingerie hanging over my shower rod. I have a thing for lacy black garter belts."

All three women looked amused. "Let me grab that scarf," Destiny said.

Lovelle looked at Annie. "This is getting out of hand. Every time I turn around I'm missing something. Yesterday Theenie accused me of taking her favorite nightgown. You've seen it, that flannel thing she wears with blue dogs and pink kittens. As if I'd be caught dead in old lady flannel," she added.

Someone knocked on the door. Annie answered it and found Lamar Tevis on the other side. "Good morning, Annie," he said. "Sorry to stop by so early, but I thought we might talk a bit." He glanced about the room. "Preferably in private."

"Is something wrong?" she asked.

"No, no. I, um . . ." He paused and cleared his throat. "I need to discuss a few things

169

with regard to your husband's, um, remains."

Wes got up from his chair. "I'd like to listen in if you don't mind."

Annie led Wes and Lamar into a large sunroom that had once served as a sleeping porch. Windows lined the room and had offered relief during hot summer months before fans and air conditioners were invented. Wes and Annie took a seat on one of several sofas; Lamar chose a chair opposite them.

Lamar pulled his small notebook from his shirt pocket and thumbed through several pages. He wore a sad smile as he regarded Annie. "I don't suppose this will come as a surprise to you," he told her, "but all the evidence we found on or near the remains that were discovered on your property proves without a doubt that they are those of your husband." He paused as though waiting for her to take it all in. "I'm sorry, Annie."

Wes reached for her hand. "You okay?"

"Yes." But she wasn't. Not really. She felt a deep sadness that the man she'd been married to had lost his life at such an early age.

"What was the cause of death?" she asked.

Lamar hesitated. "I'll get to that in a

170

minute, but first let me tell you what we *do* know. The coroner faxed his findings to me; in laymen's terms, your husband suffered a broken neck and head trauma."

Annie realized she was holding her breath. "Did he suffer?"

"I suppose he could have been unconscious at the time, but the head injury didn't penetrate the skull, so there's no reason to suspect that's what killed him."

"So he died from a broken neck," she said.

Lamar wiped his hands down his face. "We don't really know at this time."

"You *don't know?*" she asked.

"The coroner claims the vertebra was still intact, so it's highly unlikely there was damage to the spinal cord or any kind of obstruction that would have interfered with normal breathing. I know we don't have all the answers, but I'm pretty impressed with what the coroner *was* able to come up with, seeing as how he's not one of those experts. I can't think of what they're called at the moment; it'll come to me."

"Forensic anthropologists," Wes said.

Annie looked perplexed. "Why wasn't Charles taken to the Medical University in Charleston, where their methods are more advanced? I thought that was the normal procedure for suspicious deaths."

"That's true," Lamar said, shifting uncomfortably in his chair, "but our coroner insisted on taking a look, since we don't get many cases like this. Some of our law enforcement people stood in on the exam, so it was a learning experience for them."

Once again, Wes and Annie exchanged glances. She frowned. "You're saying my husband's remains were not immediately sent to Charleston because the local coroner decided to use them for teaching purposes?" She didn't give Lamar a chance to respond. "Good grief, Lamar, the man isn't even a bona fide medical examiner. Did you not consider Charles's family or how anxious we might be to find out what happened to him?"

Lamar shifted uncomfortably in his chair and stared at the floor. "Annie, I'm sorry to say it gets worse." He shook his head sadly, and it was obvious he did not want to tell her.

"Why don't we stop beating around the bush here and get to the point?" Wes suggested to the man.

Lamar continued staring at the floor. "Annie, I regret to have to tell you we've, uh, lost your husband's remains."

CHAPTER SEVEN

Annie sat there for a moment, unsure she'd heard Lamar correctly or even understood what he'd just said. "Would you run that by me again?" she said.

"An employee from the morgue left for the Medical University in Charleston last night with the remains, and, well, to make a long story short, the vehicle was carjacked."

"What?" she shrieked.

"You're not serious," Wes said. "How could something like that have happened?"

"A passing motorist found the driver unconscious on the side of the highway. He'd been robbed and hit over the head. The van was gone."

Annie gave an enormous sigh. "Do you have any idea what this is going to do to Charles's mother?"

"I plan to go over there and break the news to her once I leave here. I know it's a lot to ask under the circumstances, but I was sort of hoping you'd go with me."

"Forget it," Annie said. "She blames me for Charles's disappearance and refuses to speak to me, especially after I told her he left me for another woman. I seriously doubt she'd even let me in the door."

"Do you know who he was seeing?"

Annie shook her head.

"Hold it, Lamar," Wes said. "I don't think this is a good time to question Annie, but if you insist, then I'm going to advise her not to answer without an attorney present."

"I am *not* afraid to answer questions," Annie said, "and the sooner we get it over with the better." She looked at Lamar. "What do you want to know?"

Lamar glanced from Wes to her. "Would you mind describing your relationship with your husband?"

"I was planning to file for a divorce, if that tells you anything."

"Did Charles know?"

"We hadn't discussed it, but I don't think he would have been surprised. Our marriage had been deteriorating for months because I refused to sell this house. Charles obviously thought I'd change my mind if someone offered enough money, so he began looking for a buyer behind my back. He found one willing to offer top dollar for it, but I refused to budge. The marriage pretty much went to hell after that. It wasn't long before I learned he was seeing somebody."

"How did you find out?"

Annie was not going to drag Danny into it. "I just knew."

"And you can't think of anyone it could have been? A friend or co-worker maybe?" Lamar added hopefully.

"Annie has already answered that question," Wes said. "I think she's been through enough for one day. Besides, you and your officers have a missing corpse to find."

As Lamar closed his notebook and stood, he avoided looking at Wes. "I'm sorry to have been the bearer of bad news, Annie, and I appreciate your answering my questions. I'll call the minute we find, uh, you know. I'll just see myself out."

Theenie entered the room a few minutes later with Danny right behind. "Is everything okay?"

Annie stood and forced a smile she didn't feel. "He just wanted to touch base with me, let me know how the investigation is going." She wasn't ready to discuss all she'd learned.

"Are you sure that's all it was?" Danny asked, his gaze going to Wes.

Annie was amazed that Danny could read her so well. "I wish you'd stop worrying," she said.

Danny slung one arm over Annie's shoulder as they walked toward the kitchen. "Good news. I plan to finish the floors today," he said. "But you know how I hate to work on an empty stomach, and I just happened to notice you were getting ready to make your famous blueberry waffles."

Wes arrived at Eve Fortenberry's house later that morning. She still wore her bathrobe, and her eyes were red and swollen. "I thought I'd stop by and see how you're doing," he said.

She shrugged and stepped back so he could enter. "I've been better," she said, "but that shouldn't come as a surprise." She motioned for him to sit as she sank into a lumpy chair. "Chief Tevis came by earlier."

"I figured he would." Wes paused. "You didn't mention our arrangement to him?"

"Of course not. I'm counting on you to do the job he's incapable of." She shook her head. "I have never seen such incompetence. How am I supposed to give my son a proper burial if there are no remains?" She reached for a cigarette. Her hands trembled so badly she could barely get it to her mouth to light it. "You can bet I told Lamar exactly what I thought of him." She shook her head and smoked in silence. Every once in a while she swiped at a tear. "I think I'm still in shock."

"Is there someone I can call to come stay with you?"

"No. I'm better off dealing with it in my own way." She looked at him. "Does Annie know?"

"Yeah. She was as mad as hell, but she insisted on answering any questions Lamar had, because she's as eager to get to the bottom of this as you are." It was clear Eve didn't believe him. "You know Annie has always been convinced Charles was seeing another woman."

Eve hitched her chin high. "If he was, then Annie has no one to blame but herself. She broke her word. She promised to get rid of that monstrosity of a house, and then changed her mind after Charles went to the trouble of finding a buyer."

"Are you sure that's the way it was?"

"Charles sat right there in that chair and told me the whole thing. I've never known him to lie to me."

"Annie claimed she never agreed to it," Wes said.

"And you believe her?"

"The only thing I know for certain is that Annie Fortenberry is incapable of murder."

The woman made a sound of disgust. "I should have known she'd get to you. Annie has a way with men. Believe me, I tried to warn Charles, but he wouldn't listen." She studied Wes. "You're falling for her."

"Eve, think for a minute. As much as you dislike Annie, she may be telling the truth about another woman being in the picture. What if it's true? What if that woman had something to do with your son's death? Wouldn't you want to know?"

"The only thing I know for sure is that you've lost your objectivity, which means you're not going to do me any good. But let me warn you, you're going to look foolish when Annie gets tired of you. The only thing she cares about is that house. It's all she has now that her grandmother is gone. Her own parents didn't want her."

Wes's eyes became flat and emotionless. "I only have one goal," he said after a moment, "and that is learning the truth."

Eve's grief turned to anger. "I don't need your services anymore. You're fired. You need to go back to Columbia where you belong."

Wes shook his head. "I'm not going anywhere. I intend to stay as long as it takes to find the real murderer." He stood, reached into his pocket, and handed her an envelope that had been carefully folded in half. "You'll find my note of resignation inside," he said, "as well as a full refund of everything you've paid me. I'm really sorry about your son."

He let himself out the door without another word.

Annie was throwing on her clothes when she heard Wes leave on his motorcycle the next morning. She had slept fitfully, tossing and turning, finally dozing off as dawn approached, only to awaken after 7:00 AM, two hours behind schedule. She was still buttoning her shirt as she hurried down the hall toward the stairs. She had the mother of all headaches, and she could feel the tension in her neck building, the muscles so tight they felt as though they'd snap.

Theenie was up and about when Annie rushed into the kitchen. The woman had already made a pan of homemade biscuits, scrambled a bowl of eggs, and was in the process of slicing the ham they'd had for dinner the night before.

"Goodness," Annie said. "You've already done everything."

"I figured you could use a little help, what

with all that's going on. Now, sit," Theenie ordered, pointing to Annie's usual chair. "I'll get your coffee. From the looks of it, you could use some."

Annie was only too happy to oblige. Theenie poured a cup and carried it to the table. "Lovelle and I had a talk last night," the woman said. "From now on we're going to start pitching in more."

"Don't be silly. You two do enough around here as it is. Besides, it's my job. That's why you pay rent."

"You have far too many duties for one person, and Lovelle and I know darn good and well you don't charge us near enough to live here."

The doorbell rang. "Who on earth could that be?" Annie said, checking the wall clock.

"It's probably Danny," Theenie said, wiping her hands on a dish towel. "He said he'd stop by on his way to another job to see how the floor looked. I don't know why he'd use the front door, though." When Annie made a move to get up, Theenie motioned for her to sit. "I'll get it," she said.

Annie kept her seat and sipped her coffee and wondered what she'd done with the tablet she made her daily to-do list on. She had started to get up when an anxious-looking Theenie walked into the kitchen with Lamar. Two officers followed. One was middle-aged and balding, the other one much younger. He wore a buzz cut and looked as though he was fresh out of police academy.

"Good morning, Lamar," Annie said, noting that Theenie was already gnawing her bottom lip. "I assume you're here to tell me you found what you were looking for." She was deliberately being vague since she hadn't told Theenie.

He blushed. "We're still working on it." He glanced at the toe of his shoe. "I'm here on official police business, Annie."

"Meaning?"

He raised his head. "I just came from the magistrate's house. I have a search warrant here," he said, handing her a sheet of paper. "Me and the boys need to check the premises."

Annie stared at the warrant in disbelief. "You're going to search my house? Why?"

"We're looking for anything that might help us in the investigation of your husband's murder."

"And you think you're going to find it *here?*"

"Excuse me," Theenie said, squaring her shoulders, "but this is beginning to sound like harassment to me, waltzing in here at seven-thirty in the morning."

"Just doing my job, Miss Theenie," he said.

"Eve Fortenberry is behind this, isn't she?" Annie said. "You're trying to pacify her because she flipped out when she learned you'd lost Charles's remains."

"What do you mean he lost Charles's remains?" Theenie asked in a bewildered tone. She looked at Lamar. "Did you forget where you put them?"

"I'd rather not go into it right now," Lamar said.

"You're wasting your time," Annie told him, "but feel free to search all you like."

"But don't you dare mess up Annie's house," Theenie said, looking from Lamar to the officers. "She works very hard to keep things nice and orderly around here."

"I'll need you to round up all your guests," Lamar said.

Annie frowned. "You mean wake them?"

He sighed. "I'm sorry, Annie. Please ask them to come down."

She gave him a hard look. "You're really desperate for leads, aren't you?"

Once again he looked away. "I'm as eager as you are to get this over with."

"I'll wake the others," Theenie said in a

huff as she hurried toward the stairs.

Lamar and his men were quiet as they waited. Annie ignored them and poured another cup of coffee. She found her tablet and sat down at the table, where she began making her list, but her hands shook so badly she could barely hold her pen, much less write.

Destiny was the first to enter the kitchen, shrugging on her bathrobe. Lovelle and Theenie were right behind her. "What the hell is the meaning of this?" Destiny demanded in a hostile voice. "Why would you even think of barging into Annie's place with a search warrant?"

"That's what I'd like to know," Lovelle said, also wearing a bathrobe. "What could you possibly hope to find?"

"I'll tell you what he's looking for," Destiny said. "He's trying to find anything he can so he can pin a murder rap on Annie because he has no other leads. Fat chance, Lamar."

"I would appreciate it if you ladies cooperate and remain in the kitchen while my men conduct the search," Lamar said, not bothering to address their questions.

"We'd like to start with your bedroom if you would just show us where it is real quick, Mrs. Fortenberry," the older officer said.

Annie shook her head but stood and led them to the stairs. After reaching the second floor, the officers paused at the open door to the bathroom and glanced inside. "My room is at the end of the hall," she said as they followed her.

"What's behind these doors?" the younger officer asked, nodding toward two closed doors that were on opposite sides of the hall.

"They're bedrooms," Annie answered, not bothering to stop. "Both are presently rented. This is where I sleep," she said once they'd reached her room. "Don't let the frills and ruffles fool you; it's also where I hide my murder weapons." The younger officer looked amused.

"This is the room you shared with your late husband?" the other one asked.

"No. I moved out of the master bedroom once he, um, disappeared."

"We'd like to have a look inside that room as well."

"I just told you it's rented. The tenant isn't here at the moment."

"We'll be careful not to disturb anything," he said. "You may return to the kitchen," he added politely.

Annie knew it was useless to argue, so she

did as she was told. She found Lamar sitting at the kitchen table, a cup of coffee in front of him. Destiny sat at the other end, glaring. Lovelle sipped her coffee quietly.

Theenie looked at Lamar. "When I lose things, which is often, I usually have to write down each place I went that day."

"I beg your pardon?" Lamar said.

"I was referring to Charles Fortenberry's remains."

Suddenly a door slammed upstairs. Peaches raced down the stairs, her fur standing up on her back. She jumped onto one of the empty chairs and curled into a tight ball.

"Who else is in the house?" Lamar asked.

"Nobody," Annie muttered.

"I clearly heard —"

"It's the spirit," Destiny snapped. "If you don't believe it, go look. You won't find anyone up there. Anyone who is alive," she added.

Lamar just looked at her as if unsure what to say or do. He took a sip of his coffee, eyeing Destiny over the rim of his cup.

An hour passed. Annie thrummed her fingers on the table. "How much longer is this going to take?" she said, clearly annoyed. "I have a lot to do."

"And I need to use the restroom," Theenie

said, getting up from the table. "I've held it as long as I can." She didn't wait for Lamar's okay before she left the room.

"This really sucks," Destiny told him. "I can't wait until you ask me for help on a case, because I'm going to have a few choice words waiting for you. And don't even *think* of asking me out again, because I'll slug you. And by the way, I hope that new fishing boat of yours sinks. I hope you accidentally shoot yourself in the foot with your gun. I hope —"

"I think I get your point," a red-faced Lamar answered. He looked at Annie. "May I have another cup of coffee?"

"Let him get it himself," Lovelle said.

More time passed, and Annie could feel her anger rising with each passing minute. "You're wasting our time," she said, "when you could be out looking for the real killer."

The older officer suddenly appeared in the doorway. "Chief, could you come back here?"

Lamar nodded and got up from his chair. "I'd appreciate it if you ladies kept your seats," he said.

Peaches jumped down from the chair and walked to her empty bowl. She butted it with her nose until it was right at Annie's feet. Annie ignored her, and the cat walked away.

"Oh no!" Theenie said after a moment. "Peaches is digging in your favorite plant. I don't know why she insists on doing it when she knows she isn't supposed to."

Annie stared at the cat. "She does it because she knows I don't like it." Annie was tempted to ignore Lamar's order to keep her seat so she could toss the cat outside. Instead, Annie just sat there as dirt flew to the floor. Peaches paused and looked at her, topaz eyes unblinking. Annie wondered why the cat chose to pick on her. She had taken exceptionally good care of the animal. There were times the cat seemed to almost like her, those times when Annie awakened in the morning to find Peaches curled in the bed beside her. But mostly Peaches was a big pain in the butt.

Theenie patted Annie's hand. "It'll all be over with shortly. Why don't we discuss the rehearsal dinner for tomorrow night? There's an awful lot to do between now and then."

"I'm not in the mood, Theenie."

Lamar returned a few minutes later wearing rubber gloves and carrying several plastic bags. He held one up so Annie could get a close look. It was filled with cash. "You recognize this?" he asked.

"No. Where on earth did you get it?"

"There was a little hidey-hole in the master bedroom closet. Someone had cut out a piece of Sheetrock, stuffed the money inside, and put the Sheetrock back in place. There's almost thirty grand here."

Annie gasped. "Thirty thousand dollars!"

"Holy mackerel," Theenie said. She turned to Annie. "I thought you were broke."

"I *am* broke!"

"You're saying you know nothing about the money?" Lamar asked.

"That's exactly what I'm saying," Annie told him.

"As I recall, that's the amount of money your husband took from your joint savings. Now, why would he pack his bags and not grab the money?"

"Wait a minute," Annie said. "Before you just assume that's the money Charles took from our account, you might want to make sure it doesn't belong to my tenant Wes Bridges. How do we know that he didn't put it there for safekeeping? He paid two weeks' rent with cash." She knew it sounded dumb, nobody carried that amount of money around, but Lamar's suspicions didn't make much sense, either.

Lamar held up the second plastic bag.

"Charles's passport," he said. "We found it hidden with the money. And this bag." He paused and held it up. "There's a one-way plane ticket to Jamaica."

Annie suddenly felt light-headed. "I didn't know Charles had a passport. The few times we discussed traveling he said there were several places he wanted to see in this country before he traveled abroad."

Lamar took the chair beside her. "You know what I think, Annie? I think Charles was in the process of packing his bags when he ran into his killer."

Annie felt the room spin. She placed both hands flat on the table as she tried to clear her head. "I don't know what to think. And how come there was only one plane ticket? I can't imagine him going to Jamaica alone."

Lamar shrugged as though he didn't think it pertinent. "Annie, I'm going to have to take you in."

She just looked at him.

The younger officer stepped forward. "Mrs. Fortenberry, I'm going to have to ask you to stand."

"What?" Annie looked up. She blinked several times before pushing herself up from the chair. Destiny and Theenie stood as well. Lovelle sat there, looking from one to the other, eyes wide and disbelieving.

The officer pulled a set of handcuffs from his back pocket.

"Hold it right there!" Destiny said. "You so much as try to cuff her, and I'll claw your eyes out, and put a hex on you. Your wife will leave you, and your house will become infested with termites."

The man winced and looked at Lamar. "You know I can't afford to have my place treated for termites."

"Put those damn handcuffs away," Lamar said. He looked at Annie. "I don't know any other way to say this, Annie, but you're under arrest for the murder of Charles Fortenberry." He turned to the officer. "Read her her rights."

It was late afternoon when Wes Bridges stormed into Lamar's office. He found Jamie Swift and Max Holt sitting across the desk from the man. "I just heard the news. What the hell is going on here?" he demanded of Lamar.

Lamar leaned back in his chair. "Excuse me, but we're having a private conversation here."

"Let him stay," Max said.

Wes kicked the door closed and folded his arms across his chest. "What the hell business do you have arresting Annie?" he demanded.

Lamar opened his mouth to answer, but Max cut him off. "She's being arraigned late this afternoon. I'll see that she doesn't spend a night in jail."

Lamar shook his head. "Ain't no way a judge is going to agree to bail on a murder charge."

"Maybe I'll get lucky and find a good criminal attorney," Max replied.

"Not in this town you won't. The best criminal attorney in the entire Southeast is Cal Nunamaker from Hilton Head, but he only takes high-profile cases, and he charges a bundle. Anyway, he's semiretired. Spends most of his time on a private island off the coast of Florida."

Max didn't respond.

Wes pointed a finger in Lamar's face. "I'm sick of this bullshit, Tevis. You know damned well Annie didn't kill her husband."

Lamar blinked several times as though trying to regain his composure. "Just so happens I have evidence that puts her in a bad light."

Wes scoffed. "What evidence?"

"It's no secret," Lamar said, "but Annie's husband, I mean her *deceased* husband, withdrew all the money from their savings account the day before he disappeared. We found the money this morning after searching her house. There was almost thirty thousand dollars stashed in his closet. Annie suggested it might belong to you."

Wes shook his head. "I don't travel with that much cash, and it doesn't prove anything with regard to Annie. She obviously didn't know the money was there; she assumed her husband took it and ran."

"It boils down to this," Lamar said. "Charles Fortenberry was murdered before he had a chance to get to the money, and that same person had to dispose of his body and his luggage before driving his car to the Savannah airport."

"Once again, that doesn't prove shit where Annie is concerned."

"There's more," Lamar said. "Annie went to the bank the same day her husband cleaned out the account. She'd obviously hoped to beat him to it, but she was too late."

"That's impossible," Wes said. "She was out of town. Visiting her sick mother," he added.

Lamar shook his head. "I drove over to the bank yesterday and spoke with the teller who assisted Mrs. Fortenberry, um, Annie, with her transactions the day she claimed she left town. The woman clearly remembered the incident because Annie became real upset when she learned all the money was gone. In fact, Annie was still inside the bank when they locked the door and put up the *Closed* sign. She insisted on getting all of her important papers from the safe-deposit box."

Wes shook his head. "There's been a mistake."

Lamar handed Wes a slip of paper. "Annie had to sign this when she closed the safe-deposit box. I had the bank manager check the signature. It's Annie's all right. It's dated the same day her husband withdrew the money." He leaned back in his chair and propped his feet on his desk. "Not only that; she admitted she drove to the house to confront him. She claims he wasn't there, but she can't prove it, and we don't know what *really* happened.

"Bottom line: she lied. People don't lie unless they've got something to hide, and if she lied once, what's to say she hasn't been lying all along?" He paused. "Anything else you want to know?"

Wes tossed the slip of paper onto Lamar's desk. "I think that covers it," he said. "I'll get out of your way and let you do your job."

Chapter Eight

"No, Vera!" Jamie said, standing in the lobby of the police department. "I will absolutely *not* allow you to take pictures of Annie being led to the courthouse in handcuffs. Isn't it bad enough that every newspaper and TV station within a hundred-mile radius is out there?"

"How in Hades are we supposed to get a story without a picture?" Vera insisted while Mike shuffled his feet nervously. Vera placed her hands on her hips. "I know Annie is your friend, but we need this story, Jamie. This is hot, especially since they lost her husband's body. Folks are tired of hearing about Tim Haskin's bull busting through the fence every other day and how the hair dryer at Susie Q's Cut and Curl malfunctioned and burned Lorraine Brown's hair right off her head."

"Absolutely no pictures," Jamie said, "and that's final." She looked at Mike. "You can continue to write the stories, but as we discussed, I have full editorial control."

He nodded.

Max nudged Jamie. "I need to touch base with Muffin. I'll be back before they escort Annie next door."

"Good. She's going to need all the support she can get."

Max hurried to his car and climbed in. "Muffin, are you there?"

"No, I'm sipping a rum and Coke in Tahiti," replied a voice that Max had programmed to sound like Marilyn Monroe. Muffin was Max's high-powered voice-recognition computer that ran his business empire and personal life from the dashboard of his car. Muffin had attitude.

"I need you to run a check," he said.

"Who's the lucky person?"

Max didn't hesitate. "I want everything you can get me on a guy named Wes Bridges."

"Don't make me angry, Lamar," Jamie said. "You owe Max and me."

"I'd listen to her," Vera said. "She's on a diet."

Lamar sighed. "Let me get this straight. You want me to allow a murder suspect to attend her arraignment without handcuffs.

What if she tries to escape?"

"Oh brother!" Jamie said.

Vera patted her handbag. "I've got my .38. I'll shoot her in the kneecaps."

Lamar gaped.

"Vera's kidding," Jamie said.

"And we want her taken out through the back way," Max said.

When Lamar hesitated, Vera gave a grunt. "Lamar wants to get his face on TV," she said.

Lamar was prevented from answering when a white stretch limo stopped in front of the building. A moment later, the driver opened the back door and a blond middle-aged man climbed out. He wore a white tennis outfit that showed off his tanned, well-toned body. Reporters immediately surrounded him, but he merely shook his head and made his way toward the front doors of the police station.

"Holy smokes, it's Cal Nunamaker!" Lamar said. He looked at Max. "How in the world did you manage that?"

"I asked politely."

The man pushed through the glass doors of the police station and perused the group with sharp blue eyes. Max stepped forward, shook his hand, and made introductions. "Thanks for agreeing to take the case on such short notice, Cal."

Nunamaker smiled. "I came straight from the tennis court. Nice airplane you got there, Max. How did you know my favorite dish was lobster thermidor?"

"Just a wild guess."

Nunamaker looked at Lamar. "Nice to see you again, Chief Travis."

"It's Tevis," Lamar said, blushing.

Nunamaker checked his watch. "I want to see every piece of paper you have on my client. And don't tell me you've put her in a cell, because that's going to ruin my day."

Lamar cleared his throat. "We've got her in our nicest interrogation room. Matter of fact, we recently had it painted."

"And another thing," Nunamaker said, as though he wasn't listening. "I expect her to be dressed nicely at the arraignment. No jailhouse clothes or handcuffs, you got that?"

"I'm on it." Lamar hurried away.

"So what do you think?" Max said.

Nunamaker shrugged. "From what you said over the phone, all the evidence is circumstantial. There's no confession, no witness, no weapon. Hell, there's not even a body," he added with a wide grin.

"All they've got is probable cause," Nunamaker went on, "but that's all they need to arrest somebody. I called the DA from the plane. He was ready to charge Mrs. Fortenberry with premeditated murder, if you can believe it, but I threatened to make his life miserable, so he changed his mind."

Jamie gasped, suspecting that wouldn't bode well for Annie. "Can you get away with something like that?"

The man grinned. "Ordinarily he'd probably report me to the bar, but we're good tennis buddies, and he wants me to put in a good word for him at the Hilton Head Country Club so they'll offer him a membership. They don't let just anyone in. Do you play tennis, Max? You look awfully fit."

"Not as much as I used to. Do you think the judge will let her out on bail?"

"Normally he wouldn't, but he and I are tight."

"Is he a tennis buddy as well?" Jamie asked.

"No, he's my brother-in-law. I'll still have to argue the point, mostly so I get good press, but I don't foresee a problem. I should warn you, though: the bail is going to be high. Otherwise folks might think he's showing favoritism."

"No problem," Max said. "As long as he'll take a check."

"Hell, you're Max Holt. He'll take an IOU

on a gum wrapper. Seriously, you and I should get together and hit a few balls sometime."

Lamar returned with a file folder in his hands, a female officer beside him. "The defendant is changing clothes," he said, handing Nunamaker the folder. "My officer will escort you back in a few minutes."

"You're a good man, Tavis."

Annie paced the room and watched the clock. Only thirty minutes left before she would have to face a judge who would probably throw her in the slammer until she was old enough to use a walker. She wouldn't be able to help Max and Jamie with their wedding. She had let them down, and she had shed more tears over that than she had over being arrested.

She jumped when someone tapped on the door. The female officer who'd been so kind to her opened the door. "Your lawyer is here, Mrs. Fortenberry."

Annie blinked. "Lawyer?"

A man in a tennis outfit stepped into the room. "Mrs. Fortenberry, at last we meet, and I must say you're about the prettiest little thing I've ever seen. I'm Cal Nunamaker, your attorney. You can call me Cal. May I call you Annie?"

She nodded dumbly. "Did the court appoint you?"

"Oh no. A friend of yours, Max Holt, hired me. I promise I'll get you out of here lickety-split. Do you have any questions?"

"You're saying I won't go to jail?"

"Absolutely not. In fact, you'll be home in time for supper."

Annie couldn't hide her astonishment. "But I've been charged with murder."

He smiled kindly. "We both know you didn't kill your husband."

"I've never killed anyone in my life."

"So I want you to wipe that worried look from your face and give me a big smile."

Annie just looked at him.

"You're not smiling," he said.

She forced herself to smile.

"That's much better. Now, you just sit tight for a few minutes, and I'll be waiting outside to walk you next door to the courthouse."

Annie nodded as the officer let him out. The woman turned and gave Annie a thumbs-up before she closed the door.

"I have never been so humiliated in my life," Annie hissed to Jamie when they exited the courthouse more than an hour later. Annie blinked several times when she saw the crowd that had doubled in size during her brief arraignment, where she had actually been charged with murder and given a court date. Several news vans waited out front, men and women stood on the steps holding microphones, and they raced toward Annie as soon as they caught sight of her. "Oh no," she said.

"Trust me, we want the publicity," Nunamaker whispered. "I'll handle everything." He stepped forward as microphones were thrust at him. "Ladies and gentlemen, I'm sure all of you know me, but for the record, I'm Cal Nunamaker, and I'm representing Mrs. Annie Fortenberry. I am only going to comment briefly on the case, and if you're nice I'll take a few questions." He gave them a movie-star smile.

"Mrs. Fortenberry is absolutely and unequivocally not guilty of the preposterous murder charge that has been brought against her by a police force that is either too stupid or too lazy to perform a real investigation." He paused to catch his breath. "Once this silly matter is behind us I plan to take measures to see that reparations are made."

"Are you saying you plan to sue?" one of the reporters asked.

"I'm planning something more formidable," he said. "My client is an honorable, law-abiding citizen, and I refuse to allow her name to be tarnished by frivolous charges that can't be backed up with solid proof."

Annie perked up when she spied a smartly dressed woman she recognized from a Charleston TV station. The woman stepped right up to Nunamaker.

"Excuse me, Mr. Nunamaker, but aren't you jumping the gun here, if you'll forgive the cliché? After all, I understand the police chief searched Mrs. Fortenberry's residence and found incriminating evidence."

"It could easily have been planted," Nunamaker said. "Chief Tavis is desperate to find a suspect after yesterday's debacle regarding the loss of Mr. Fortenberry's remains."

"Has there been any news on that?" the woman asked.

"Not that I've heard."

"From what I understand, the suspect lied as to her whereabouts the day of her husband's disappearance," the woman went on smoothly. "There's also talk of a troubled marriage and adulterous affairs. That, combined with the fact the remains were found buried in the backyard, is pretty damaging in my opinion."

"And that, young lady, is precisely why

I'm representing her and you're not," Cal said, earning a dark look from her. "That's all I have in my opinion."

The reporters called out more questions, even as Annie was led away with Max, Jamie, and Nunamaker surrounding her. The crowd was so thick that Annie didn't see Wes standing at the very back.

Annie was feeling better by the time she arrived home. Cal had insisted on giving her a ride in the limo Max had sent for him. He'd gone over the case briefly with Annie, discussed his strategy, and given her his private cell phone number in case she needed to reach him. He didn't stop talking until they arrived at her mansion, at which time his mouth fell open.

"Well now, I've never seen anything like *that*," he said.

"And you probably never will," Annie assured him.

Annie barely made it to the front steps before Theenie threw open the front door. She rushed out, followed by Lovelle and Danny. "Oh, thank goodness you're home!" Theenie cried, throwing her arms around Annie's neck. "Lovelle and I have been sick with worry. I don't know what we would have done had Danny not stayed with us.

And, bless her heart, Jamie called several times with an update."

Annie gave Danny a grateful look and he smiled, but she could see the deep concern in his eyes. It was the same look he'd worn as he waited with Annie during her grandmother's final hours, the look he'd worn when he told her about Charles's infidelity and afterward, when Annie realized her husband was gone, along with their savings.

Theenie pulled away slightly and reached for a tissue as Lovelle gave Annie a quick hug. "It's going to be okay," Annie said.

Theenie took Annie's hand. "Come inside, dear. We decided to hold off serving dinner until you got here."

"Welcome home, Anniekins," Danny said, leaning over to kiss the top of her head. "It's good to have you back."

Annie's kitchen had never looked more inviting to her. Theenie and Lovelle ordered her to take her seat at the table while they put the finishing touches on the meal. Although Annie had not eaten all day, she had little appetite, but she forced herself to eat so as not to hurt the women's feelings.

"Where is Erdle?" she asked.

"Who knows?" Lovelle said. "He hasn't been home all day."

"And Wes?"

"He came back a couple of hours after you were arrested," Theenie said. "He left as soon as I told him. He didn't say where he was going."

Annie wondered if he'd gone to the police station, if he'd spoken with Lamar, if he knew the truth.

Lovelle glanced up from her dinner. "Destiny called Lamar to check on you, then lost her temper on the phone, and then Danny grabbed the phone, and it went from bad to worse. You should have heard all the names he called Lamar. Even used the *F* word," she added proudly.

"I'm sorry to have put all of you through this," Annie said.

"It's not your fault," Danny said. "The good news is the ballroom floor looks great."

Annie smiled. "Thank you." She looked from one to the other and was touched to have such good friends. "By the way, where is Destiny?"

"She had to go into the office and help out, since Max and Jamie were at the police station. It probably saved Lamar's life." Theenie touched Annie's hand. "Did they lock you up with one of those, you know, *big* women?" she whispered.

Annie laughed. "No, Theenie. I never even saw a jail cell."

The woman gave an enormous sigh of relief. "Oh, thank goodness!"

"Everything is going to be okay, you guys. I promise." Annie hoped she sounded more convincing than she felt.

It was late when Max and Jamie left the newspaper office. Muffin had news for them the minute they climbed into his car.

"I have information on Wes Bridges," Muffin said.

"I'm listening," Max said.

"He used to be a cop in Columbia, graduated to detective and pretty much ran the homicide unit. Now he's a private investigator." Max and Jamie exchanged looks. "The man doesn't come cheap, but he's supposed to be the best in the business. Charles Fortenberry's mother hired him to look into her son's disappearance after she collected insurance money on her husband's death."

"That explains why he rented a room from Annie," Jamie said. "Eve Fortenberry suspected Annie had something to do with Charles's disappearance." She looked at Max. "I don't like it. I think we should drive over and tell Annie right this minute."

"I don't think that's a good idea," Max said.

"How can you say that? I think Annie has

feelings for this guy."

"She's also up for murder. If he's that good, he just might find out who killed her husband."

"I don't want to see her hurt, Max. Again," Jamie added.

Max reached for her hand and squeezed it reassuringly. "It'll be a whole lot easier getting over a broken heart than doing prison time," he said. "I'm going to have to ask you to go along with me on this one, Swifty."

Jamie was quiet for a moment. "That doesn't mean I have to like it."

It was late when Wes arrived back at Annie's. She was sitting on the piazza, a candle burning on the wicker table beside her. "'Bout time you got home, Bridges," she said once he'd cleared the top step.

He glanced her way. "Do you make a point of sitting up until all your tenants arrive back safely?" he asked.

His tone was as cool as the breeze that whipped across her face and ruffled her thick hair. "I was worried about you."

"How was jail?"

Annie frowned. "That's a helluva thing to ask."

"Yeah? Well, I'm not feeling very sociable tonight."

He had learned the truth. She had been naive to think he wouldn't eventually find out. She should have known that even Lamar would learn that she'd withheld information. Wes crossed the piazza and reached for the door.

"I was scared," she said. "Afraid that Lamar would think the worst if he found out I was in the bank that day."

"Well, he *does* think the worst, and now you're in a shitload of trouble. You weren't where you said you were, meaning you don't have an alibi for what, a week?"

She scooted forward on the swing. "I went to my mother's house just like I said. But when I arrived, she took one look at my face and knew something was wrong. I told her I had an appointment with a divorce attorney the following week, and she insisted that I return to Beaumont immediately and clean out the savings account. I was only planning to take half of the money, but I was too late."

"So you confronted him?"

"That was the plan, only Charles wasn't home. I was so outraged that I didn't think to check to see if he'd packed his clothes until I was on my way back to my mother's. I just figured what the hell, he was well on his way to wherever he was going."

"Lamar found the money."

"And you think I knew it was here?"

"I don't know what the hell to think, Annie. I'm having a real problem distinguishing fact from fiction."

Finally, she stood. She didn't know if she was angry or hurt at his response. "Fact," she began. "I wouldn't have spent the last few years struggling financially if I'd had that kind of money to fall back on. Fact: if I *had* found the money and Charles's passport and ticket, I would have immediately suspected something was wrong and gone to Lamar."

Wes looked at her, and the hard lines on his face relaxed. "I'm sorry you had a shit day, Annie, but look at the good side. You were on CNN."

As Annie watched him go in, she pictured throwing her rolling pin at him and it bouncing off the back of his head. Like she needed to be reminded that she had made CNN. The telephone hadn't stopped ringing since the story had first aired, only to be replayed every hour on the hour, as if the staff feared that one person in the town of Beaumont might miss it.

Annie had finally taken the phone off the hook after her mother called from West Palm Beach, having watched the whole sordid thing unfold after headlines announced that the remains of a South Carolina man were missing due to a carjacking. Not only had they mentioned Charles Fortenberry by name; they'd also given a brief history of the case, beginning with the unearthing of his bones. There was a goofy picture of Lamar Tevis standing at the site pointing toward a mound of dirt, followed by footage of Annie at her best, in an old chenille bathrobe, hair out to there, yelling and shaking her fists at a TV camera. The next shot showed Annie trying to duck behind Cal Nunamaker on the courthouse steps after her arraignment.

"I just want you to know I'm here for you, Annie," Jenna Worthington had said. "I'll catch the first plane out if you need me. I'll even sleep in that god-awful house if I have to."

Annie had thanked her but said it wasn't necessary. Still, the fact that she had offered to come had taken some of the sting out of being hauled off to jail that morning.

Annie had been hard at work since dawn, getting things ready for the rehearsal dinner and trying to sidestep Peaches, who obviously hoped something edible would come her way.

Annie looked down and shook her head. "You've already had two cans of cat food this morning. I think you have an eating disorder."

The cat meowed.

"Sorry, all I have is lettuce." Annie resumed her work. A moment later, she heard a noise, turned, and found Peaches digging in her plant.

"No!" Annie said firmly, unaware that Wes was standing at the bottom of the stairs. She hurried toward the plant and reached for the fat ball of orange fur, but Peaches dived to the floor in the opposite direction. Annie turned so quickly she lost her footing and fell, butt-first on the plant. It toppled over and dumped potting soil on the kitchen floor. Annie sat there for a moment, muttering four-letter words under her breath as Peaches walked to the braided rug in front of the refrigerator, slumped on it, and began grooming herself.

"Problems?" Wes said.

Annie looked at him. "What makes you ask?"

He grabbed a coffee mug, filled it, and sipped in silence. Peaches got up, walked over to him, and rubbed against his leg. Wes reached down and scratched the animal lightly behind one ear, and she began to purr. Finally, he belted down the rest of his coffee, placed the empty cup in the dishwasher, and started for the door.

He paused and looked down at Annie. "Do you need help getting up?"

"Nope. I like it here."

He nodded, unlocked the door, and opened it. "Just so you know, that plant is a goner."

Annie heard him fire up his bike, and a moment later he roared away. He no longer trusted her. At this point, she wasn't even sure he liked her. And she didn't have the foggiest idea how to make things right between them. It was her own fault. She should have told Lamar everything when he'd questioned her shortly after Charles's disappearance. But she hadn't. And that was only going to make things worse.

Erdle arrived home as Annie was serving breakfast, and she and Theenie watched him stagger across the backyard and upstairs to his apartment. "I guess he fell off the wagon," Theenie said.

Annie looked at her. "You think?"

Danny pulled up in his car, climbed out, and walked toward the carriage house, opening the door on the first floor that led into the garage. He emerged a moment later with the rake. "Oh, he's going to tidy the yard for you," Theenie said. "How sweet."

Annie nodded. She would take him a cup of coffee and invite him up for breakfast. "Yeah, he's a good guy," she said. "I don't know what I'd do without him."

"Maybe it's high time you gave it serious thought," Theenie replied. "But I suspect it's too late now, since you've already got it bad for Wes."

Max's plane touched down on the small airstrip that afternoon. Jamie stood beside Max and Frankie as it taxied in while Dee Dee and her personal assistant, Beenie, waited in the stretch limo. Fleas, who'd insisted on following Jamie from the car, had immediately found a sunny spot on a patch of grass next to the building. He was presently sprawled on his back, eyes closed, snoring loudly.

Max glanced at the animal. "I swear I think that dog has sleep apnea."

"He snores louder than Dee Dee," Frankie said, and immediately punched his fist lightly against his forehead. "Please don't tell Dee Dee I said that."

The plane rolled to a stop, and a few minutes later Nick and Billie Kaharchek descended. Billie's children followed them: Christie, a dark-haired beauty in a smart dove gray business suit, and younger brother Joel, who had the same hair color as his sister but obviously lacked her sense of style. He wore khakis, a kelly green dress shirt, and the ugliest plaid jacket Jamie had ever seen. He was a good two inches taller than Nick and had an easy lopsided smile.

Everyone hugged and Nick and Billie praised the smooth flight while Joel extolled the awesome in-flight cookie tray and Christie complained good-naturedly that she had probably put on five pounds by eating her weight in brownies.

"You two amaze me," Max told Nick and Billie. "You never age."

Billie laughed. Despite having a little age on her, she had maintained the youthfulness and zest for life that had drawn Nick to her some twenty years ago.

When Max had flown Jamie to Virginia to meet Nick and Billie, she had taken an instant liking to the handsome couple who had practically raised Max. Jamie was equally fond of Christie and Joel. She liked that Billie was down-to-earth and unpretentious despite having married a multimillionaire.

"Where's Dee Dee?" Nick asked Frankie, who was in the process of checking Joel's muscles and planning their first arm-wrestling match.

"In the limo. She's having problems with her feet."

"I need to give her a big hug," Billie said.

"Just don't tell her she's fat," Frankie whispered to the group.

Billie smacked his arm, and they started toward the vehicle as the last piece of luggage was placed inside the trunk. "I plan to smother her with a lot of TLC while I'm here," Billie said.

Jamie glanced in Fleas' direction. He rolled over, pulled himself up, and shook, his big ears and sagging jowls flapping from side to side. He started toward them in slow gear.

"Check out that cool bloodhound," Joel said. "I think he's following us."

"He belongs to Jamie," Max said. "Although I've agreed to adopt him after we're married."

Everyone paused and waited for the dog to catch up. Christie reached down and stroked his head. "What's his name?"

It was the question Jamie always dreaded. "Fleas."

Instead of jerking her hand away like most people, Christie laughed loudly. "Poor baby," she said. "No wonder you look depressed. Who stuck you with a name like that?"

"Not me," Jamie said, noting that Fleas was giving Christie his most pitiful look, having perfected it when he'd discovered it was usually followed by Jamie-the-sucker pulling his favorite butter pecan ice cream from the freezer. "And he always looks like a candidate for Prozac."

"What happened to his fur?" Joel asked, reaching down to pet Fleas as well.

"Hey, you guys are looking at a champion and silver-cup raccoon hunter," Max said, although the looks he received were dubious. "He's since gone into retirement, living off his 401-K now."

"Well, if you ask me, it looks like the last coon kicked some hound dog butt," Joel said.

Frankie opened the back door of the limo and climbed in next to Dee Dee as the others began opening doors, waving off the chauffeur's offer to assist. A subdued Beenie sat beside Dee Dee and nodded as Frankie made introductions, trying to talk above the compact TV set where a woman was kneeling before a toilet bowl singing the praises of a new product. Frankie hit the remote control button, and the woman disappeared as quickly as she had assured the toilet bowl stains would.

"You look wonderful," Billie said, reaching across the seat to hug Dee Dee. "Except I thought you'd have put on weight by now."

"She's already gained fifty pounds," Frankie said. He winced the moment the words left his mouth. "Although you'd never know it to look at her," he added sheepishly.

It wasn't until they were all seated that Jamie noticed Dee Dee and Beenie were behaving oddly. They had said very little, and there was tension on their faces. "Dee Dee, are you okay?" she asked.

When Dee Dee hesitated, Beenie spoke for her. "We just saw your friend on CNN."

CHAPTER NINE

Annie was wearing a bright smile when she answered the doorbell shortly before 6:00 PM and found Max, Jamie, and Max's family standing on the other side. "Welcome to my home!" she called out gaily to the crowd, wondering how many of them had seen her on CNN. The only thing she had going for her was the fact that she looked 100 percent better than she had on TV in her shabby bathrobe.

She had purposefully chosen to dress like an old-maid librarian: conservative dark gray skirt that fell below her knees, rose-colored cardigan and shell, sensible pumps, and her grandmother's antique cross pendant. Lovelle had offered her rosary, but Annie figured that would be overkill.

"Please come in," Annie said, stepping aside so the group could enter.

Jamie and Max gave Annie a hug. Jamie had called earlier in an obvious attempt to cheer Annie and make light of her CNN debut, and in the end they were laughing hysterically, just like old times.

Max began making introductions.

"I've already met our mayor and his beautiful wife," Annie said, offering Frankie and Dee Dee a warm handshake. Frankie and Dee Dee were infamously fun-loving and colorful, though Dee Dee was known to be a bit of a drama queen and prone to hysterics. And with her late-in-life pregnancy, these personality traits were becoming increasingly pronounced.

Dee Dee's bottom lip trembled when she smiled, and she didn't quite meet Annie's gaze. "I've heard so much about you," she said. "From Jamie," she added quickly.

They all knew, Annie told herself. Probably everyone in Beaumont knew by now, which explained the traffic jam out front. Theenie had caught several people snapping pictures.

"Pregnancy becomes you," Annie said. "You must be very excited."

"Yes." Dee Dee's voice squeaked and she edged closer to Frankie.

Finally, Max turned to an older couple. "This good-looking twosome is my cousin and best man, Nick Kaharchek, and his lovely wife, Billie. They took me in when I was dangerous," he added with a grin.

"He's still dangerous," Nick said.

Annie greeted them. She could see the resemblance between Max and Nick, even though the older man's face bore a few lines that gave him an air of distinction. His wife was lovely and exuded a feeling of warmth as she smiled and shook Annie's hand.

"And these are my children, Christie and Joel," Billie said.

Annie offered her hand, and the young woman shook it and gave her a quick wink that suggested Annie was all right in her book. Joel held Annie's hand longer than necessary and flirted shamelessly.

"Enough already," Billie said as she pulled him away and told him to behave. "I'm still your elder," she said, trying to sound stern and failing miserably because she couldn't quite hide her smile.

Annie noted an anxious-looking dark-haired man standing at a distance. He stepped forward and shook hands, but Annie could see that his smile was forced. "I'm Beenie," he said. "I sort of take care of Dee Dee."

"He spoils her rotten," Max said.

"I could use someone like you," Annie replied jokingly. "How would you like to come to work for me?"

"I can't!" he blurted, drawing stares from those around them. He blushed. "I mean, Dee Dee needs me. Especially right now with the baby due soon," he added. "I'm her personal assistant, so I can't leave her side. Not for five minutes, even if it means sleeping at the foot of her bed like a Chihuahua."

"Jamie was right about the house," Billie said, taking in the living room. "It's unlike anything I've ever seen. In a good way," she added.

Jamie nodded enthusiastically. "I told you you'd love it. How many people get to tie the knot in a pre–Civil War bordello?"

"Red is Dee Dee's favorite color," Frankie said. "She wants the name of your decorator before we leave, right, honey?"

"Um . . ." Dee Dee looked at Beenie.

"I don't think red is a good color for babies," Beenie said. "The person who decorated the nursery thought red was an angry color."

Annie laughed. "I suppose that explains my bad temper," she said. "Because I'm surrounded by red."

Annie had already served cocktails and hors d'oeuvres by the time Vera Bankhead arrived. "Saw you on CNN," she whispered. "I'd rethink that chenille bathrobe."

"I'll keep that in mind," Annie said. She was about to close the door when she spotted the minister hurrying up the front walk. She was glad Theenie had removed some of the more risqué objets d'art, although she suspected her grandmother was frowning down at her.

Reverend Lester Tuttle had presided over a number of weddings in Annie's house. She introduced him. He sat close to Max and Jamie, obviously wanting to get to know the couple before the wedding. Destiny entered by way of the dining room, wearing a purple ankle-length dress that hugged her curves and breasts and brought a bright blush to the minister's cheeks as they shook hands.

"I'll hang out here and see to the refreshments," Destiny whispered to Annie. "I know you have things to do in the kitchen."

Annie thanked her and hurried through the dining room and the swinging door that led to the kitchen, where Theenie and Lovelle were checking the two prime rib roasts with meat thermometers. "How do they look?" Annie asked.

"Everything is right on schedule," Theenie proudly announced. "We should be ready to serve the first course as soon as the rehearsal is over."

"Has Wes come in?" Annie asked.

Theenie shook her head. "Haven't seen him."

Annie tried to hide her disappointment as she worked to get things ready. When she was certain all was in order, she returned to the living room and led the group into the chapel. For the next half hour Reverend Tuttle instructed the wedding party as to when they would come in, where they would stand, and Annie coached Jamie and Dee Dee as they practiced walking down the aisle.

"Would you just look at me," Dee Dee said to Jamie. "I'm waddling like a duck."

Jamie and Annie lied, insisting that was not the case.

"Are you still planning to use Fleas as your, um, flower dog?" Annie asked Jamie.

She nodded. "I know it sounds totally crazy, so go ahead and say it."

"It *is* crazy," Vera said. "The craziest thing I've ever heard."

"Yuck!" Dee Dee said. "You're going to have that —"

"Don't you dare call him ugly," Jamie said.

Dee Dee clamped her lips together but shook her head sadly.

"I tried to talk her out of it," Vera said to Annie, "but she treats him like her first-born."

Annie chuckled, noting the wide-eyed look on Reverend Tuttle's face. "Trust me: having a dog in the wedding is tame compared to some of the things couples have asked for."

"Thank you for defending me," Jamie said. "I've never had a pet before, and I know I've spoiled him, but . . ." She paused and sighed. "I think his previous owner mistreated him, so I guess I'm trying to do all I can to make up for it."

"That's so sweet," Christie said. "Mom and I are big-time animal advocates, so we admire people who take such good care of their pets."

"I still think it's dumb," Vera said.

Afterward, while Annie ushered the group into the dining room, Dee Dee asked Jamie to show her where the restroom was located. They started down the hall.

"Psst! Psst!"

Jamie glanced over her shoulder to see who was making the sound and found Beenie hurrying toward them.

"Here comes Beenie," Dee Dee said. "The man just won't leave my side."

He closed the distance between them. "What? Why are you staring at me?"

"Because you've been sticking to me like

glue since we arrived."

Beenie planted one hand on his hip. "I'm your personal assistant. It's what I do."

"I have to pee. I don't think following me into the bathroom is part of your job description."

"I think Dee Dee is asking for breathing room," Jamie said.

He looked hurt. "Okay, if you insist on knowing, this place creeps me out."

Jamie made a sound of disgust. "Oh, for Pete's sake! I don't believe you said that."

"Honey, I don't want to hurt your feelings," Dee Dee said to her, "but this place gives me the heebie-jeebies, too. Why, there's a grave in the backyard, and everybody suspects Annie killed her husband. If I weren't a strong woman I would probably faint just thinking about it." She pulled a linen handkerchief from her pocket and mopped her brow. "I might faint anyway."

"You *do* look pale," Beenie said.

"She's pale because she refuses to let the sun touch any part of her body." Jamie crossed her arms. "Annie is perfectly innocent of the crime with which she's been charged. She is no more capable of murder than we are. She's also a very good friend of mine, and I don't want her feelings hurt,"

Jamie added. "She has been through enough."

Dee Dee looked contrite. "I'm sorry. I don't know what's gotten into me. I am so emotional these days. I seem to cry over everything."

Beenie nodded. "Me, too."

"We wouldn't think of doing anything that might embarrass you at your wedding," Dee Dee said, and Beenie nodded in agreement.

Jamie looked relieved. "Thank you." She motioned to the bathroom door. "We need to hurry. I'm sure Annie has begun serving."

Dee Dee turned for the bathroom door, then paused and turned. "Just one question," she said. "Her husband didn't die from food poisoning, did he?"

Annie noticed Jamie ate very little dinner and refused dessert, although Max convinced her to take a tiny bite of the almond torte.

Annie smiled as she refilled coffee cups. She had specifically chosen not to serve anything chocolate, knowing Jamie would find it hard to turn down. Annie and Jamie had once shared an entire bag of Snickers candy bars. It had been well worth the stomachache they'd had afterward.

Vera looked at Jamie's plate. "You barely touched your food."

"How many more pounds do you have to lose?" Dee Dee asked.

Jamie looked proud. "I'm down ten pounds. But I don't want to eat anything fattening and risk blowing it."

"Don't be surprised if you gain back a few pounds on your honeymoon," Billie said. "I kept something in my mouth the whole time."

All eyes turned her way, and Billie blushed profusely, but nobody said anything in deference to Reverend Tuttle.

"It's this house," Destiny whispered to Billie. "I haven't stopped thinking about sex since I walked through the door."

"Jamie, you should take up horseback riding," Billie said as though hoping to change the subject. "Once Max moves his horses down," she added. "That's how Nick and I keep in shape."

Dee Dee gave a shudder. "I could never understand how you could tolerate those smelly horses."

"I must be used to it by now." Billie looked at Jamie. "Before I met Nick I didn't even know how to climb on a horse."

"She didn't know how to get off, either," Nick said. "First time I tried to help her dismount she slipped and fell on me, and we both ended up on the ground." They shared a private smile.

Annie noticed the loving exchange between the two as she began to clear away the dessert dishes. She had caught Max and Jamie looking at each other the same way, and she'd felt sad that she and Charles had never experienced that degree of intensity. She wondered what it would feel like to be madly in love with someone, to fall asleep and wake up in that person's arms year after year and still share that depth of feeling.

"Max told me it was love at first sight for the two of you," Jamie said, addressing Billie and Nick.

"I guess you could say that, considering the fact we got married after knowing each other only two weeks," Billie replied.

Vera gaped. "Two weeks! Goodness, it takes me longer than that to break in a new pair of shoes. I'll bet everybody thought you were crazy."

Billie and Nick nodded in unison. "I think sometimes you just know from the beginning that it's right," he said. "At least that's the way it was for us."

"That is so sweet," Beenie said, dabbing moist eyes with his napkin.

"We had a double wedding," Frankie said.

He winked at Nick. "Remember the bachelor's party and Billie jumping out of that cake half-naked?"

Annie, holding a tray of empty dessert dishes, paused at the swinging door and turned around. She didn't want to miss this one.

Billie hitched her chin high. "Excuse me, but I was wearing a T-shirt over my tassels and G-string."

"A very *sheer* T-shirt," Nick corrected.

"Mother!" Christie looked shocked. "You never told me about that."

"You should have seen the men tossing money at her," Dee Dee said.

"That is so cool," Joel said. "My mom the stripper."

"I made a gigantic fool of myself," Billie confessed. "I slipped and fell across a table of cold seafood. My hair smelled like fish for days."

"I'd like to have seen that," Max said.

"You were busy at the time," Nick reminded, "taking my Mercedes apart piece by piece."

Annie grinned, pushed through the door, and entered the kitchen. Jamie joined her a few minutes later, smiling broadly. "Everything was perfect," she said. "I can't thank you enough."

"I couldn't have done it without Theenie and Lovelle," Annie said, and was pleased when Jamie praised their efforts as well. Annie's face softened. "You're going to make a beautiful bride."

"I think I'm going to cry," Theenie said, sniffing loudly.

Jamie's smile faltered when Wes walked through the back door, but she quickly regained her composure. "We're getting ready to leave," she said. Annie had noticed the change in Jamie the minute Wes had come in and had wondered at it, but didn't have time to think about it, since her guests were leaving. She hurried out front, where they thanked her for a wonderful dinner, said their good-byes, and filed out the door. Once they were gone, Annie smiled, knowing it had gone exceptionally well.

Theenie and Lovelle helped Annie clean up. As though reading her mind, Theenie looked at her. "I offered Wes something to eat, but he said he'd grabbed something earlier. I think the man lives on junk food."

Destiny entered the kitchen. "Great dinner," she said. "I would have enjoyed it even more if *she* hadn't been there."

"Who, dear?" Theenie asked.

"The spirit. She stood across the room giving Max goo-goo eyes the whole time.

The woman has no shame."

Theenie shook her head. "Well, I hope you told her Max is soon to be married." She stretched and yawned. "I don't know about the rest of you, but I'm pooped." She cut her eyes toward the stairs. "Lovelle, are you coming up?"

"I'm right behind you," Lovelle said. They wished Annie and Destiny a good night and started up the steps.

Destiny stood there for a moment watching Annie. "Are you okay?"

"Yeah. I was nervous in the beginning, but everyone was so nice they put me at ease."

Destiny was quiet for a moment. "Annie, I know how your husband died."

Annie almost dropped the coffeepot she was filling with water. "What!"

"I saw it in a vision. He died falling down those stairs." When Annie simply looked at her, she went on. "There was an argument." She'd no sooner gotten the words out of her mouth before she sneezed.

Annie reached for the box of tissues and handed it to her. "Who was with him?"

"I don't know, but I'm certain *she* saw the whole thing."

"The spirit?"

Destiny nodded. "I've asked her a dozen

times, but she refuses to communicate."

"You said she was mute."

"I've been able to pick up bits and pieces telepathically, but she won't open up completely. I don't know if it's a physical or emotional problem or both, but the woman is terrified." She paused. "Here's what I think. I'm almost certain she saw her lover hanged, but she's blocked it. She had already been through the trauma of being murdered, and the hanging was too much to bear. Until she remembers I don't think she's going to talk *or* go to the light." She sneezed twice.

Annie was trying hard to keep an open mind, but it all sounded outlandish. "Can you help her?"

"I don't know."

Annie turned back to filling the coffeepot. "Is there anything else you can tell me about Charles?" she asked.

Another sneeze. "He was definitely seeing another woman, and I'm almost certain she was somebody you knew. Although I haven't actually seen it in a vision, it's logical that the person he was arguing with pushed him. I don't know if it was this woman or if it was a jealous boyfriend or husband."

Annie heard a noise and glanced up as Wes came down the stairs.

"I was going to get a glass of ice water," he said. "Am I interrupting?"

Destiny shook her head. "I'm on my way to bed." She glanced at Annie. "Thanks again for a great dinner." She disappeared up the stairs.

Wes was quiet as he leaned against the counter and sipped his water. Annie could feel his eyes on her, and she thought it best to go upstairs. "I've locked the doors," she said. "Would you turn off the light before going to bed?" She started for the stairs.

"Annie?"

She paused and turned.

"I'm sorry for being such a . . ." He paused.

She waited. "If you can't think of a word, I'll give you my list and you can choose several from that."

"Jerk," he finally said.

"That's pretty tame and has less syllables."

He almost smiled. "I probably don't want to know. Thing is, I can understand that you were afraid, what with Charles's mother making accusations and having someone like Lamar Tevis in charge of the investigation."

Annie was thoughtful. "I just want you to know I'm not a liar by trade."

He glanced at the stairs. "I accidentally overheard some of what Destiny said. Do you believe her?"

Annie shrugged. "I believe she has visions. I don't know how accurate they are."

Wes indicated the table. "Can we talk a minute?"

He waited until Annie had taken a seat before pulling a chair out for him. "I've been checking around. I know who Charles was seeing."

Annie sucked in her breath. She almost dreaded hearing it. "Someone I know?"

"His boss's wife."

Annie frowned. "Donna Schaefer? Who in the world told you that?"

"You sit in enough bars, you're bound to hear something sooner or later. Folks are talking about the murder, finding the body." He paused and grinned. "Losing the body," he added. "By the way, about that bathrobe you were wearing on CNN —"

"I've already put it in a box to go to the women's shelter."

"Man, you're not doing those poor women any favors."

"Could we please get back to what we were discussing?"

"I heard a guy mention he'd seen Charles at the Hilltop Steakhouse a couple of times with a pretty brunette. I already suspected it was the wife after looking over Charles's cell phone bill. He placed a lot of calls to his boss's house. During the day when he would most likely be at the office," Wes added, "but I decided to dig a little deeper just to make sure, so I got a picture of her and —" When Annie arched one brow, he shook his head. "Don't ask. I took the picture to the Hilltop, along with Charles's picture, and the bartender recognized them."

"From more than three years ago?"

"The bartender accidentally spilled a drink on your husband's favorite suit one of the times he and Mrs. Schaefer came in. Bartender said Charles made a big deal out of it, so he gave him twenty bucks to have it dry-cleaned."

"I'm stunned."

"Were you and she friends?"

"Not *close* friends, but Charles and I socialized with them now and then, and Donna and I usually planned the company Christmas party together, which was always held at the country club. She spent one Saturday here, only a few months before Charles disappeared, so we could decide on the menu and discuss decorations. She and Norm, her husband, had come to dinner here a couple of times before that, but it was pretty boring because the guys talked shop the entire time." Annie paused. "I do remember feeling disappointed that she didn't call after I'd assumed Charles had left me, but I figured she didn't want to get involved in our personal problems."

"I plan to question her, of course," Wes said.

"Then I'm coming with you." When Wes started to argue, Annie held up a hand. "I want to hear it from her own lips. The sooner the better," she added.

"We can leave in the morning after breakfast."

Jimbo Gardner shook Erdle Thorney hard. "C'mon, Erdle, you gotta wake up."

Stretched out in a booth at the back of Jimbo's Bar and Grill, Erdle mumbled something unintelligible in his sleep. He opened his eyes, made to sit up, and groaned. "Head hurrs like hell," he said.

Jimbo handed him a glass of whiskey. "Here's a little hair of the dog," he said. "Double shot, it ought to cure what ails you."

Erdle tossed back the drink, winced, and set the glass on the table. "Wha' time is it?"

"Eight AM. I couldn't wake you last night,

so I decided to let you sleep it off. But I got to start cleaning this place in time for the lunch crowd."

Erdle pressed his hands on either side of his head as though he feared it would explode. "Wha' do I owe?"

"You paid your tab last night. Don't you remember?"

"Naw."

"Man, you're shaking all over. You okay?"

"'Nother shot o' whiskey might help." Erdle slurred his words badly. "I'll pay for it."

Jimbo gave a grunt of disgust. "I'll give you one more, but that's it." He went behind the bar and filled a shot glass.

Erdle gulped it and shuddered.

"I've already called a cab," Jimbo said, "but it's going to be a while before it gets here on account Otto has several people ahead of you. You'll have to pick up your car later."

Erdle didn't put up an argument as he lay back in the booth. "Lemme know when he gets here."

Annie stared tentatively at the massive black and chrome bike. She took a step back. "I've, uh, never ridden a motorcycle before," she said, wishing Wes had taken her sugges-

237

tion to use her car. "What if I fall off?"

"Don't." Wes handed her a spare helmet, then put his on. "You're not afraid, are you?"

The look in his eyes challenged her. "Of course not."

"Let me help you with the strap." He tilted her head back and fastened the strap beneath her jaw. "Okay, Red, you're all set." He swung one leg over the bike and sat on the leather seat. "Your turn. Grab my shoulders and hop on."

Annie hesitated. She should have known it would require bodily contact. She did as he said, climbing on.

Wes showed her where to put her feet and started the engine. "Which way?"

The Schaefer residence was a two-story colonial with long porches and a perfectly manicured lawn. Wes parked his bike, shut off the engine, and waited for Annie to climb off.

She looked at the house as she stood and unfastened her helmet. "Let's get this over with."

Wes rang the doorbell. A moment later a striking brunette opened it, holding in her arms what appeared to be a newborn baby. She took one look at Annie, and her mouth formed a large *O*.

"Hello, Donna."

"Why, Annie Fortenberry, you are the absolute last person in the world I expected to see."

Annie smiled tightly. Donna looked considerably older, her facial bones prominent, deep creases embedded between perfectly formed eyebrows. She had lost weight and appeared as fragile as a china teacup. "I'm sorry to bother you this early," Annie said, "but it's important."

The woman's smile faded as she caught sight of Wes, but she quickly disguised it. She hesitated, as if uncertain whether to invite them in. Finally, she stepped back so they could enter.

The oversize foyer held an antique pedestal table that shone like a new penny, on top a crystal vase with fresh flowers and beside it the mail that had been precisely stacked, larger envelopes on the bottom, the smaller ones on top.

"Gosh, how long has it been?" Donna asked, but didn't wait for an answer. "You look great."

"I see you have a new addition to the family," Annie replied. "I didn't know you'd recently had a baby or that you were even pregnant."

Donna's eyes clouded. "We haven't kept in touch like we should have," she said. She held the baby up for inspection. "This is Kevin. He's six weeks old today," she added proudly.

Annie stepped closer to get a better look at the infant, so close, in fact, that she thought she smelled alcohol on Donna's breath. "Congratulations. He's adorable."

Donna stood there a moment as if wondering what to do or say next. "Why don't we go into the den?" she suggested. "I was just about to put Kevin down for a little nap."

Annie and Wes followed the woman to the back of the house and into a large, picture-perfect room. Annie knew that a professional had decorated the room. The French doors looked out onto a covered patio where several tables and chairs sat among lush plants. Annie and Charles had attended a number of cookouts at the Schaefers'.

"Please make yourselves comfortable," Donna said. "I'll be right back."

Annie and Wes sat on the sofa. "I think she's been drinking," Annie whispered.

He looked at her. "I thought her mouthwash smelled funny."

Donna returned a few minutes later. "May I offer you refreshments?"

"No thank you," Annie said. "We can't stay long." She thought she saw relief in the woman's eyes.

Donna smoothed her wool slacks and sat in a chair directly across from them, her back ramrod straight. "Annie, Norm and I read about poor Charles in the newspaper. We were just sick over it and everything else that has occurred since. Please accept our sincere condolences. If there's anything we can do —"

"I'm fine," Annie interrupted, thinking either Donna was a damn good actress or Wes had his information wrong. Annie glanced at Wes, who seemed to be studying the woman closely. "Donna, I need to ask you something," Annie said, "and I thought it would be best if we came by while you were alone."

The woman plucked a piece of lint from her slacks. "It sounds serious."

Annie shifted on the sofa, feeling more uncomfortable by the minute. "There is talk that you and Charles were romantically involved."

Donna looked incredulous. "Who would say such a thing?"

"I have proof," Wes said.

Donna tossed a dark look his way. "I don't believe you," she said stiffly.

He nodded and stood, as did Annie. "We'll be back," he said. "With pictures."

The color drained from the woman's face. She clutched the arms of the chair. "Wait!" she said. When they faced her once more, she looked sadly resigned, and her voice was strained when she spoke. "Please." She motioned to the sofa. "Don't leave. Not yet."

They both sat.

Donna looked directly at Annie. "Why are you doing this?" she asked. "Charles has been gone for more than three years. What do you hope to accomplish by coming here now?"

"Someone murdered my husband," Annie said simply.

"And you think that person might be me?"

"Somebody who knew about the affair could have killed him," Wes said.

"If you're insinuating that my husband killed Charles, you're wrong. He didn't know about . . ." She turned sad eyes to Annie. "The affair," she added.

"So it's true," Annie said simply. She sighed heavily, trying to take it all in.

Donna began to fidget with her hands. "Charles told me the two of you were divorcing. Norm and I were having serious problems as well. Things just sort of happened, and before I knew it, Charles asked me to leave with him."

"How could Norm not have suspected?" Annie asked, and then realized what a dumb question it was, since she hadn't either.

Donna shrugged. "Who knows? Perhaps Norm was having an affair as well. He was out of town the night Charles and I were supposed to leave together. As planned, Charles and I each spent the day getting things ready, tying up loose ends. Supposedly, he had a late-afternoon appointment for an oil change. We'd planned to drive to Atlanta, spend the night, and fly out early the next morning —"

"To Jamaica," Annie said.

"Yes," Donna said, so softly it was barely audible. She took a deep breath. "I was packed and ready at the designated time, only he never showed up."

"What time was that?" Wes asked.

"Seven pm." Annie had left for her mother's that morning.

"What did you do?" Wes asked. "When he didn't show up?"

"What *could* I do? I just assumed I'd been duped." Her shoulders sagged; she seemed to sink within herself. "I should have known something was up. We'd planned the trip well in advance, but Charles stopped calling as often as he had before. Even when I knew it was safe to call his cell, he didn't always answer. When he did answer, he acted rushed." She gave a rueful smile. "I knew there'd been other women . . ." She paused as tears sprang to her eyes. "But you know how it is: you keep thinking you're different from the others."

"No, Donna," Annie said coolly. "I don't know how it is."

More tears. Donna swallowed. "I was desperate." It took her a moment to pull herself together. "Anyway, Norm and I managed to get our marriage back on track, and a couple of years later I became pregnant with Kevin. Things are going well for us, Annie." Her eyes seemed to plead for understanding, even as tears ran down her cheeks.

"I'm happy for you both," Annie said, "but the fact remains, my husband *was* planning to leave. He'd packed his bags. Only he never made it because somebody murdered him."

Donna shook her head. "I don't know anything about it other than what I read in the newspaper like everyone else. And, of course, heard on CNN."

Annie closed her eyes. Just her luck that her husband's mistress had seen her in that damn bathrobe.

"You say your husband was out of town at the time," Wes said. "Where was he?"

"I don't remember. We own a couple of other real estate companies outside of Beaumont, one in Hilton Head and the other in Savannah, so he could have been at a sales meeting or assisting one of the brokers."

The front door opened and footsteps sounded in the foyer. Donna jumped at the sound. Norm Schaefer stepped into the den. He looked from Annie to Wes and finally at his wife. "What's going on, Donna? Why are you crying?"

CHAPTER TEN

Nobody said anything right away. Finally, Annie stood. "Hi, Norm," she said. "It's so good to see you again." She paused and introduced him to Wes, and the men shook hands, even though Norm still looked confused.

"Wes is a professional photographer and is taking pictures of Beaumont. He's renting a room from me. I asked him to bring me over on the off chance you'd be home so I wouldn't have to bother you at the office." Annie hated to tell even more lies, but for some insane reason she didn't want to give Donna up. "Naturally, Donna and I began reminiscing about Charles, and I'm afraid we both let it get to us. I should have known better than to discuss it with a new mother who's going through hormonal changes."

Norm nodded as though it made sense. "Donna and I were both saddened to learn of Charles's death," he said as though loath to use the word *murder,* "and the charges brought against you. I don't know what Lamar Tevis is thinking. If he weren't related to half the big shots in this town he never would have been hired in the first place."

"Honey, what are you doing home this time of day?" Donna interrupted.

"Kevin has his six-weeks checkup in half an hour," Norm said. "I thought I'd go with you, see how the boy is doing. Don't tell me he's napping again. You promised to keep him awake as much as possible today so he'd sleep tonight."

"It's not as easy as you think," Donna said.

Annie heard the tension in their voices and suspected the couple wasn't getting much rest these days, what with a newborn in the house.

"That boy eats every two hours like clockwork," Norm said. "By the time we finally fall asleep again he's crying to be fed."

"I have a cat like that," Annie replied. She glanced at her watch. "Wes and I should be going so you and Donna can make your appointment."

"Why did you want to see me?" Norm asked.

"Huh?" Annie blinked. "Oh well, it's

probably going to sound silly. It's about Charles," she said. "I just wanted to ask you whether you know if he was having problems with anyone at work. Or any of his customers," she added, wondering if Norm would fall for her story.

"You want to know if he had any enemies," Norm said. "Absolutely not. He was well liked at the office, and a genuine asset to the company." Norm looked thoughtful. "We miss him, Annie, even after all this time."

She smiled. "Thank you. It's nice to hear. But if you think of something that might help —"

"I'll call right away," he said.

Donna and Norm walked them to the door. Norm put his hand on Annie's arm. "Annie, I don't mean to sound insensitive, but now that Charles has been officially declared dead, I want you to know he had a sizable life insurance policy. Once you get this legal business behind you, and I have no doubt you will, you'll be eligible to collect."

Wes drove the motorcycle to a small park and pulled into an empty slot. "Why are we stopping?" Annie asked once he'd cut the engine.

"Climb off. I want to talk to you."

Annie did as she was told. "If this is about Charles's life insurance policy, I know nothing about it."

"How can you not know about your husband's life insurance?"

"I mean, I knew he had it, but I don't know what Norm means by 'sizable.' Charles was in perfect health. I can't see him paying out-of-pocket for a larger policy than what his company provided."

Wes remained silent.

"Think about it, Wes. If I was hoping to collect on Charles's insurance, why would I have buried him in the backyard, where he wasn't likely to be found? If I had killed him, knowing there was money to collect, I would have put his body in his car before driving it to the Savannah airport. You can't collect insurance on a person who has been listed as missing. Jeez, even I know that. And why all these questions?" she demanded. "I feel like you're accusing me."

"Because sooner or later you may have to face a jury. You'd better get used to it."

Jimbo and Otto from Otto's Cabs managed to rouse Erdle. "Man, you look like shit," Otto said.

"I think he's still drunk," Jimbo said. "I

249

probably shouldn't have given him anything else to drink, but he had a bad case of the shakes."

"You're killing yourself, Thorney," Otto said. "Come on; let me help you up." Together the men managed to get Erdle outside and into the cab. "You're not going to puke in my cab like last time, are you?" Otto asked.

Erdle shook his head.

Otto took his place in the driver's seat and started the engine. "I'll have you home in no time."

"My lan'lady is goin' t'kick me out for sure this time," Erdle managed weakly.

Otto gave a grunt. "I doubt it. She has too many problems of her own."

"Huh?"

Otto glanced at Erdle in the rearview mirror. "Don't you ever read the newspaper?" When Erdle shook his head, Otto went on. "She's been charged with murdering her husband."

Erdle just stared.

"Yeah, man. They took her to jail. She's out now, but there's going to be a trial and everything." When Erdle didn't respond, Otto glanced up at the rearview mirror once more. "You're sweating like a pig. Hang in there, okay?"

"Take me to the p'lice department," Erdle said.

"Say what?"

"Take me," Erdle demanded. "I got t'clear up some biz-ness. I's impor'ant."

Ten minutes later Otto pulled up in front of the police station. Erdle opened the back door, stepped out, and tripped on the curb. He fell facedown on the sidewalk. Blood spurted from his nose.

"Dammit to hell!" Otto said, slamming out of the car. He pulled Erdle to his feet. "Hold on." Otto yanked the door open on the passenger side and grabbed a box of tissues. He yanked out several and handed them to Erdle. The blood soaked through the tissue in a matter of seconds. "Here, take the box," Otto said, frowning. "Man, I ain't never seen you look this bad."

Erdle swayed. "I'm 'kay," he said. He turned and slowly staggered toward the double doors.

Inside, the dispatcher gaped as Erdle stepped up to the counter. "Sir, are you okay?"

Erdle swayed again and grabbed the ledge to keep from falling. "I need to see Tevis."

The woman sniffed. "You have been drinking."

"I know who murdered that fellow."

On the other side of the counter, an officer looked up from a file cabinet. He joined the dispatcher. "What's your name, sir?"

"Erdle Thorney. *T-h-o-r-n-e-y.*"

"And you're here to discuss a murder?"

Erdle nodded, the box of tissues tucked beneath one arm, a wad of tissue pressed to his nose. His bottom lip was beginning to swell.

"The victim's name?" the officer asked.

"Fortenberry. Y'all just dug him up the other day."

The dispatcher picked up her phone and punched a number. "Chief, you need to get out here. There's a guy says he has information on the Fortenberry case."

Tevis wasted no time. "Erdle?" he said. "What in tarnation happened to you? Do you need to go to the hospital?"

Erdle shook his head. "You arrested the wrong person. I'm the man you want."

Tevis frowned in confusion. "What are you talking about?"

"I'm the one who did it. I murdered Charles Fortenberry."

Theenie raced out the front door and down the steps the minute Wes pulled up on his bike. From the look on the woman's face,

Annie could see that something was terribly wrong.

"Erdle's in jail!" Theenie said.

"In jail?" Annie groaned. "Please tell me he wasn't driving drunk! He knows better."

"No, nothing like that. You're not going to believe it. He confessed to murdering Charles."

"What!" Annie almost fell off the bike. "But that's impossible. He wasn't even here that week."

"Well, of course he wasn't," Theenie said. "Don't you see what he's trying to do?"

Annie slumped. Finally, she climbed from the bike. "He's taking the rap so the charges against me will be dropped. What did Lamar say?"

"I didn't talk to him. Delores, the dispatcher, called me with the news. She and I used to play bingo together at the VFW once a week, until people started getting greedy and buying five and six cards at a time. I can barely keep up with one card. There's just no fairness in that if you ask me."

Annie went on before the woman could go off on a tangent. "Has Erdle actually been charged?"

"Delores said he was too drunk to answer questions. Said Lamar put him in a cell to

253

sleep it off. After Erdle threw up in the lobby."

"Oh, Jeez. I suppose I should go get him."

"Won't do any good," Theenie said. "Delores says he's out cold. Said she'd call when he woke up. After Lamar questions him," she added. "You ask me, they ought to take him over to the hospital and throw him in the detoxification unit." Theenie began to fidget with her hands. "Oh, and Jamie called. I told her you and Wes were checking out a lead." She looked from one to the other. "Did you find out anything?"

"Still looking into it," Wes said.

Danny Gilbert pulled into the driveway and parked his truck. "What's going on?" he asked, making his way toward them. "How come everybody looks worried?"

Annie told him what was going on.

Danny shook his head sadly. "I'm not surprised Erdle would try to protect you," he said.

"I need to call my attorney," Annie said. All three followed her into the house, where Tchaikovsky blared from the ballroom. Annie did an eye roll. "Lovelle's practicing her dance routine." She dialed Nunamaker's cell phone number and got his voice mail. After explaining the latest events, she hung up.

The music stopped and Lovelle came into the room in a hot pink leotard and skirt. "Guess you heard the news," she said to Annie, shaking her head in disgust. "I'm beginning to think Lamar earns bonus fishing days for everybody he locks up. Too bad he can't find the real killer."

Wes excused himself and went upstairs.

"This is probably bad timing," Danny said to Annie, "but I was thinking maybe you'd like to see a movie tomorrow night. Might take your mind off your problems," he added. "I'll even buy you dinner beforehand." When she didn't respond, he leaned closer. "Annie?"

"Uh? Oh, I'm sorry. I'm just worried about Erdle. I need to drive over to the police station and find out what's going on."

"I would drive you myself if I had time," Danny said, "but I'm in the middle of a job. What do you say?"

"You should go," Theenie said. "You haven't done anything fun in a long time. Maybe Lovelle and I will go out for a bite to eat." Lovelle nodded in agreement.

Annie smiled. "Sounds great, Danny," she said, although it was the last thing on her mind at the moment. But she knew Danny wouldn't give up until she agreed, and she had promised. "I should be paying *your* way after all the work you've done," she said. "We had a deal."

He ruffled her hair playfully. "I just told you that so you'd agree to let me take care of the floors," he said, "so I'm covering it." He checked his wristwatch. "I'd better run. How about I pick you up tomorrow around five-thirty so we'll have plenty of time to eat before the seven o'clock movie?"

"I'll be ready," Annie said as Wes cleared the stairs. His camera hung from his neck.

"I'm going out for a while," he said. "Thought I'd take a few pictures since it's such a nice day."

"What about lunch?" Annie asked.

"I'll grab a hot dog if I get hungry." He started for the back door.

"I'll follow you out," Danny said, telling the others good-bye. He waited until they'd cleared the back stairs. "You got a minute?" he asked.

Wes paused and turned. "What's up?"

Danny hesitated. "I know it's probably none of my business, but is anything going on between you and Annie?"

Wes's gaze turned cool. "Why do you ask?"

"Simple. I don't want to see her hurt. She's been through a lot."

"What makes you think I'm interested in

hurting her?"

Danny frowned. "Do you always answer questions with a question?"

"I appreciate your concern for Annie, but even if we were involved, I wouldn't discuss it with you."

Danny's jaw hardened. "I've already had to clean up after one man," he said. "You have no idea how hurt Annie was when she found out Charles was cheating on her."

"Yet you didn't waste any time telling her," Wes said, and walked away.

Wes parked his bike and pulled out his cell phone. He dialed a number, and a woman answered from the other end.

"Hello, gorgeous. Do you miss me?"

"Yeah, like a gunshot wound to the head," she replied.

"I need you to run a check on several people."

"And I'm going to do this because?"

Wes grinned into the phone. "'Cause you're hot for me."

"That would mean I have exceptionally bad taste in men. Give me their names."

Shortly after lunch, Annie walked into Lamar's office without an invitation and found him admiring a new rod and reel.

She planted both hands on her hips and gave him a no-nonsense look that told him she was not in a good mood. "I've come for Erdle."

"Look what my brother sent me for my birthday," Lamar said, holding up his new toy. "Got a seventy-five-pound test line. Can you imagine pulling in a seventy-five-pound fish?"

"Nope. And I don't want to."

"Well, it would probably have to be a shark," he said thoughtfully.

Annie simply looked at him, thinking how scary it was to have someone like Lamar Tevis protecting the town. "I don't have all day, Lamar."

"Oh boy, I can tell you're still mad over that incident several days ago."

"Incident?" she said in disbelief. "You mean the one where you searched my home from top to bottom or the part where you arrested me for murder?"

"Aw, Annie, I was just doing my job. Do you think I enjoyed it?" He shrugged when she remained silent. "Hey, if you're here to yell at me I may as well tell you that Jamie Swift beat you to it. She and the mayor have already given me an earful."

"Frankie Fontana visited you?"

"Oh yeah. I'll probably lose my job before

this mess is over. 'Course I'll have more time to pursue my dreams."

Dreams? Lamar? Annie blinked. "That's real special, Lamar, but why did you lock up Erdle?"

"The man could barely walk when he came in, so one of my officers suggested he lie down. He confessed to your husband's murder, but he couldn't remember the details. When he woke up he had no idea where he was or how he'd gotten there."

"So you don't consider him a suspect?"

Lamar practiced casting his rod. "I'm undecided. I know how protective he is of you. If he thought Charles Fortenberry mistreated you in any way —"

"You're barking up the wrong tree, Lamar. Again," she added. "Have you bothered to investigate the case further or are you just going to pin the murder on me and be done with it?"

"The DA was the one who insisted on bringing you in, not me. It's all about politics, Annie, but you didn't hear it from me. As for your question, the answer is yes, I am considering other possibilities."

"But I'm still the main suspect."

"Technically, yes. But you got a dang good lawyer, so I wouldn't lose any sleep over it. Which reminds me, Cal Nunamaker said he has a ton of friends who love deep-sea fishing, and that I should dock my boat over on Hilton Head because people are willing to pay whatever it costs to catch the big one, especially if it's business-related and they can write it off."

"Great. In the meantime, have you found my husband's remains? And when are you going to take down that ugly crime scene tape? I'm losing business; I've got strangers running through my yard taking video —"

"Annie, do you have any idea how much stress I'm under?" he said. "Eve Fortenberry calls some three or four times a day, yelling in my ear as loud as she can because she can't have a funeral for her son without his remains. And when she doesn't feel like yelling, she blows a whistle into the phone, and now I think I've got tinnitus. And did you know she's offering a ten-thousand-dollar reward to the person who finds her son's, um, body parts?"

"I could use ten grand," Annie said to herself.

Lamar pressed one hand against his forehead. "I've got TV and newspaper reporters hounding me day and night, crackpots calling saying aliens took Charles's remains, and now CNN wants to do a special on me. They're tired of focusing on big-city crimes and gangs. They want one of those touchy-feely stories about small towns with low crime rates, only we're going to look bad on account everybody thinks you killed your husband and buried him in the backyard. That's the kind of coldhearted big-city stuff CNN is trying to get away from. Dang, I wish this had never happened."

Annie sank into a chair and covered her face. Lamar leaned his fishing rod against the wall and paced. Annie wondered if Lamar would consider bringing in extra manpower to help with the investigation, wondered if he had even *thought* about the investigation. She sighed. "So what's the plan?"

"I'm going to let my agent handle it."

Annie looked up. "What?"

"The CNN deal. If they want me they're going to have to fight for me. They aren't the only big dog in town; know what I mean?"

Annie just looked at him, noted his gun. She wondered if he was allowed to keep real bullets in it. "I'd like to take Erdle home now."

Lamar shrugged. "You may as well. He's so hung-over he can't think straight, and he's too sick to think of leaving town. I'll question him once his stomach settles."

Ten minutes later, a slow-walking, slow-talking Erdle Thorney followed Annie to her car.

"Are you out of your damn mind?" she demanded when he climbed into the front seat beside her and closed the door.

"Please don't yell," he said, leaning his head against the side window. "I've had a rotten day. I think."

"It's going to be a whole lot worse if you end up in prison for confessing to a crime you didn't commit. Not that I don't appreciate what you were trying to do," she added.

"How do *you* know I didn't do it? I had just as much opportunity as you did. I never liked Charles anyway."

"Just do me a favor and stop trying to help me, okay? I'm in enough trouble."

"How do you think Annie is holding up?" Jamie asked Destiny when she arrived at the office to pick up her mail.

Destiny shrugged. "As well as can be expected considering most of the town thinks she murdered her husband." She looked at Max. "It meant a lot to her that you retained a lawyer for her." Destiny paused and shot a glance toward the door. "Please don't just stand there." She pointed to the sofa.

Max and Jamie followed Destiny's gaze. "I take it your spirit is with you?" he asked.

"Like I have a choice? But I'm going to solve the problem once and for all. We have an appointment with a therapist in an hour."

Max and Jamie exchanged looks.

"Hold it, Destiny," Jamie said, "and let me get this straight. You're actually taking a *spirit,* an entity that no one but you can see, to a psychologist? Do you think that's wise?"

"She needs help. I can't just stand by and do nothing."

"What kind of help does she need?" Max said.

"I think she's suffering from post-traumatic stress disorder."

Max nodded as though it made complete sense. "I know I'm going out on a limb here, but what if this therapist doesn't believe you?"

"He will. I mean, what kind of person would admit to this sort of thing unless it's for real?"

"A delusional person?" Jamie suggested.

Destiny glanced at the sofa. "Don't start shaking your head. We've already discussed this, and you agreed to go." She turned back to Max and Jamie. "Believe it or not, most, if not all, of my friends have been in therapy for years. Trust me; I know what I'm doing."

"May I borrow your muscles for about ten minutes?" Annie asked Wes when he returned from his outing.

"Sure. How can I help?"

"I need to set up some tables in the ballroom for the wedding on Saturday."

"Lead the way." He followed her toward the living room and through a door that led into a massive room with highly polished wood floors, ornate woodwork, bronzed statues, and the tallest ceiling he'd ever seen, on which fat white clouds had been painted. Wes gazed up at them, so realistic, and for a moment they seemed to be moving. He wasn't aware that Annie was watching him, a smile playing on her lips. It was impossible for him to look away. He thought he saw something in the clouds, but the harder he stared the more difficult it became.

"Don't try so hard," Annie said. "It's like looking at one of those three-D illusion pictures."

Wes relaxed his shoulders, neck, and eyes and simply waited. He had an odd sense of the clouds being alive somehow, as though something pulsed in their centers. The clouds seemed to expand and contract, the edges becoming crisp and distinct, and their roundness began to take on human forms, Rubenesque women and powerfully built men, and from behind, a radiant light somehow seemed to pass through them and purify their nakedness so that it was a thing of beauty. Wes blinked, and the forms faded once more into the clouds.

He looked to Annie for answers.

"One of my ancestors commissioned a French artist to paint something on the ceiling," she said. "He spent three years on the project. Most people can't see what's really there."

"What is it about this house?"

"I'm not sure. I just know it's important to preserve it. That's why I could never sell it."

Wes was quiet as Annie led him to an adjacent storage area where a number of tables, legs folded inside, were propped against one wall. Dozens of metal folding chairs with padded seats had been stacked around the room as well.

Annie selected seven large round tables, and she and Wes carried them into the ballroom and placed them near the wall. "I need to make sure there's enough room for dancing," she said.

Annie was breathing hard by the time

they'd lugged some fifty-plus chairs into the room, placing eight at each table. "Boy, I must be out of shape," she said.

Wes looked her up and down. "Your shape looks fine to me."

"Anybody ever tell you you've got a silver tongue?"

He grinned. "As a matter of fact, I have received a few compliments with regard to dexterity —"

"Never mind," Annie said. "I don't think we're talking about the same thing."

"Perhaps it's time we should. Too bad you're already involved."

She knew he was referring to Danny, but she shrugged it off because it was difficult to explain the relationship she shared with him and because she was beginning to sense a subtle change in Danny. Perhaps it had been there all along and she'd simply been too wrapped up in other things to notice. Like with the clouds, she thought. One had to pause and look closely to see what was really there.

"The guy is in love with you, Annie."

"I can't think about that right now, Wes. Not with everything else that's going on."

"You might have to," he said. "I suspect he has been in love with you for a long time. The question is: what would he be willing to do to have you all to himself?"

Annie frowned. "Are you saying what I think you're saying?"

"It hasn't crossed your mind?"

"Not even once. Danny would never."

"People will do almost anything to protect the person they love," Wes said.

Annie suddenly laughed. "If I didn't know better I'd think you were jealous of him."

He grinned. "I'm not the jealous type, because I always get the girl in the end."

"You are so full of yourself, Bridges."

He stepped closer and toyed with a lock of hair. Annie met his gaze. "How about it, Annie?" he said softly. "How about you and me? Don't you ever wonder what it would be like?" He traced the lines of her mouth with one finger. "Think about it."

She watched him go. Holy hell, she thought. How could he possibly not know that she hadn't stopped thinking about *it* since the minute she'd laid eyes on him? It was Destiny's fault. All the woman talked about was sex. Sex, sex, sex. Anyone who thought about sex that much had a serious problem. Of course, Destiny would never admit to it; she blamed it on the house.

Annie looked around the room. With all the naked statues and titillating art filling the rooms, it was impossible *not* to think of sex. But maybe there was more to it, she thought. What if Destiny was right and there was something about the house itself that caused people to feel more sensual?

Annie walked over to one of the walls and pressed an open palm against it. She waited. She didn't feel any different. She tried the other palm. The wall was surprisingly warm. Why had she not noticed it before? It warmed her hand and slowly moved past her wrist and up her arm. Annie wondered if she was just imagining it, even as the tension seemed to drain from the muscles in her shoulders and on either side of her spine. Her body became loose, and she was filled with a sense of well-being. Her mind floated.

She thought of Wes. The two of them locked together, embracing. Warm and naked in her bed, Wes's hands caressing her, deft fingers seeking. And suddenly his mouth on her, tasting, and her breath becoming rapid. Her reaching out, grasping him tightly as he filled her.

"Oh, my Lord!" she said, and snatched her hand from the wall.

The bearded man sitting across from Destiny read the form she had filled out. Finally, he looked up. Kind eyes peered out from beneath bushy gray brows. "Okay, Miss Doe," he began.

"You may call me Jane, Dr. Smithers."

"How may I help you, Jane?" he asked.

"I know this is going to sound strange," she began.

"Please feel free to speak your mind. You're safe here."

"I have a problem with dead people following me around. Sometimes there are more than just one of them; they just latch on to me and won't let go. It's driving me crazy."

"I'm sorry you've been having such a hard time," he said.

"The problem is *convincing* them they're dead and pointing them to the light. Like this redneck named Ronnie who got drunk and fell out of the back of a pickup truck while coon hunting," she said. "He died instantly, but he was too dumb to realize it. Followed me everywhere, even came into the shower with me. He was a pervert."

"That must have been awful for you."

"Took me forever to get rid of him. I finally lied and told him there was a strip bar on the other side of the light, and let me tell you, he hauled ass the minute I said it."

Dr. Smithers looked sympathetic and he

made notes on his tablet. "Tell me about your childhood, Jane."

Destiny frowned. "My childhood? Listen, Doctor, we don't have time to go into that. I have more immediate problems. There's a new spirit following me, and I haven't had a good night's sleep since she showed up.

"She was a prostitute many years ago. She met her death violently, and that's why she's still hanging around. But I can't help her, because she won't talk. I'm pretty sure she's a mute." Destiny leaned closer. "There are other problems that I can't discuss with you in her presence because she's blocking them."

One hairy brow arched high on Smithers's forehead. "She's in the room with us?"

"Yes. I'm hoping you'll hypnotize her and help her remember these things in her past that are too painful for her to face alone."

Dr. Smithers put down his pen and studied Destiny closely. "Let me make certain I understand what you're asking," he said. "You want me to provide counseling and hypnotherapy for a spirit. So she will go to the light."

"Right. But first she has to help solve a murder. See, a friend of mine has been charged with murdering her husband and burying his body. If I could get this spirit to talk — her name is Lacey, by the way — she might be able to tell us who the real killer is. Oh, and if you could convince her to stop stealing our underwear in the meantime, that would be great," Destiny added.

He took a deep breath. "Okay, back to this friend of yours who has been charged with murder," he began patiently. "Is this person a spirit as well?"

"No, she's real."

"So you're able to differentiate between what's real and what's not?"

Destiny gave him an odd look. "Excuse me?"

He smiled gently. "I believe I can help you, Jane."

Annie was setting the table for dinner when Max and Jamie arrived. "Bad news," Jamie said. "Destiny called as we were leaving the office. She's been locked up in a psychiatric ward."

Annie, Theenie, and Lovelle just stared back at her, looks of astonishment on their faces. Finally, Theenie spoke. "I'm not surprised. I suspected her elevator was one floor short."

"I don't know what that means," Lovelle said.

"It's all my fault," Jamie said. "I knew

271

what she was planning to do, and I didn't stop her."

"I'm equally responsible," Max said. "I should have tried to talk her out of it."

Annie finally found her voice. "What did she do?"

Jamie sighed. "She took the spirit to see a psychologist, hoping he could help her overcome her fears of what happened that traumatized her. I don't know the whole story, because Destiny and I only spoke briefly. She's pretty upset, says she's surrounded by crazy people."

"Jeez Louise," Annie muttered. "They're going to throw away the key. What else can go wrong?"

"Don't ask," Theenie and Lovelle said in unison.

"What should we do?" Annie asked.

"Nunamaker is going to take her case," Max said. "He can't do anything tonight, but he promised to check on it first thing in the morning. I personally want to know how it all came down. You can't just lock someone up without going through the proper channels." He looked at Jamie. "We need to get going."

"Are you sure you can't stay for dinner?" Annie asked.

"We're dining tonight with Max's family,"

Jamie said. "We wanted to tell you about Destiny because we knew you'd worry when she didn't come home tonight."

Wes came through the back door soon after Max and Jamie left. He glanced about the kitchen. "Uh-oh. How come every time I walk into this house I sense another catastrophe? A new drama?" he added.

"I don't know what you're talking about," Annie said. "Everything is fine."

"Couldn't be better," Theenie said, obviously following Annie's lead.

Lovelle nodded. "Life is good."

"Not only that," Annie said brightly. "Dinner is ready."

"Isn't Erdle eating with us?" Theenie asked once everyone was seated at the table.

"He's probably embarrassed," Annie told her. "I lowered the boom on him after the stunt he pulled."

"Maybe it wasn't a stunt after all," Wes cut in.

All three women just looked at him.

Wes shrugged. "It's a thought. He could have had his buddy lie for him."

"I don't think Erdle could stay sober enough to get away with murder," Theenie said. She looked at Annie. "We really should get him some help."

Annie nodded. "I worry about him, too.

I'll take a plate over after dinner."

"He's probably out cold and won't hear you," Lovelle said. "You'll have to climb through his kitchen window like before. Maybe this time he won't have his underwear soaking in the sink. Maybe he got rid of that mouse and you won't sprain your ankle again running from it."

"It won't be easy climbing in a window with a plate of food in your hand," Theenie said. "I would help you if I wasn't afraid that mouse was still in his house." She shuddered.

Something hit the cabinet door and everyone jumped. Peaches sat there looking at Annie. "You've already eaten," she said. Peaches began batting the door with her paw, never taking her eyes off Annie.

"We should drop that cat through Erdle's kitchen window," Lovelle said. "She'd sober him up right quick."

"That's mean," Annie said, although she grinned at the thought.

The garbage can toppled to its side and dumped trash to the floor. Peaches stuck her head inside searching for food. Annie pretended not to notice.

"I'll clean it up," Wes said, shoving his chair from the table.

"It can wait," Annie said. "Go ahead and

finish your dinner."

"She's making a big mess," he said.

"Trust me. It's best to ignore her when she gets into a mood."

The garbage can rocked back and forth. Inside, Peaches kept digging, and before long all the litter was on the floor. The garbage can began to roll. It rolled through the open swinging doors and into the dining room and kept going. Something shattered in one of the rooms. The women didn't look up from their meals.

"Is there ever a peaceful moment in this house?" Wes asked.

Annie looked at him, remembering he once had referred to it as a crazy house. "All the time."

Lovelle nodded. "It's usually real quiet around here."

"Boring, you might say," Theenie added.

Wes went back to eating. "By the way, where's Destiny?"

"Locked up in a mental hospital," Annie replied, concentrating on her food once more.

CHAPTER ELEVEN

It was after 10:00 PM by the time Annie showered and climbed into bed. Theenie and Lovelle had turned in early, and Wes, who'd selected a Ludlum book from a stack in the sunroom, had gone up shortly afterward. Annie set her alarm clock, turned off the light, and snuggled deep beneath the covers, not because she was cold but because she needed to feel the heaviness of the blankets on her, the sense of security their weightiness evoked.

Moonlight peeked through her window and cast a soft glow in the room. Annie had slept in this room the very first time she remembered visiting her grandmother, and it had become her own when she moved in. She'd felt safe and loved, knowing the woman was just next door. Annie had remained in her small room even after her grandmother had died. She'd closed off the grand master suite with its ornate furnishings and mirrored ceiling, slipping inside from time to time for a nap on the tall rice bed, covering herself with the woman's favorite shawl.

Shortly before Annie was to be married to Charles, she had packed her grandmother's clothes and personal items and moved them to the attic, and eventually the woman's scent had faded, replaced with Charles's Aramis cologne and Annie's simple White Linen perfume. Their lovemaking was squeezed in between *Larry King Live* and *David Letterman.* When their marriage began to sour, Charles channel-surfed during the hour-long gap and Annie spent her evenings reading magazines on "How to heat up your sex life," "How to drive your man crazy in bed," and "Satisfying him every time."

She obviously hadn't gotten it right, or so she thought at the time, because one day Charles was there and the next day he was gone. Annie moved back into her old room and read magazines on "How to survive the split," "Life after divorce," and being "Happily single."

Annie jumped when something hit her door, and she heard Peaches mewing on the other side. She thought of putting a pillow over her head to drown out the sound, but she was afraid the cat would wake the others. Annie dragged herself from her bed and opened the door, but the cat started down the hall toward the steps leading to the kitchen. Darn cat, she thought. It would be easier if she just stuffed a feeding tube down her throat.

"Peaches," Annie called out softly as she tiptoed down the hall. "Come here, Peaches." The cat made a sound low in her throat and dashed away.

Annie saw it before she felt it, something light and wispy hovering several yards away, coming toward her slowly. She froze as she caught sight of a woman's face and long swirling hair, barely visible but there nevertheless. Then, a brush of cool air against her cheek, the smell of flowers, and the feeling that something was swirling around her. The air shifted and became icy cold.

"Holy crap!" Annie staggered forward, trying to escape whatever it was, but she fell to one side, hitting her elbow on the wall. She tripped on her own feet, grasped an armchair to break her fall, and stubbed her sore toe. A multitude of four-letter words came to mind, but she was too scared to speak. She had to get back to her room. She turned and hit something solid. The ghost was bigger than she'd thought.

She was screwed.

"Annie?"

"Outta my way, Wes. Can't you see I'm running for my life?" Annie bypassed him and raced to her room, closing the door behind her. She made a mad dive under her covers.

Wes poked his head inside. "Problem?"

Annie mumbled from beneath the covers.

"What's a gust?" he asked.

Annie peered out. She could barely see him in the shaft of light from her bedroom window. "Not gust. Ghost." It was hard to talk with her teeth chattering.

Wes closed the door, walked to the bed, and pulled the covers aside. "Good thing I'm here to protect you." He slid beneath the sheets. "The things a guy has to do." He slipped one arm beneath her head. "Come closer."

Annie snuggled against him.

"You're shivering. What did you see?"

"A woman's face and hair. She just came at me, and everything got cold."

"Did she appear menacing?"

"No, but it still scared the hell out of me." Annie was quiet for a moment. "You know, I think I've seen her before. Maybe when I was a little girl," she added. "Or maybe I just dreamed of her." When Wes didn't say anything, Annie lifted her head and looked at him. "Do you believe me?"

"I think you were just trying to get me in your bed." There was a smile in his voice. "I may start hiring people to scare you so I can sleep here every night."

Annie grinned. "Sorry about the flannel gown," she said. "I wasn't expecting company."

Wes ran his finger across the material. "Feels nice."

"It's been known to send ice water through a man's loins."

"Trust me, my loins are feeling just fine. If they start feeling any better one of us is going to have to leave."

Annie liked the timbre of his voice against her ear. She had to admit snuggling against Wes's warm body was a lot more fun than lying beneath a pile of blankets. "I'm glad you're here," she said after a moment. "I was feeling sort of lonely."

"I would have been here a lot sooner if I hadn't been afraid you'd kick me out."

"It's been a long time since I shared a bed with a man," Annie confessed.

"After one night it'll be old hat."

"You're assuming I'll invite you back."

"I'm assuming you won't let me leave."

She punched him lightly. After a moment she grew serious. "Wes, I'm scared. About being convicted of a crime I didn't commit."

"I know."

"I'm not afraid for myself, but if something happened to me, if a jury actually found me guilty and I had to go to prison, I don't know what would happen to Theenie and Lovelle. Or Erdle, for that matter," she added. She remembered how bad the man had looked when she'd delivered his dinner and a short sermon on his drinking.

"Do you trust me, Annie?" Wes asked.

Oddly enough, she did. "Yes."

"Then take my word for it: I'm going to do everything in my power to keep you out of jail."

"You don't really think Erdle killed Charles, do you?"

"I have a friend running checks on several people. So why don't you try not to worry, and let me handle it?"

Annie lay there quietly, wondering who else Wes thought might have killed her husband, but she was tired of thinking about it. All she did these days was worry; now she simply wanted to enjoy being held. Her mind drifted; the real world with its problems soon felt very far away. The only thing she was conscious of was the man beside her, his chest beneath her cheek, his steady heartbeat, and the way his long legs felt against hers.

Annie placed one hand flat against his chest, enjoying the sturdy feel of him. She ran her hand slowly across Wes's stomach, found it hard and flat. His muscles tensed beneath her fingertips. He pressed his lips against one temple. She raised her head, and he kissed her chin, the tip of her nose. He pulled back slightly, and for several seconds neither of them moved, even though Annie knew his mouth was only a breath away. Somehow she knew that Wes was waiting on her to make the next move. If she played it safe, closed her eyes and went to sleep, he would simply lie there for as long as she needed him.

But she had played it safe all her life, and look where it had gotten her.

Exactly nowhere.

Besides, who was she fooling? There was no way in hell she was going to fall asleep with Wes Bridges lying beside her.

She shifted on the bed and very tentatively touched her lips against his. They bumped noses, laughed softly. Wes's lips parted, and she tasted him.

Wes rolled to his side, and Annie found herself on her back. The kiss deepened, and Wes slipped his tongue inside, found hers, and their tongues mingled. How long they kissed, Annie couldn't have said, but it felt as if their lips had somehow fused together and she no longer knew where hers began and his left off. What had started out as tender and sort of dreamy, a kiss that she had wanted to sink deeply into and rest her tired soul in, had turned hot and urgent.

Wes pulled off her nightgown and smiled at the sight of her breasts in the moonlight. "Pretty," he whispered. He explored lower with gentle fingers. He covered her with his mouth and tasted her. Annie was almost certain her eyes crossed when he slid inside.

Afterward, he held her. Annie closed her eyes and slipped into a mindless sleep. When she opened them again, the room had lightened and Wes was nuzzling her throat. Their lovemaking was unhurried as they touched and explored and shared heated sighs until they finally shuddered in each other's arms.

The next time Annie opened her eyes, the sun shone through her bedroom window and the birds, which had mistaken the warm winter for spring, chirped and sang. Downstairs she heard someone, most likely Theenie, searching through the pan cabinet, probably in the early stages of preparing breakfast. Annie could not remember when she'd slept so soundly, and it almost didn't matter that she had awakened late. She smiled and stretched.

And froze when her leg brushed against another leg.

Her eyes popped open. Holy cow! She turned and found Wes beside her, a satisfied grin on his face.

" 'Morning, Red."

"Omigod! You're still here."

He cocked one brow. "Am I not supposed to be?"

"No! The others might find out."

"Afraid they'll get jealous?"

"That's not funny. I mean, what will people think? And believe me, news spreads fast in this town. Everyone already thinks I'm a murderer; they'll think I'm loose as well."

"You are loose, but that's a good thing."

She blushed. She was no longer Wild Woman; she was Annie Fortenberry who ran a respectable bed-and-breakfast. She heard footsteps on the stairs and bolted upright on the bed. "You have to get out of here. Now!"

"Only if you'll let me come back tonight."

Annie tried not to stare, but it was damn difficult.

He grinned. "Like what you see?" He dropped a kiss on her forehead and started for the door.

"Wait!" she said. "You can't go out that way. Somebody might see you."

He paused and looked at her. "What do you suggest?"

Annie frantically searched for the gown and panties that Wes had removed the night before. She found them crumpled at the foot of the bed. She dressed quickly, feeling a bit self-conscious under his watchful eyes.

"Sexy," he said.

She didn't feel sexy; she felt desperate. She pointed to the pair of French doors that led to her balcony. "You'll have to go out that way."

"In my underwear?"

"Yes!"

Wes sighed and shook his head as he pulled the doors open and looked out. "Did you forget there aren't any stairs leading down?"

"You can climb from my balcony to yours," she said.

He shot her a look of utter disbelief. "You're kidding, right?"

"They're only about three or four feet apart. You can easily make it."

"This is the dumbest thing I've ever

heard, and I've seen some pretty dumb things in my life. It's downright crazy, Annie. Are you sure all that hot sex didn't jiggle your brain?"

Annie joined him on the balcony. "Piece of cake," she said.

He stood there for a moment, studying the situation as though gauging the distance. "If I don't make it, I want to be buried with my Harley."

Annie heard voices downstairs. "Hurry!" she whispered. She held her breath as he climbed over the wrought-iron railing and planted his feet on the narrow ledge on the other side of the pickets. Taking great care, Wes held on to the wrought-iron banister and had started to step across the three-foot gap to his own balcony when a section of iron leaned toward him, yanking bolts from the stone base and taking Wes by surprise.

Annie watched in horror as the iron gave way completely. Wes twisted around and reached for the railing on his balcony, missing it by several inches. Annie screamed as he fell, landing in the thick holly hedges below.

She darted inside, raced from her room and down the stairs, almost slamming into Theenie and Lovelle, who'd obviously heard her scream and were on their way up.

"What happened?" Theenie asked.

"Wes just fell from my balcony."

The three did a little dance on the steps, trying to get out of one another's way. Annie managed to get past them. Her hands trembled as she turned the lock in the door and flung it open. She took off in a dead run.

Theenie and Lovelle looked at each other.

"What do you suppose the man was doing on Annie's balcony?" Theenie asked.

"Oh, wise up, Theenie," Lovelle said.

Annie found Wes struggling to get out of the hedges, cursing each time the spiky leaves jabbed him. Finally, he rolled out and hit the ground, giving a loud grunt.

Annie knelt beside him. The fact that his eyes were open had to be a good sign. "Are you hurt? Should I call nine-one-one?"

Wes pushed himself into a sitting position, glanced at all the pricks on his arms, and shook his head. "I think I'd like to take a hot shower."

Annie winced at the sight of his face and arms where the tiny pricks were already beginning to bleed. "I'm sorry," she said. "I didn't know about the balcony."

Doc suddenly appeared in his bathrobe, a newspaper tucked beneath one arm.

"What's all the racket?" he demanded in a cranky tone. His eyes widened at the sight of Wes. "Uh-oh." He looked at Annie. "You didn't clobber him again, did you?"

In response, she pointed to the balcony outside her room.

Rounding the corner of the house, Theenie and Lovelle came to a halt. "Is he okay?" Lovelle asked.

Annie nodded.

Doc gazed down at Wes. "You need to find another place to live, son. *I* need to find another place to live. It was so much quieter at my daughter's house, even with four kids."

"What are you doing back so soon?" Theenie asked Doc. "I thought you were going to stay with your daughter while she recuperates."

"I was just in the way," he said.

"And how come you always get your newspaper and we don't?" Theenie asked.

Doc didn't answer. "You sure you're going to be okay?" he asked Wes.

"Yeah. The bushes broke my fall."

Doc grinned. "Good. I won't have to put you down."

A sleepy-eyed Erdle suddenly appeared. "I heard someone scream. What happened to him?" He nodded toward Wes.

Theenie explained. Erdle looked up and studied the damaged wrought iron, scratching his head as though trying to decide how much work he was going to have to do to fix it. "I can't believe the stuff that goes on around here," he said. "It's just one dang thing after another. I can't take much more." He wiped his hands down his face. "I need a drink." He turned and walked away.

"What's wrong with him?" Doc asked.

"We had a terrible time while you were gone," Theenie said, wringing her hands. "I just shudder every time I think about it. You would not *believe* what we've been through. And poor Annie," she added.

Doc waited. "Well, *what?*" he asked.

Theenie gave a sorrowful sigh. "I could tell you, but you wouldn't believe me."

"Well, *somebody* needs to tell me," he said loudly.

"It all started the day you left," Lovelle said, beginning with his gardener finding Charles's body. She quickly filled him in on the rest.

Doc frowned at Annie. "You were *arrested?*"

The last thing Annie wanted was for Doc to worry about her. "It'll be okay," she said.

"Max Holt hired a big shot lawyer who is confident I'll get off."

Doc's ninety-year-old face suddenly took on more creases. "Are you sure?"

"Do I look worried?" she asked lightly. "My lawyer has already told me that no jury would convict me because there is absolutely no proof." Annie hated to lie, but she didn't want Doc losing sleep over her problems.

"You let me know if you need money, you hear? Or anything else," he added.

"Let me help you up," Annie told Wes. "We need to get you inside."

He stood on his own. "Am I going to have to scale the walls and climb through the attic window or am I allowed to use the back door like everybody else?"

"Your Honor, this is the craziest thing I've ever heard," Nunamaker said to his brother-in-law, who'd agreed to hear Destiny's case first thing that morning. A male nurse and a social worker had driven Destiny to the courthouse, and the social worker had handed the judge a sheaf of papers and Dr. Smithers's report.

The judge glanced over the report. "Dr. Smithers seems to think your client is dangerous and delusional." He frowned.

"Something about a spirit and a murder?"

Nunamaker waved it off. "The whole thing is preposterous. Dr. Smithers only saw my client once and for a very brief period. I have highly credible witnesses who are prepared to attest to the fact that Miss Moultrie is perfectly sane."

He motioned toward Max and Jamie, who were sitting in the front row in the small courtroom. They both nodded. "Furthermore, my client is not involved with any murder, nor is she under investigation." He paused and squared his shoulders. "I resent these frivolous accusations against Miss Moultrie, as well as the unorthodox measures Dr. Smithers took to have her committed. The magistrate who signed the commitment papers never even spoke to my client."

"Dead people following her around?" the judge said. He arched one brow.

Nunamaker shrugged. "Miss Moultrie has psychic abilities. It's common knowledge that those with her gifts are more perceptive to these phenomena. Miss Moultrie donates her time to helping others through a newspaper column. She writes as the Divine Love Goddess Adviser."

The judge looked at Destiny. "So that's where I recognize you from. My wife and I read your column. Your advice always seems to be right on-target."

"Thank you, Your Honor," Destiny said, speaking for the first time since she'd entered the courtroom. "I'm very proud of the work I do, for both the living and the dead."

The judge leaned forward. "I'm not going to pretend to understand everything you do, Miss Moultrie, but you seem perfectly sane to me." He turned to the social worker. "I'm going to deny Dr. Smithers's recommendation to hold Miss Moultrie for further observation." He smiled at Destiny. "You're free to go."

"Thank you, Your Honor," she said.

The judge stood, brandishing a brand-new tennis racket in one hand.

Annie was dressed and waiting for Danny when Wes came downstairs in his denim jacket, his camera hanging from his neck. Theenie had treated the needlelike puncture wounds and applied small, round Band-Aids to the worst of them.

"Where are you headed?" Annie asked.

"I have work to do."

"Are you sure you're up to it?"

"Hey, you're looking at one tough guy here. Want to see my muscles?"

292

Annie would have enjoyed reminding him she had already seen his muscles and she liked them just fine, but she knew Theenie and Lovelle were taking in every word. She tried to hold back her smile as they exchanged looks, and Annie knew he was thinking about how they'd spent the previous night.

"We all have plans for tonight," she told him, "but there are plenty of leftovers in the refrigerator."

"I'll grab something while I'm out," he said, although he didn't seem to be in a hurry to leave. He just stood there looking at her, a half smile playing on his lips.

Annie tried not to remember what those lips were capable of.

"Oh, look at the time," Theenie said. "If Danny doesn't get here soon, the two of you won't have much time to eat before the movie."

Annie knew Theenie had mentioned the fact she was going out with Danny for Wes's benefit.

Wes looked Annie over. "I'd better let you go so you can fix yourself up for your big date."

Annie glanced down at her neat slacks and best white blouse. She'd even taken special care with hair and makeup. "I *am* fixed up."

"Oh well, my mistake." He winked once and walked out the back door.

"Very funny," Annie mumbled under her breath.

Danny arrived shortly after. "So how about a nice, thick steak?" he said.

"You want to know what I've been dying for?" she said. "A big, fat, juicy hamburger, onion rings, and a thick strawberry milk shake."

"You mean Harry's Place? I offer you steak and you'd rather eat grease?"

"Yeah, ain't it sinful?"

They arrived at Harry's Place a few minutes later and found the parking lot packed. "Hope we can get a table," Annie said as they made their way to the entrance. Inside they found a long waiting line.

Danny looked at his wristwatch. "We're doing okay on time as long as we don't have to wait too long to get served once we get a table." He glanced around the room. "Oh, look, there's your pal. What happened to his face?"

Annie glanced in the direction Danny was looking. She froze when she spotted Wes sitting in a booth in the back, across from him a pretty blonde. They were leaning forward talking, their heads so close they almost touched. "Um, he fell," Annie managed, trying to keep her voice from wavering, but the sight of Wes with another woman almost made her ill. She resisted the urge to bolt out the front door.

"The guy certainly has good taste," Danny said, looking amused. "He must like 'em young; she barely looks old enough to vote. I'd ask to join them, but they look pretty intense."

"You know what?" Annie said. "I think I'd like to have a good steak after all."

It was all Annie could do to remain cheerful and attentive as they waited for their waitress, but she was determined to give it her best shot, since Danny had taken her to a nice steak house. Because all of the other tables were taken, they'd been seated at one in the bar where mostly men sat on the tall stools watching a sports program on a widescreen TV.

The waitress appeared, and Danny ordered each of them a glass of red wine and the filet mignon with béarnaise sauce. He waited until the waitress hurried off. "If you're a good girl and eat all your vegetables, I'm going to order you your favorite dessert, Death by Chocolate."

"You're so bad," Annie said.

"I know all your weaknesses, Anniekins."

Sometimes she wished he wouldn't be so nice, and she wondered if maybe Theenie was right, that Danny wanted more out of the relationship. She looked up and found him watching her intently, his eyes telling her things he had never said out loud. Annie averted her gaze and reached for her wineglass. She raised it to her lips, and it slipped through her fingers, splashing wine across her blouse, and shattered on the table. "Oh no!" she cried, reaching for her linen napkin to blot the mess she'd made. "I'm so clumsy!"

"Watch out for the glass," Danny warned, using his own napkin in an attempt to help. The waitress arrived with a damp cloth.

"I need to run to the ladies' room and see if I can get the wine off my blouse before it stains," Annie said, and hurried away. Inside the restroom she wet a paper towel and pressed it against her forehead. Jeez, what was wrong with her? She was losing it, that's what. She was making a fool out of herself over a man. She tried to scrub the stain from her blouse, but it was no use.

She looked up, spied her reflection in the mirror, and saw the pain and disappointment in her eyes. "Boy, you really know how to pick them," she muttered to her reflection, her mind filled with the image of Wes and the blonde.

Annie had almost forgotten how bad she could hurt, and she hadn't even known Wes long. She thought of Nick and Billie Kaharchek. Love at first sight. Annie sighed. That sort of thing only happened to other people.

She arrived back at the table to find the waitress had cleared the glass from the table and delivered their food. "The stain didn't come out, huh?" Danny said.

"I'll try to treat it with something at home," Annie said.

"You'd better eat before the food gets cold."

Annie picked up her steak knife and considered falling on it. What did it matter? Her blouse was already ruined. Instead, she grabbed her fork and began the process of eating.

"How's your steak?" Danny asked.

"Great," she said, giving him an appreciative smile. She suddenly spied the widescreen TV and saw her own reflection. The local news station was enjoying a real heyday thanks to her problems. Her smile faded.

Danny followed her gaze. "Oh, hell," he muttered. "Let's get out of here."

Annie waited until they were in his car to say anything. "It's okay, Danny," she said.

"I'm getting accustomed to my new-found notoriety. Look on the bright side. I could be discovered and end up on *Star Search*. And you can tell everybody you knew me *when*."

He shook his head. "Only you could crack jokes at a time like this."

"The least you can do is look amused. I'm using my best material."

"Do you realize there isn't anything I wouldn't do for you?"

"Of course I do. You've already proven it time after time."

"I'm not talking about sanding floors or making household repairs. I'm telling you that there are no limits, no line I wouldn't cross, to protect you."

Annie felt herself frown. "Please tell me you're not planning on doing anything dumb like Erdle did."

"We should get away," Danny said. "Spend a few days in the mountains. Theenie and Lovelle wouldn't mind. It would give us time to think. And talk," he added.

Annie looked out her side window and wondered when things had changed between them, wondered why she hadn't seen it coming despite Theenie's warnings. She had counted on Danny's friendship for so long, what would become of them now?

"Annie?"

She couldn't look at him. "You know I can't."

He gave a sigh. "I thought things would be different with Charles out of the picture. I kept hoping. But I guess deep down I knew it wasn't going to happen." He looked thoughtful. "And now there's Wes."

"I'm sorry." She finally looked at Danny.

His face was weighted with disappointment, but he didn't say anything. Instead, he reached for the key and started the car. "What do you say we skip the movie tonight?"

Annie walked into the kitchen and skidded to a halt when she found Wes sitting at the kitchen table reading the newspaper. And she thought things couldn't get worse. "What are you doing here?"

"Last time I checked, I had a room here."

"You're home early. Why are you home early? What time did you get here? And where did you get that newspaper?" She had to pause to catch her breath.

"I've been here a couple of hours, and I found the newspaper in the bushes. Have you been drinking a lot of caffeine? Is that a wine stain on your blouse?"

"Why are you interrogating me? I haven't

done anything wrong."

Wes studied her for a moment, a perplexed look on his face. "Could we start over?"

"I want you out of here, Wes. I'm evicting you as of this moment. I'll give you all your money back."

"I don't want money. Besides, I like it here."

"This is my house, and if I say you're out, you're out." She turned and marched up the stairs.

Wes just sat there, shaking his head in confusion. Finally, he stood and started up the stairs. He found Annie in his room stuffing his clothes in his backpack.

"What the hell are you doing?"

"What does it look like I'm doing? I'm throwing you out. I should never have rented to you in the first place. You'd think I would have learned my lesson by now where men are concerned."

He shoved his face in hers. "Lady, what *is* your problem?"

"I saw you tonight. With the *blonde.* Really, Wes, isn't she a little young for you?"

He looked surprised. "She's not as young as she looks. Her brother is a plastic surgeon."

Annie grabbed his pack and lugged it from the room and down the stairs.

Wes followed.

Annie opened the door, dumped the backpack on the piazza, and crossed her arms. "See ya."

"Red, we need to talk." He closed his arms around her waist and locked his fingers together.

"Take your hands off of me!" she shouted.

"Not until you calm down and listen to what I have to say."

"What is going on here?" Theenie demanded from the doorway.

Annie turned and found Theenie and Lovelle standing there, each holding her purse. "Wes was just leaving."

Destiny walked through the back door. She paused, glanced at Wes and Annie, and then made her way to the refrigerator. She nodded at Theenie and Lovelle. "Does anybody want a sandwich?"

"How was the funny farm?" Wes said.

"It sucked; how do you think it was?"

Wes looked at Annie. "You weren't kidding."

Annie picked up his backpack, stepped out on the piazza, and raised it high over her head.

Wes hurried after her and reached for it. "Hey, don't throw that," he yelled. "My camera is in there."

They struggled.

The women huddled at the door and watched.

Erdle staggered up the back steps. "Who's doing all the yelling?" he asked. His eyes were red-rimmed, his words badly slurred. He took one look at Annie's face and staggered back. "Uh-oh, she's at it again."

"Let me go!" Annie shouted, trying to wrestle the bag from Wes.

"Miss Annie, please stop!" Erdle pleaded. "You can't keep acting like this. You're only going to end up killing someone else."

CHAPTER TWELVE

All eyes turned to Erdle. Wes and Annie stopped struggling.

Annie realized her mouth was hanging. "Erdle, what the hell are you talking about?" she demanded.

He covered his mouth as though only just realizing what had come out of it. "Uh, I need to lie down." He stumbled toward the door.

Annie grabbed his arm. "Oh no, you don't. Not until you explain what you just said."

"I don't r'member."

"Then you'd better search your memory, because I'll call Lamar and have you thrown into detox if you don't finish what you started."

He looked hurt. "You'd do that?"

"Damn right. Now, start talking."

"I don't want to cause no trouble," the man said, glancing at Annie. "I could be wrong, but I thought, um . . ." He glanced down at the floor.

"What did you think?" Annie said. "That I killed Charles?"

Erdle shrugged. "I just wondered, that's all. I mean, I knew the two of you didn't get along. Far as I'uz concerned, he was a no-'count husband, and I didn't much care what happened to him. 'Sides, I figured you had a damn good reason. So I kept quiet." He looked up. "Reckon I was wrong."

Annie was clearly stunned.

Theenie had begun picking her nails.

"I think he's had too much to drink," Wes said to Annie. "Why don't I help him to bed?"

"I can make it," Erdle said. "I've had a lot of practice." He looked at Annie. "Can I go now?"

She shrugged and turned away.

He let himself out the back door.

Theenie was the first to speak. "You can't take Erdle seriously. He's a drunk."

"Who else in this room thinks I murdered my husband?" Annie asked.

Theenie gave a snort of disgust. "Don't be ridiculous."

"It never crossed my mind," Lovelle said. "I wouldn't have moved in if I had thought you were responsible for his disappearance."

304

"I know damn well you didn't do it," Destiny said.

Annie looked at Wes. "And you?"

"Would I be looking for the real murderer if I thought you'd done it? Erdle is just whacked-out on booze."

Annie went to the table and sank tiredly onto a chair. "My life sucks. I've got a drunk for a handyman, a crazy, senile neighbor, and a spirit in my house stealing everything."

"Speaking of which . . ." Destiny carried her sandwich to the table. "I think I'm finally gaining Lacey's trust. I had a long talk with her when they threw me in the rubber room. She stayed with me most of the time to keep me company."

Theenie gasped. "You were in a padded cell?"

Destiny's look was deadpan. "The Hyatt was full."

"She wasn't in a padded cell," Lovelle said. "They only put dangerous nutso cases in those kinds of places."

Destiny went on. "I met with a guy from the historic foundation, Mr. Hildenbiddle, this afternoon, and he gave me some interesting information. Also told me about some of your more colorful ancestors," she said to Annie. "But you already know, because

Mr. Hildenbiddle said he'd shared the information with you a long time ago."

Annie's face pinked. "Okay, Destiny, you insist on airing my dirty laundry, so I may as well tell it all. Your spirit, Lacey Keating, was my great-great-grandmother, and madam of the bordello which she named Passion's Fruit. In her diaries, she claimed she got the idea because at the time there were dozens of peach trees on the property."

"Why didn't you tell us, dear?" Theenie asked.

"I didn't particularly want to share that information with anyone, but I suspect a lot of people already know."

"People aren't going to think badly of you because of what your great-great-grandmother did," Lovelle said. "My brother married a lesbian stripper, and nobody held it against our family."

Theenie looked confused. "He married a lesbian stripper? How does that sort of thing work?"

Lovelle shrugged. "Beats me."

Destiny reached into her pocket. "I don't know if this means anything, but Lacey gave it to me. I have a feeling it's significant." Destiny set a single sapphire earring on the table. Tiny diamonds surrounded the blue stone.

Annie's eyes widened, and she reached for it.

"Don't touch it," Destiny said. "I'm hoping if I hang on to it a couple of days I might get some vibes. Find out who it belongs to and why Lacey seemed to think it was important."

"Don't bother," Annie said. "I recognize it. It belongs to Donna Schaefer."

Annie and Wes remained at the kitchen table as, one by one, the others drifted off to bed. Although Annie was embarrassed that the entire household had witnessed what Theenie referred to as Annie's "hissy fit," she was still hurt over seeing Wes with another woman.

It was no wonder Erdle had suspected her of killing Charles; she *had* to do something about her temper.

But right now she needed to accept the fact that Wes did not feel as strongly about her as she did about him. She had only been a diversion.

"Annie, I can see the wheels turning in your head," he said finally. "We need to talk."

She shook her head. "It's late, and I don't want to discuss our relationship. . . ." She paused. "Correction: what I *thought* was a relationship. I'm not going to insist that you leave tonight, but I would appreciate it if you would vacate the room as soon as possible. Preferably in the morning."

"No."

She looked up. "Excuse me?"

"I'm not going anywhere. Not until your name is cleared." When she started to object, he held up his hand. "But right now, you're going to listen to what *I* have to say."

She crossed her arms. "Five minutes."

"There is absolutely nothing going on between me and the woman you saw me with tonight."

She did an eye roll. "Jeez, where have I heard that before?"

"Probably from your dearly departed husband, and by the way, I don't appreciate being compared to him. The blonde, Peggy Aten, is my ex-partner from when I was a cop."

Annie gazed back in disbelief. She remembered how nervous she'd been at the thought of him living there, recalled Destiny telling her Wes Bridges was not what he seemed. "You were once a cop and you never mentioned it to me?"

He shrugged. "I didn't see the need. I got out a while back because I could tell I was getting burned-out after spending ten years as a homicide detective. I needed a change."

"So you became a photographer?" she said, thinking it an odd choice.

Wes gazed down at his hands for a long moment, his eyes troubled. He looked at Annie, opened his mouth to say something, and then closed it as though he'd changed his mind. "I'd rather not talk about that right now," he said. "I need to concentrate on the problems before us. I'm just asking you to trust me. And know that I have your best interests at heart."

Annie pondered it. Trust didn't come easy for her. Not when men were involved. But the concern in Wes's eyes, as well as the numerous unanswered questions about her husband's murder, told her it was best not to press him for more information.

"I wish you had told me about the cop part earlier," she said. "I would have worried less knowing I had an expert investigating the murder. Instead of someone who made his living taking pictures," she added.

He almost smiled. "Peggy was able to get her hands on some valuable information. You might be interested to know that Norman Schaefer never checked into his hotel the night of the murder. The night his wife claimed he was out of town."

"Oh yeah?"

"He was supposed to be at a real estate seminar. It wasn't listed on his expense reports, charge card, or checking account. In other words, he never showed."

"How did this Peggy person find out all of that?"

"She has friends in all the right places. The less you know, the better. If the case was to go to court and Norm was a potential suspect, Nunamaker would naturally ask him to produce proof of his whereabouts the night his wife claimed he was out of town."

"What do you think it all means?"

"It sounds suspicious as hell, if you ask me. But it gets even better. Norm had an oil change the week before your husband came up missing, and they recorded his mileage. A week later he had a small fender bender, and the mileage was included in the report. Had Norm attended a sales meeting in Savannah or Hilton Head, he would have put at least a couple of hundred miles on his car, only the odometer listed less than one hundred miles during that period."

"So he never went out of town," Annie said. "Wonder what he was doing?"

"Following his wife, maybe? I'm going to pay Lamar Tevis a visit tomorrow. Tell him what I know."

"I'll go with you."

"Maybe, maybe not," he said.

"Huh?"

"You obviously haven't read today's paper."

"No."

"You might want to take a look at the obits." He handed it to her. "Your husband's memorial service is being held tomorrow at two o'clock."

"Tomorrow?" she asked, her eyes round and wide. "Does that mean his remains have been located?"

"I spoke with Lamar. Nothing so far, and Mrs. Fortenberry isn't convinced they'll ever be found. She said she needed some kind of closure on this and if they *do* find the remains she will have a private burial."

Annie's face drained of color, and her emerald eyes looked as though they'd turned to stone. "And she didn't bother to *tell* me? She thinks she can just plan a memorial service for my deceased husband and not *tell* me?" Tears filled her eyes; Annie was suddenly furious. "I don't believe it."

"Come with me, Annie," Wes said, getting up from his chair. She looked dazed as he pulled her up. "We're going for a walk. We're going to practice what's called anger management. And at this moment you look like the perfect candidate."

Annie waited until he'd slipped on his denim jacket before going into the living room and pulling her lined windbreaker from the coat closet. "I hope none of my neighbors see me lurking in the night," Annie said as she and Wes stepped outside. "They'll think I'm looking to break in and kill somebody in their sleep. I'll be hauled off to jail again."

"You do look pretty dangerous in that Mickey Mouse jacket."

"Theenie, Lovelle, and I went to Disney World last year. They chipped in and bought me this." She tossed him a dark look. "Don't try to cheer me up; I'm still mad as hell."

"You have every right to be. I'm just trying to teach you ways to deal with it better. Before you discover where Theenie hid the rolling pin."

Annie sucked in the cool night air as they crossed the piazza and cleared the front steps, passing the fountain where the cherubs stood in repose. They crossed the yard and started down the sidewalk. Streetlights lit the way, and tall oaks, their massive roots jutting through the sidewalk, formed a high canopy over the cobblestone road that the residents of the historic district had refused to let the city replace with asphalt.

"I'm going to Charles's memorial tomorrow, Wes," Annie said after they'd walked a while.

"I figured as much." But he sounded worried. "I think you should maintain your distance with the woman; avoid her altogether."

"Eve Fortenberry has never liked me."

Wes tried to match strides with Annie, but she was walking fast. "I'm going out on a limb here, but I'll bet she likes you less since you were arrested for her son's murder."

"Let her think what she likes. She has suspected me of doing something to her son since he first turned up missing."

"I wonder why?"

Annie shook her head. "I don't know. Maybe it was easier for her to think I'd done something to him than to imagine him leaving without even telling her or contacting her in all that time.

"And now it's easier for her to hate me than to . . ." Annie paused and shrugged.

"Accept the death of her son?" Wes finished for her.

"Yeah."

They walked in silence. After a while, Annie felt the tightness in her stomach dissolve, and the muscles in her neck and shoulders no longer felt like rubber bands pulled tight enough to snap. She continued to breathe in the night air. Here and there she caught the unmistakable scent of gardenia, another reminder that winter had somehow escaped them. Wes had been right to get her out; the air had cleared her head, and she felt, oddly enough, rejuvenated.

"Better?" he asked as if noting the change.

"I must be. I no longer feel like driving to my mother-in-law's and slicing all of her tires. I think I'm even beginning to feel sorry for her. Just don't tell anyone; I don't want to lose my edge." She realized they had walked quite a distance. "We should turn back," she said.

"Getting tired?"

"Not really. I've caught my second wind. I should do this every night. But that would make it seem like exercise."

They turned around and headed for the house. Wes took her hand. "I forgot to ask. How was your evening with Danny?"

"We had a good time," she said, trying to keep her tone light. She didn't want to have to think about Danny right now. She looked at Wes, noted how dark he looked in the moonlight. Mysterious. "I'm, uh, sorry I lost my temper earlier. I haven't always had a temper. I don't even know when I got it."

"You'll work it out."

They'd arrived at the house. Wes released Annie's hand once they reached the front steps. "How does hot chocolate with marshmallows sound?" she said.

Ten minutes later Annie carried two steaming cups of hot chocolate, piled high with marshmallow topping, to the kitchen table. She'd put out a small plate of chocolate chip cookies that Theenie had made a few days before.

Wes and Annie sipped their cocoa in silence, but she felt his eyes on her. "You're staring."

"I can't help it. You look so pretty with your cheeks flushed from the walk and your hair all mussed. Like you just spent the last hour or so making love," he added, and drained his hot chocolate.

Annie felt something stir inside of her. The attraction she'd felt for him before had intensified into full-blown lust. And something else she wasn't ready to put a name to. She finished her hot chocolate and carried both cups to the sink, where she rinsed them and stuffed them into the dishwasher. She heard Wes get up, and a few seconds later he slipped his arms around her waist and kissed the back of her neck.

"How about a shower?" he said.

She turned. "You mean together?"

"It'll be more fun that way. Besides, you know what they say: it's cheaper if two people shower at the same time."

"Oh yeah?"

He stepped closer and gathered her in his arms, tilted her head up, and kissed her. He ran his hands through her hair, across her shoulders, and down her back before sliding them over her hips and pulling her closer.

Annie tasted the chocolate on his tongue, felt the strength of his arms. She laid one cheek on his chest. He felt safe, like an anchor holding her in place even with all that was going on in her life. At the same time, his kisses turned her thoughts to mush and sent logic right out the door.

After a moment, he pulled back slightly. "Is my timing off?" he asked. "I know you have a lot on your mind."

She took his hand and led him toward the stairs, where he paused to take off his boots, as though realizing they would make too much noise on the bare steps. Nevertheless, the wood creaked beneath his and Annie's feet, and she winced, hoping they didn't wake Theenie. Inside the bathroom, Annie grabbed a couple of towels and washcloths from the linen cabinet.

"We don't need washcloths," he said. "I'd rather wash you with my hands."

Annie's stomach did a little dance at the thought. She put the washcloths back. When she turned, she found him pulling off his shirt.

Wes reached for the buttons on her blouse, undoing them slowly, pressing kisses against her neck and shoulders as he pushed the material aside and let it fall to the floor. He gazed at the lacy bra she wore. "Nice," he said, cupping her breasts with his hands.

Annie could feel the heat of his touch through the fabric, and she stifled the moan low in her throat. Wes reached around and undid the clasp. He tossed the bra aside and pulled her against him once more. Skin touched skin.

He lowered his head and took one nipple in his mouth and tongued it until Annie felt it harden. He moved to the other nipple and teased it as he reached for the button on her slacks.

Annie slipped her arms around his neck and sighed as her body reacted; her lower belly warmed. Wes leaned down and pulled off her shoes. Her slacks joined the rest of her clothes on the floor. Finally, he removed her panties, and his bold stare drank in the sight of her naked body.

Annie could not help feeling self-conscious. She and Charles hadn't showered together often. Their first time in bed had not been at all romantic; he'd simply suggested they strip down and crawl beneath the sheets, where they could "fool around." His caresses had not been slow and light like Wes's. She'd felt rushed and, afterward, an enormous sense of disappointment and frustration as Charles held her in his arms stiffly for a few minutes before turning over and reaching for the remote control and turning on *Letterman.*

Wes kissed her once more, and his big hands felt like heaven on her body. "Undress me," he said against her lips.

Annie was only too happy to oblige. Her knuckles grazed his hard belly as she unfastened his jeans and tugged the zipper. Freed from their clothes, they simply stared at each other.

"You're beautiful," he said. His smile was lazy and sexy as hell.

"You're not so bad yourself, big guy."

Wes turned on the water, tested it, and motioned for Annie to step in first. He joined her and pulled the shower curtain closed.

The warm water felt good against Annie's shoulders and back. Wes wet the soap, made lather, and then spread it across her back. He put the soap aside and began kneading her neck and shoulder muscles until Annie felt them go lax. He massaged her back as he washed. Annie sighed.

"Feel good?" he asked.

She nodded. "I guess I was a little tense."

He chuckled and turned her around. "There are other ways to relieve tension, you know." He soaped her from head to toe before slipping his hand between her thighs. Annie cried out softly as he brought her to orgasm. She grasped his shoulders, buried her face against his chest, and shuddered.

"Sweet," he said.

Once she stopped trembling, Annie washed his back and hips. She soaped his chest and stomach before moving lower. He was already erect. Palms slick with soap, Annie closed her fist around him and brought him to full arousal. Wes laughed softly as he stilled her hand, rinsed himself, and turned off the water. They dried quickly and moved into the bedroom.

He wasted no time, running his tongue lazily across her body, to her center, until Annie clutched at the covers and bit back the moans that accompanied the burst of pleasure that was as powerful as the first. Wes moved over her, and she arched high as he filled her. They moved together fluidly. Annie felt her eyes tear with emotion at the beauty of their coupling, the exquisiteness of their joined bodies, and the sound of her name on Wes's lips when he lost himself in her.

Afterward, he gathered her close and they lay there quietly as their heartbeats slowed. Wes glanced down. "Why the sad look?"

"I'm just tired," she said. "It's been a long night." She couldn't tell him the truth: that she was beginning to care about him too much too soon, and that it terrified her.

Wes arrived at Lamar Tevis's office shortly after 10:00 AM and found the police chief sipping coffee and reading the newspaper, both feet propped on his desk. He looked up. "What happened to your face?"

"I cut it shaving."

"Holy cow!"

"I have information on the Fortenberry case," Wes said.

"Can I get you a cup of coffee?" Lamar asked. "We also have cheese Danish. Home-made, I might add, by our dispatcher. Yesterday it was cinnamon rolls, and the day before that —"

320

"No thanks," Wes interrupted.

"Grab a chair and tell me what you got," Lamar said.

Wes told him what he knew about Donna and Norm Schaefer.

"So Fortenberry was having an affair with his boss's wife. Sounds like trouble waiting to happen."

Wes reached into his shirt pocket, pulled out the sapphire and diamond earring, and placed it on the desk. "She lost this at Annie's place."

Lamar pulled his feet from the desk. "Hey, this is nice," he said, picking up the earring and studying it closely. "Are these real diamonds?"

"Yeah. I just had it checked out at the jewelry store down the street. You've got a full karat sapphire and another karat of diamonds, all high-quality stones."

"I'm confused," Lamar said. "What does this have to do with anything?"

"It puts Donna Schaefer at the house during the time Annie was away."

"Was that the only time she went to the house?"

"Mrs. Schaefer visited at Christmas, months before Charles came up missing. It was the same Christmas her husband bought the earrings. Annie said the woman loved them so much she wore them all the time. She and Charles had planned to leave together, but he didn't show."

Lamar reached for a notebook and began scribbling.

"Here's my theory," Wes said. "Although she denies it, I think Mrs. Schaefer was angry when Charles didn't arrive at her house as planned and she drove over to confront him. They got into a bad argument, and it became physical."

"Why do you suppose Fortenberry changed his mind?"

"Maybe he met someone else in the meantime. He had a reputation for cheating on his wife."

"Did Mrs. Schaefer's husband know about the affair?"

"I've got information that suggests he did."

"Okay," Lamar said, scratching his head as though he was having trouble taking it all in. "It sounds like you might have something here. So if you don't mind, I'd like to back up and start from the beginning. Just so I get my facts right."

"No problem."

"By the way, how in the world did you get this information?" Lamar asked.

"From a very reliable source."

Annie and Theenie slipped into River Road Baptist Church and sat in the very last row. Several people glanced at them, and Annie wondered if her oversize sunglasses offered the disguise she'd hoped for. Under normal circumstances she would have sat up front with the immediate family, but the current circumstances were anything but normal. Eve Fortenberry walked into the church, pain etched into the deep lines on either side of her mouth, making her shoulders sag with the burden of it. Annie's heart went out to the woman who'd never really welcomed her into the fold despite all Annie had done to be a good wife.

On a table at the front of the church was a portrait of Charles, young, handsome, and smiling. More regret.

As though sensing Annie's deep sadness, Theenie covered one hand with hers. Annie was glad Theenie had insisted on attending the service with her. She looked about the church and saw Norm Schaefer sitting across the aisle, staring at her. He looked angry; Annie suspected he'd already been questioned. He was alone. Obviously Donna had chosen not to attend.

"Scoot down," Theenie said, interrupting

Annie's thoughts.

Annie looked up. Jamie and Max stood at the end of the row. She immediately made room for them. "Thanks for coming," she said, relieved to find two friendly faces in the crowd.

Jamie reached around Theenie and took Annie's hand. "We thought you'd need a little moral support, but we have to leave as soon as the service is over. A couple of employees are out sick with the flu, so we're covering for them."

Annie smiled and nodded as a woman began singing "Amazing Grace." Afterward, people walked to the podium and told of warm and sometimes funny experiences they'd shared with Charles. Annie found herself smiling from time to time. She had forgotten that side of her husband.

Once the service was over, Annie made her way toward Eve, hoping to catch up with her before she was ushered toward the limo that had been provided by the funeral home. Annie touched Eve's shoulder lightly, and the woman turned. She had obviously been so caught up in her pain that she hadn't noticed Annie in the crowd, because her face suddenly became as cold as a barren winter ground.

"Eve, I'm so sorry," Annie began. "I can

only guess how hard this is —"

"What in the name of God are you doing here?" Eve hissed. "How can you even show your face?"

Annie had never seen such contempt. "I was his wife."

"You're a cold-blooded murderer is what you are."

"We should go," Theenie said, nudging Annie.

"I did *not* kill your son," Annie insisted. "I can't believe you'd even think it."

"Go home, Annie. I can't bear the sight of you. Go back to that new boyfriend of yours that I paid for."

"What are you talking about?" Theenie asked when Annie merely stared back at the woman in utter confusion.

Eve looked at Annie, eyes narrowed. "You don't even know, do you?" When Annie shook her head, Eve almost smirked. "You poor little fool. He's a private investigator. I hired him to find out what you'd done to my son."

CHAPTER THIRTEEN

"I should drive," Theenie insisted as they approached Annie's car. "You're far too upset."

Upset didn't come close to describing how Annie felt. *You poor fool.* Eve's words echoed in Annie's head. And that's exactly what she was. Wes Bridges had been hired by her mother-in-law to look into her claims that Annie was responsible for Charles's disappearance. Renting a room in her B & B had made it easy. Sleeping with her had provided the intimacy Wes thought would make her more open to a little pillow talk.

"You haven't driven in years," Annie said. Her face and limbs felt numb and her chest tight. She gulped in several breaths. A horn blew and Theenie pulled her from the path of a car.

"Are you okay?" Theenie asked.

Annie nodded.

"Give me the car keys."

"It's a stick shift."

Theenie shrugged. "It's been a while, but I can do it. You need help getting into the car?"

Annie shook her head and climbed into the passenger seat as Theenie took her place behind the steering wheel. She started the car, and it leaped forward and died.

"Clutch," Annie said.

"Oh yeah. It's all starting to come back to me now." Theenie tried again, and the car lurched forward. "You want me to take you home?"

"No. I can't face Wes right now. Take me to a bar."

"Come again?"

"I need a drink."

"Oh dear, I've never really been in a bar. We might look like a couple of sluts, walking in by ourselves."

"I am a slut," Annie said. "A fool *and* a slut."

"You're not a fool."

They drove a distance, the car bumping along as Theenie tried to reacquaint herself with a four-in-the-floor. "There's a bar," Annie said, pointing to a place called Jimbo's Bar and Grill. "Pull in."

"It looks a little rough to me," Theenie said, but did as she was told.

Annie climbed from the car and marched toward the door. Theenie had to move quickly to keep up with her. They stepped inside and blinked, trying to adjust their eyes to the dark interior. It smelled of stale cigarette smoke. The bartender, a big man in a stained white T-shirt, paused and stared. "We want a drink," Annie announced.

"Have a seat."

"Let's sit in the booth in the back," Theenie whispered, "so nobody will see us."

They headed in that direction, still trying to maneuver their way in the dark. Theenie started to sit, then gave a little yelp and jumped up. "There's a man lying here. He's probably dead. Somebody probably shot him last night and forgot to remove the body. We should leave. You don't need to be seen around dead people on account of you're already up for a murder charge."

Erdle Thorney sat up and blinked. Annie and Theenie blinked back. "What are you two doing here?" he asked.

"Annie needs a cold one," Theenie said. She and Annie took the seat across from him. Theenie began picking at her fingernails. "You look awful," she told Erdle.

The bartender arrived. "This is Jimbo," Erdle said. "He owns the place."

"I need something strong," Annie said. "I've had the worst day of my life." Well, maybe the second worst day, she thought, the first being when Charles's remains were discovered buried in her backyard.

"Give her a tequila straight up," Erdle said, "and as long as she's buying, bring me the usual."

"And you?" The bartender looked at Theenie.

"I'll just have a glass of tea."

"All we got is Long Island iced tea."

Theenie looked thoughtful. "Well, I usually drink Lipton, but I'm open to new experiences."

This brought a smile to Jimbo's face. "I'll be right back."

The front door opened, and a man stood there for a moment, silhouetted by the light streaming in from the outside. He closed the door behind him, blinked several times as though trying to see, and then headed toward them.

"It's Norm Schaefer," Annie whispered.

Theenie squinted. "I didn't know he was a worthless drunk, too."

Norm approached the booth, a menacing look on his face. He pointed to Annie. "You and I need to have a little talk."

"How did you know where to find us?"
she asked.

"I followed you from the church." He
looked at Theenie. "Where'd you learn to
drive? I've never seen such bad driving in
my life. Somebody needs to take your li-
cense."

Theenie hitched her head high and
sniffed. "That would be difficult, seeing as I
don't have one."

Norm gave a grunt of disgust. "You old
people need to get off the road."

"Would you like to sit down?" Annie
asked, trying to be polite but hoping he
wouldn't take her up on her offer. She had
never seen Norm act so rude, but she was
determined not to make a scene.

He ignored her invitation. "What the hell
did you tell the police?" he demanded, his
eyes boring into hers. "They came to my office this morning and questioned me about
your husband's murder. I don't like having
cops show up at my place of business."

"I haven't told the police anything," Annie replied. "It's not my favorite place right
now."

He sneered. "Then it must have been your
biker boyfriend."

Annie hated sneers. She had an urge to
slap it right off his face, but she was in no

hurry to go back to jail. "Wes is not my boyfriend. He's just somebody I have sex with." The sneer disappeared, and Annie decided it was worth having Theenie and Erdle openly gape at her.

"I don't care if he's your damn plumber," Norm said after he'd composed himself. "Tell him to mind his own business or you're both going to be sorry."

"Are you threatening me?" she asked.

"Don't threaten her," Erdle said. "I'm too drunk to kick your ass."

Norm put his finger in Annie's face, and she decided she liked that even less than sneering. But she wasn't about to let him upset her; that's exactly what he was looking for, and it would be her first time practicing anger management on her own. "Did you have something else you needed to say?" she asked lightly. "Before I ask the owner to throw you out?"

"Yeah." Norm put his hands flat on the table and leaned closer. "Don't blame me because your husband had problems keeping his zipper closed."

Theenie gasped. "That's a *terrible* thing to say on the day of Charles's memorial service. Especially to his widow," she added. "Didn't your mother teach you any manners? Why, if I had children, which I don't,

I would have raised them to be more sensitive to other people's feelings."

Jimbo arrived with their drinks and set them on the table. "Y'all want to run a tab?"

"That's fine," Annie said. She waited for him to leave before she addressed Norm. Instead of lashing out as she was tempted to do, she decided to take the high road. "I'm sorry that you were embarrassed by the police, Norm," she said, trying to sound sincere, "but they're questioning all of Charles's friends. That doesn't mean you're a suspect."

"She's right," Theenie said as though hoping to diffuse the man's anger. "Annie's the only one they want to fry."

With those words, Annie picked up her shot glass of tequila and tossed it back like she'd seen people do on TV. It took her breath away. "Holy crap!" she managed, and then began to wheeze.

"Bite into the lemon," Erdle said.

Annie did as he said, but it didn't help. "I can't feel my tongue."

Norm shook his head, muttered a four-letter word, and walked away.

"Here, dear," Theenie said when Annie's eyes began to roll around in her head. "Drink some of my tea. It's not bad."

Annie took the glass and gulped thirstily.

Beads of perspiration oozed from her pores. She drained the glass.

"Uh-oh," Erdle said.

"It's okay," Theenie told him. "I'll order another." She motioned for Jimbo. "Would you be so kind as to bring us two more iced teas?"

"Uh-oh," Erdle said.

Two hours and three Long Island iced teas later, Theenie's head was on the table and Annie was still telling Erdle how sorry Wes Bridges was. "Did I tell you he's a private investigator hired by my mean ol' mother-in-law to snoop on me?" she said, her words badly slurred.

Erdle nodded. "I believe you mentioned it once or twice or maybe ten times." His words were equally slurred, but then, he'd drunk nonstop since Annie and Theenie had arrived.

Jimbo delivered their check. Annie picked it up, and her mouth dropped open. "Holy marolly!" She looked at him. "I believe you gave us somebody else's check. We didn't have this many drinks."

"Long Island iced tea has four different kinds of booze in it, lady," he said.

Annie looked at Erdle. "Did you know that?"

"Uh-huh. But you and the old gal seemed to like it."

Annie swallowed. That explained why she could barely see. She leaned closer to Erdle. "I don't have this much cash."

"Don't look at me. I'm flat busted."

Annie smiled at Jimbo. "My credit card is at its limit. Do you take personal checks?"

"Nope." He pointed to a big sign in bold letters that read: Absolutely No Personal Checks. Despite the size of it, Annie had to squint to see it, only to realize she was seeing double.

"Aw, c'mon, Jimbo," Erdle said. "I can vouch for her."

The man made a sound of disgust. "Look, Thorney, I don't care if she's the pope's sister; you know the rules. If I had a dollar for every bounced check I've gotten over the years I could walk away from this dump a wealthy man."

"Well, what do you expect me to do?" Annie asked.

"Hey, I don't care if you have to go from table to table and give lap dances; it's your problem. Let me know when you figure it out."

"This is not good," Erdle said.

"You're right," Annie said. "Because I don't know the first thing about lap dancing." She recounted her money in case she'd made a mistake. She was way short. "Will Jimbo call the cops on us?" she whispered to Erdle. "I can't afford to get busted again."

"I've seen it happen," he said. "First Jimbo takes 'em out back and slaps 'em around; then he calls the cops."

"Uh-oh. I can't afford to get slapped around, either. I have to give a wedding day after tomorrow. I mean, how would it look?" She glanced at Theenie, who was snoring. "Maybe she can lend me some money." She tried to wake Theenie, but the woman didn't so much as budge. Annie shook her harder. "Wake up, Theenie, I need money," she shouted in her ear, causing the other customers to look their way.

"You're making a scene," Erdle hissed.

Annie sank into the booth. From the looks of the other customers, it was hard to believe that she could possibly say anything to offend or embarrass them.

"I have no other choice but to check Theenie's purse," Annie said. She pulled out the woman's wallet, looked inside, and frowned. "She has less cash on her than I do."

"Uh-oh," Erdle said.

"What are we going to do?" Annie asked. "We can't pay this tab."

He thought for a minute. "I'll call for backup." He slid from the booth and almost landed on the floor. He grabbed the edge of the table to steady himself. "I'll be back."

Danny Gilbert arrived fifteen minutes later. He scratched his head and perused the threesome. "What happened to Theenie?"

"She's taking a nap," Annie said.

"So you ladies decided to drop in for a couple of drinks, huh?" he said, glancing about the room, now filled with bikers and construction workers.

Jimbo suddenly appeared. "The guy across the room wants to buy the redhead a drink," he said.

Annie was flattered. "Oh yeah?"

"I think we're leaving," Danny said. "Do you have the check?"

"Sure do." Jimbo handed it to Danny, who arched both brows. "Wow," he said, reaching into his back pocket for his wallet. "When you guys decide to tie one on, you don't mess around."

"It wasn't our fault," Annie said. "We didn't know the bartender was putting extra booze in our drinks." She looked at Jimbo as though she held him personally responsible for the condition they were in.

"They were drinking Long Island iced

tea," Jimbo told Danny.

Danny looked annoyed. "Did you inform them in advance how much alcohol was in each drink?"

"I don't run a babysitting business," Jimbo said.

Danny counted out the money and handed it to him.

The man didn't look pleased. "What, no tip?"

"Yeah, I have a tip for you," Danny said. "Next time tell people what they're getting when they order a drink they've never heard of."

Jimbo pocketed the money. "Just get them out of here, okay?"

"What are we going to do about Theenie?" Annie asked. "She's passed out."

"Good question," Danny said.

Jimbo gave a disgusted sigh and motioned for Annie to get out of the booth. "Grab the old broad's purse," he said.

"Excuse me, but did you just refer to my friend as a broad? Why, you're nothing but a —"

"Annie, let's just get out of here," Danny said. "Now."

Annie reached for her and Theenie's purses and slid from the booth. Jimbo leaned over, pulled Theenie across the booth, and threw her over his shoulder. "Just tell me where you want her."

Annie fell asleep as soon as Danny helped her into the backseat of his car. "We'll pick up your car in the morning," he said, but she and Theenie were both out cold. "Guess you're not really worried about it right now," he said as he closed the door.

"What happened?" Danny asked Erdle when he joined him in the front seat. "I've never seen Annie in this condition."

Erdle told him how Eve Fortenberry had treated Annie at Charles's memorial service.

Danny looked incredulous. "Wes is actually working for Eve?"

"I don't know what's going on between them now. All I know is that Eve hired him to find out if Annie was responsible for her husband's disappearance and obviously got a great deal of pleasure announcing it to Annie at the memorial."

"Does Wes know that Annie's on to him?" Danny asked.

"Not yet. But he will the minute Annie sets foot in that house, buh-lieve you me." He paused and glanced over his shoulder at the two women. "Unless Annie is still unconscious."

Danny chuckled. "You know, I think I'd

like to hang around and see that."

Annie and Theenie awoke as soon as Danny cut the engine. "Where am I?" Theenie asked. "What day is it? And how come my head hurts like the dickens?"

"It was the tea at Jimbo's Bar and Grill," Annie said. "It was spiked with tons of alcohol."

"Oh my. And it went down so easy."

The two women climbed from the car and stumbled up the front walk. The front door was thrown open by a worried-looking Wes. "You two look terrible," he said. "Where have you been?"

"They got all liquored up," Erdle slurred.

Annie walked past Wes without a word and headed for the kitchen to put on a pot of coffee. He followed. "Are you okay?"

She glared at him. "Are you asking out of personal concern or is this just part of your job?"

"What?"

"Annie knows the truth," Danny said. "Her mother-in-law gave her an earful at the memorial service."

Wes sighed and raked his hands through his hair. "I was planning to tell you."

"I don't want to hear anything you have to say. I don't even want to look at you.

What I *do* want is for you to leave this house immediately."

"I don't work for Eve anymore, Annie. In fact, I gave her a full refund, including her retainer. I'll bet she didn't bother to tell you that, did she?"

"I don't care if you gave her the Hope Diamond. You're a liar and a phony, and I don't ever want to look at your face again." She staggered from the room and up the stairs.

"I think she means it," Danny said. "I'd start packing if I were you."

"That's going to make things real convenient for you, isn't it, Gilbert?"

"Don't blame me, friend," Danny said. "You managed to screw up all by yourself."

When Annie opened her eyes the sun had gone down and her bedroom was bathed in shadows. She could barely make out Danny's form in the corner chair. "Is he gone?"

"Yes. I stayed with him while he packed so he wouldn't be tempted to knock on your door."

"Thank you."

"How do you feel?"

"Like I should be in ICU."

Danny moved to the bed, sat down, and

took her hand. "Listen, I've got some time off, so I'm going away for a while."

"How long is a while?"

"Actually, I've had a job offer in Charleston."

"I didn't know."

"I'm supposed to report to work in a couple of days."

"So you've already decided."

He nodded. "I think a change would be good for me."

"How will I reach you? Will you still have the same cell phone number?"

"No, I'm going with a different plan." He paused. "How about I call you once I find a place to live and get settled in?"

"That'll be great. Charleston's only a little more than an hour away. I can come on a Saturday or Sunday morning and stay all day."

"Yeah." He reached up and mussed her hair. "Be good to yourself, Anniekins."

Annie watched Danny leave through her bedroom door, and instinct told her he would not be calling anytime soon, if at all. She sat in the growing darkness, knowing she had never felt more alone. Wes was gone, and one of her very best friends had just said good-bye.

She had a choice: she could either sit in

bed and feel sorry for herself or move on.

She would move on, because that's the way she was.

Annie entered the kitchen some minutes later, once she'd run a brush through her hair and brushed her teeth. She needed to eat; maybe the food would absorb whatever alcohol remained in her stomach. She found Theenie, ice pack pressed against her head and a bottle of Extra Strength Excedrin in her hand. Her other hand held the phone to her ear. She glanced at Annie.

"Thank you for calling," Theenie said. "I'll be sure to pass the news to Annie. . . . No, she's not mad at you." Theenie hung up.

"I hope that wasn't Doc. If he sees us like this he'll put us down for sure."

"Guess what?" Theenie said as she opened the bottle in her hand.

"I could use a couple of those," Annie said. "Maybe three."

Theenie shook two tablets into her palm and passed the bottle to Annie. "That was Lamar Tevis on the phone just now. And guess what?"

"Okay, *what?*"

"Donna Schaefer just confessed to murdering Charles. The charges against you have been dropped."

CHAPTER FOURTEEN

Wes checked into a motel, grabbed his knapsack from the bike, and went inside the room. He dropped his bag on the bed, switched on the TV set, and went into the bathroom, where he threw cold water on his face. In the mirror over the sink a tired, haggard man looked back at him. Wes paced the room, picked up the remote, clicked on several channels, and turned off the TV. Finally, he kicked off his boots and lay down on the bed.

He awoke shortly before 11:00 PM with an empty stomach.

Some ten minutes later Wes pulled into a diner where a neon sign flashed the words: *We Never Close.* Inside, a jukebox wailed a Patsy Cline song, competing with the loud, steady hum of voices and occasional laughter.

Wes glanced about, noted the full booths, and took a seat at the long counter. A TV set anchored to the ceiling played the eleven o'clock news. He tried to listen once the Patsy Cline song came to an end, but Jimmy Buffet took her place.

A young waitress with hair that had been bleached one too many times sauntered toward Wes, the gleam in her eyes making it clear she liked what she saw. Her uniform was short, the top button undone, giving Wes an unimpeded view of plump, youthful breasts. "What'll you have?" she asked.

He averted his gaze. "Large milk and a stack of pancakes."

"Want hash browns with that? We're running a special."

"No thanks."

She stood there for a minute, tapping a pencil against her bottom lip. Her mouth was slick with gloss. "You're new in town, aren't 'cha?"

He glanced up at the TV. "Yeah. Just visiting."

She smiled. "I saw your bike when you pulled in. Awesome. I love motorcycles, but I've never ridden on one."

Wes kept his eyes glued to the TV. "Will my order take long? I'm in a hurry."

"No problem. I'll put a rush on it." She scribbled something on her pad and turned.

Wes blinked and straightened on his stool

when Lamar Tevis's face suddenly flashed on the screen. "Hey, wait, can you turn up the volume on the TV real quick?"

"We're not supposed to."

Wes smiled. "Please."

She ambled toward it, reached for the remote control, and turned it up a notch. Lamar's face disappeared, was instantly replaced with a photo of Donna Schaefer, followed by what appeared to be a home video of her leaving a hospital with a baby wrapped in a blue blanket tucked in her arms. She pulled the blanket back, and there was a close-up shot of the baby, red-faced and squint-eyed, his tiny fist pressed to his mouth. A smiling Norm Schaefer stepped into the frame, wearing the look of a proud new father.

Wes strained to listen, but the jukebox drowned out the sound. "I still can't hear the TV," he told the waitress when she delivered his milk.

"You wouldn't be able to hear a freight train coming through with that music blaring," she said. "Just hold on." She disappeared through a swinging door. In less than a minute, the jukebox died. Several people began to complain.

"I'm sorry," the waitress shouted, arms flailing as though she had no idea what was going on. "I'll bet the dang thing blew another fuse."

Wes grinned and slapped a ten-dollar bill in her palm.

Annie, Theenie, Lovelle, and Destiny were crowded around the TV set in the sunroom as the newscaster gave the latest details on the investigation of the murder of Charles Fortenberry. Jamie and Max had called only minutes ago to let Annie know the local news station was airing a news conference.

All four women were quiet as they watched Lamar step up to a microphone while one young officer in the background did his best to make sure the camera got a shot of his face. He smiled, waved, and mouthed the words, *Hi, Mom.*

"Ladies and gentlemen," Lamar began in an authoritative voice. "As you know, this office has been investigating the murder of thirty-year-old Charles Fortenberry, who was found buried in his wife's backyard less than two weeks ago. Mr. Fortenberry had been missing for more than three years. Thanks to the hard work of my excellent investigative team, we have solved the case. In record time, I might add."

"Excellent investigative team, my butt," Jamie muttered.

Lamar glanced down at his notes. "At approximately three *pm* today, thirty-five-year-old Donna Schaefer, a lifelong resident of Beaumont, was admitted to Beaumont Memorial Hospital for fatigue and depression. A staff physician immediately saw her, and our office was contacted. Mrs. Schaefer gave a statement to me from her hospital bed, admitting that she was responsible for the death of Charles Fortenberry."

"Well, now we know," Theenie said.

"Mrs. Schaefer's husband has retained an attorney," Lamar went on, "so I'll answer a couple of questions, and then I'll give him the microphone."

"Chief Tevis," one of the reporters called out. "Does this mean Mr. Fortenberry's widow has been cleared of murder charges?"

"Yes." Lamar pointed to a reporter nearby.

"Has anyone located the missing remains?" another reporter asked.

Lamar looked uncomfortable. "I'm sort of hesitant to talk about it until I am one hundred percent certain, but the van was very recently discovered abandoned less than one hundred miles from here in Baxter County. It has been searched, and it is my understanding that it is indeed the van, and the contents inside are intact. I'm waiting for verification from the Baxter County sheriff."

"Oh my gosh!" Annie said. "Lamar finally did something right."

"Chief Tevis," a female reporter called out. "Does anyone know at this time the actual cause of death to the victim?"

A camera swung in the woman's direction.

"She's the reporter from Charleston," Annie said.

Lamar hesitated. "Well . . ."

"Isn't it true Mr. Fortenberry's injuries were not life threatening?"

Lamar looked surprised. "We don't know that for sure."

"I understand the medical examiner was unable to state the cause of death," the woman continued.

"Boy, she's a real ball buster," Destiny said, drawing raised brows from Theenie.

Lamar was clearly flustered. "We don't have all the answers right now," he said. "That's why the remains were being sent to the Medical University in Charleston to begin with. I have nothing more to say." He stormed away from the microphone.

Lamar was replaced by a balding man with oversize glasses who wasted no time getting started and spoke quickly. "My name is Randolf Pierce, and I've been retained to represent Mrs. Schaefer in this case. I met with her only briefly before she made her statement to the police. I do not share Chief Tevis's optimism that this is a cut-and-dried case, so to speak; this investigation is ongoing."

The camera flashed to a frowning Lamar.

"Because we still have many questions, most of which will have to wait until my client's condition is stable, I will not be answering questions specific to the case." A disgruntled murmur rose from the crowd. "All I'm prepared to say is that Mrs. Schaefer is being treated by a fine group of doctors, and it will be up to them as to how long she remains in the hospital and when she can answer further questions." He paused and looked through the crowd. "I would like to say, on my client's behalf, that she willingly came forward and insisted on talking to the police, despite serious medical problems. Thank you for your time."

Several reporters voiced questions, but they went ignored as Pierce stepped away from the microphone.

The telephone rang and Lovelle rolled her eyes and picked it up. She immediately put her hand over the mouthpiece and looked at Annie. "It's Wes. He says it's important."

Annie took the phone and gently placed the receiver in the cradle.

Wes was waiting for Lamar in the reception area the next morning when he came in at seven. "I need to talk to you," Wes said.

"Hey, did you see me on TV last night?" Lamar asked.

"Yep."

"How about that smart-aleck woman from Charleston? Boy, I ripped her a new one, didn't I?"

"Oh yeah."

Lamar checked his watch. "Now, where is Delores? She's supposed to bring in sausage biscuits. I'll spend the rest of the day fighting heartburn, but it's worth it. By the way, several of my friends taped the news conference last night in case you want to watch it again. You know, in case you have company or something. Let's grab a cup of brew and go into my office."

Wes waited until they had their coffee and were seated in Lamar's office before he pulled out his wallet, flipped it open, and handed it to the other man.

Lamar arched both brows. "A PI, huh? I should have known."

"Before that I was a cop. Worked homicide for a number of years."

"Someone from Beaumont hired you for a job?" When Wes hesitated, Lamar handed him his wallet, got up, and closed the door. "Everything you say stays in this room."

"Eve Fortenberry contacted me a few weeks ago," Wes said. "Asked me to look into her son's disappearance."

Lamar reclaimed his seat. "I'm not surprised. She's taking it pretty hard." He stared into his coffee cup for a long time. He looked sad. "The more I look at this case, the more questions I have."

"Such as?"

"Fortenberry was alive when Donna Schaefer left the scene; she saw him blinking his eyes. But like I said, he didn't die from injuries sustained in the fall."

"Fall?"

Lamar nodded. "When he didn't show up she drove over and confronted him. Even went into his bedroom to see if he'd packed, which he hadn't. Hell, I don't know if he changed his mind about leaving or if he met someone else. Sure can't ask him." He shrugged. "Anyway, she says the whole thing was an accident. Charles told her he didn't love her and never had. They got into some kind of tussle, 'cause she said she left a bad scratch on his face.

"So he told her to get the hell out, and

when she wouldn't, he stomped out of the room toward the stairs. She caught up with him and grabbed his arm to stop him from leaving. He struggled to pull free and fell. She flipped out and ran."

"Does Mrs. Schaefer know she wasn't responsible for his death?"

"She's in the psych ward and in no condition to talk. She was a mess when she came in, but it was obvious she was trying to hold herself together long enough to get it all out. It must've been eating at her." He shook his head sadly.

"So what do you think killed him?" Wes asked after a moment.

"Don't know. At first I wondered if he could have had a heart attack, but he had a complete physical less than a month before his death, and he was in excellent health. We also don't know who buried the body. Mrs. Schaefer swears she didn't do it."

"Are you thinking there was more than one person involved?"

"Had to be. Fortenberry was six foot two and weighed one-eighty at his last physical. And get this. Mrs. Schaefer has back problems from a car accident some years ago. Has to see one of them chiropractors every so often," he added. "Bottom line is, nobody is going to convince me that some one-hundred-and-ten-pound weakling with back problems dragged that body from the house, across the backyard, and buried it."

"You're wrong," Wes said. "The bottom line is we still have a murderer out there."

Annie was hard at work in the kitchen when someone knocked on the back door. She washed her hands and dried them, then hurried to answer. She was surprised to find Wes standing there. Okay, maybe *surprised* didn't aptly describe her, because her stomach gave an immediate lurch and her heartbeat quickened. Not a good sign. Definitely not good. Best to get rid of Wes fast, before some other body part went haywire on her. She started to close the door, but he pressed one hand against it, holding it fast.

"We need to talk."

She wished he didn't have to look so good. "When pigs fly, Bridges." She tried once more to close the door, but he continued to block it.

"I'm prepared to stand here as long as it takes."

The determined look on his face told her he meant it. "This is a bad time, okay?" she said. "The wedding of the century is being held here tomorrow, and I've got a ton of work to do." She gave him a tight smile. "Now, why don't you run along? Surely you can find somebody to spy on."

"I'm not going to apologize for renting the room under false pretenses," he said. "I'm a professional, and I was hired to do a job, namely find out what happened to your husband."

"Which meant snooping on me," she reminded. "You got a lot of nerve coming here, you know that?"

"You're still mad at me."

"Duh. If I weren't practicing anger management I'd pull out my rolling pin. I might just have to have a relapse and do it anyway."

"Put yourself in Eve's place."

"No thank you. The woman is nutso." But she *had* put herself in Eve's place as much as she could, and her anger and resentment toward the woman had cooled. Not all of it, though.

"Her son and only child had been missing more than three years when she hired me, Annie. She was sick with worry."

"And positive I was behind his disappearance. That stinks. At least I don't have to feel guilty for all the mean things I've said about her."

"I think some of the blame should fall on her son for telling her how unhappy he was in his marriage."

"Don't worry; I've said plenty of bad things about Charles, too."

Wes looked like he might smile and then seemed to think better of it. "What would you have done differently, Annie? Had it been your son? And knowing Lamar Tevis was in charge of the investigation," he added.

"I certainly wouldn't have accused *me*."

"It took me about five minutes after meeting you to realize you weren't responsible for his disappearance. I would have decided sooner had I been conscious."

"I think that would have been a perfect time to tell the truth."

"I wanted to."

"What you wanted was to get me into bed."

"That, too."

Annie glanced at the clock on the wall. "Are we done yet?"

He stepped closer. "Darlin', we haven't even started."

Her toes tingled at the endearment, at the look in his eyes that made her stomach feel like warm taffy. "I'm busy, Wes."

"I have to tell you something," he said. "About Charles."

Annie couldn't hide her irritation. "I'm

tired of talking about Charles, okay? I just want to get on with my life."

"Donna Schaefer didn't kill him, Annie. I think someone else came in after she left. Probably the same person who dragged him to the backyard and buried him."

Annie felt a chill race up her spine. "Norm?"

"Could be. I want you to be careful. He's already mad because I pulled him into the investigation, and because you made him look stupid at Jimbo's. Erdle told me."

"I can take care of myself," she said.

"You won't have to. Danny is so love-sick over you he'll come running every time you call."

"Danny is gone."

Wes's brows drew together. "Gone where?"

"He had a job offer in Charleston."

"Where in Charleston?"

"I don't know," she said impatiently. "He just left, okay? I don't have any way of reaching him." She felt a lump in her throat. "Can we not talk about it right now?"

"Annie —"

"Look, I'm not mad anymore, okay? And I appreciate your giving me the heads-up about Norm. But I really have a ton of work to do, and I just need to be alone for a while." What she needed was to be away from him. So she could think.

Wes nodded. "I'm, uh, on my way to Columbia," he said. "Something came up with a case that I thought was over and done with."

Annie felt a sinking sensation in her stomach. He was leaving. "I see," she said, keeping her voice even.

"I'll be back."

"Of course."

"I'm coming back because I don't want to be away from you."

She tried to look away, but she couldn't let go of his eyes, and the thought of him leaving, even for a day, made her want to reach out to him and ask him to stay.

"My timing is probably way off, but I want you to think about something while I'm gone, Annie," Wes said softly. He reached into his pocket and pulled out a small velvet jeweler's box.

Annie's stomach dived to her toes and her lips went numb. "Oh, shit. Oh, shit. Oh, shit." She looked at his face. "Is that what I think it is?"

He smiled. "Only one way to find out."

Annie started to reach for it and then snatched her hand away. "Um, I don't think —"

"Afraid?" he said gently.

All the air had been sucked from her body. She gulped in a mouthful. "Terrified," she managed.

"Take a chance, Annie. Take a chance on me. On us."

"It feels like things are moving so fast."

"I think sometimes you just know," Wes said.

She had heard those words before. Annie opened her mouth to speak, but no words came out.

"Why don't you think about it?" He set the box on the table. "You know how to reach me."

When Lovelle and Theenie came downstairs some time later, they found Annie sitting at the kitchen table staring at the box.

"Holy cow, is that what I think it is?" she said, echoing Annie's own words.

"I think so," Annie said, "but I'm afraid to look."

Theenie put a hand to her mouth. "Wes asked you to marry him?"

"Uh-huh."

"Well, what did you say?" Lovelle demanded impatiently.

Annie was prevented from answering when Destiny plodded down the last couple of stairs, groaning aloud. "I'm exhausted," she said. "I was up half the night talking to Lacey, but I *finally,* after Lord knows how many hours, got through to her."

"How did you manage that?" Theenie asked.

"Well, the name Fairchild kept popping up in my mind, and I kept getting a funny feeling about it, so I did a little research and discovered the Fairchild family lived in this area when the house was a bordello. I suspected Jonathan Fairchild was a customer. I managed to get a picture, and when I showed it to Lacey she became agitated. Finally, she pointed to the marks on her neck."

"So he killed her?" Theenie asked.

Destiny nodded. "I don't know why. Maybe he had a thing for Lacey and resented her sleeping with other men. Or maybe he just got rough with her. It'll probably come to me later, but the good thing, once Lacey saw that picture, she suddenly realized she was dead. And *then* she remembered her lover being hanged, and she couldn't wait to go to the light. I hope they're happy, because I'm so far behind with my mail I'll never get caught up."

"You mean she's really gone?" Lovelle said, sounding disappointed.

"Yup. Now I'll be able to get some sleep."

Destiny sighed. "Damn, I'm good."

"I'm going to miss her," Theenie said. "It was so nice having a spirit in the house. And kind of sexy, too, what with her stealing our underwear."

"Cotton underwear is not sexy, Theenie," Lovelle said. "Face it."

Theenie ignored her. "At least we know she's finally at peace."

"I need coffee," Destiny said, "and lots of it." She started for the coffeepot, paused, and looked at Annie. "You haven't said a word. What's wrong?"

"She's contemplating," Theenie whispered, stepping aside so Destiny could get a look.

Destiny crossed the room and stared down at the box. "Hmm, let me guess."

"She's afraid to open it," Lovelle said.

Destiny frowned. "That's nonsense. A jar of pickles is hard to open, a stuck window is hard to open, but we're talking jewelry here. I can rip that lid off with my bare teeth from the other side of the room. Come on, Annie, give it up."

Annie knew she would have to look sooner or later. She took a deep breath and lifted the lid. The ring flashed at her.

"Oh, my Lord!" Theenie said.

Lovelle sighed. "Boy-oh-boy."

"Very nice," Destiny said. "A full karat, great clarity, no visible flaws, perfect Tiffany setting. I take it Wes gave it to you?"

Annie nodded. Her heart was pounding so loud she was certain Doc could hear it next door. "I can't think. I must be in shock."

"It's beautiful," Lovelle said.

Theenie began picking her nails. "Yes, but it's likely to snag on the blankets when she makes the beds."

"So, does this mean you're engaged?" Destiny asked.

"Um."

"Not that I'm surprised," Destiny said. "I've been having visions. Max and Jamie aren't the only ones getting married in this house. I didn't want to say anything on account I wanted it to be a surprise. When is the big event? No, don't tell me; I already know. You're going to be a May bride. Better start making plans."

"I didn't give him an answer," Annie said. "He just left the ring here and told me to think about it."

"At least try it on," Lovelle said. "See if it fits."

Annie was tempted. Finally, she pulled the ring from the box and slipped it on her left finger. All three women leaned forward to

361

get a closer look.

"That's one big rock," Theenie said.

Annie nodded. "It's a little loose."

Destiny waved the remark aside. "It can be sized. I think you should wear the ring while you're considering your answer, though. Do you get to keep it even if you say no?"

"Why would I do that?" Annie asked.

"You can always put it in a different setting. I should know these things after five marriages."

Theenie looked at Lovelle. "If she marries Wes, we'll have to move. You know how newlyweds are."

Lovelle nodded. "They stay naked a lot." She looked thoughtful. "That might not be a bad thing, seeing how Wes is so hot."

Theenie's mouth flew open. "Lovelle, I don't believe what I just heard come out of your mouth!"

"Hey, old ladies have needs, too. That's why they make adult toys."

"I shouldn't be hearing this." Theenie pressed her hands to her ears. "La la la la la. Is she done yet?"

"Nobody is moving anywhere," Annie said. "Besides, I can't get married right now; I just buried my husband."

Theenie nodded. "Oh yeah. You're supposed to be in mourning."

Destiny took a sip of her coffee. "See, that's the thing about diamonds. They go with any color. Especially black."

"Do you love him?" Lovelle asked.

All eyes went to Annie. She suddenly felt a lump in her throat. "Yeah. I just need to think."

Lovelle patted her on the back. "Well, now that things have settled down, your mind will be clearer."

Annie and Destiny exchanged looks. Neither of them spoke. Annie went back to work. Destiny refilled her coffee cup and sipped in silence. Peaches stretched and yawned in one of the chairs and jumped to the floor. She walked over to her bowl and swatted it hard. Water sloshed over one side as the bowl sailed a good three feet. Nobody noticed. Peaches walked over to the cabinet, sat, and stared at Annie. Finally, Theenie and Lovelle disappeared into the sunroom to watch their favorite morning show.

Destiny sneezed. "Donna Schaefer didn't kill him."

Annie went on with her work but said nothing.

Peaches rubbed up against the cabinet, never taking her eyes off Annie.

"She only thinks she's responsible for his

death because he was alive when she ran out." Destiny wiped her nose.

Peaches smacked the cabinet with her paw. *Bam, bam, bam.*

Annie looked up and gazed out the window over the sink.

"Somebody came in afterward and did it. I just have to figure out who." Sneeze, sneeze. *Bam, bam, bam.*

Peaches took several steps back and hurled herself against the cabinet and then slumped to the floor, tongue lolling from her mouth.

Destiny gaped.

Annie glanced at the cat, turned, and continued to stare out the window. "She's faking."

It was late in the afternoon when Annie allowed herself to take a break. She poured a glass of iced tea and decided to drink it in the sunroom. As she made her way through the house, she smiled. Theenie had polished the antiques until they shone like a dime, and Destiny had run a damp mop over the wood floors and vacuumed the rugs. The tables in the ballroom wore crisp white tablecloths and were set just so, thanks to Lovelle.

Annie wasn't sure how she would have managed without their help; she'd spent the entire day preparing hors d'oeuvres, baking traditional wedding cookies, as well as layers for the French pound cake that she would later frost and decorate. Salad plates, asparagus, stuffed cherry tomatoes, champagne, and wine were chilling in the restaurant-sized refrigerator at the back of the large walk-in pantry. She had wanted to get as much food preparation behind her so she could concentrate on the main course tomorrow. The two women she often hired for large occasions would arrive an hour before the food was to be served so that she would be able to concentrate on last-minute details.

Everything was under control.

Yeah, right. Her guts had not stopped shaking since Wes had arrived bearing an engagement ring and the latest news on Charles's death.

She missed Wes. Her bed had been a lonely place without him the night before. She longed to have his arms around her because he made her feel safe and cared for, something she had only recently begun to realize that she'd spent most of her life craving. She missed his smile, the laughter in his eyes that told her he refused to take life so seriously. She missed the tender looks and kisses, and the taste and smell of him.

And she regretted sending him away that morning instead of admitting that somehow, in just two weeks' time, she had fallen in love with him, too.

"Annie?"

She jumped at the sound of Theenie's voice. "I didn't hear you," she said.

"Are you okay?"

"Yeah. I'm just trying to think of everything I need to do before tomorrow. Right now I'm on break."

Theenie followed her to the sunporch, where they each claimed a chair. "You're thinking of Wes."

"He deceived me."

"He was hired to do a job. Once he was convinced of your innocence, he began looking elsewhere."

"He's probably all wrong for me, Theenie."

"That's what I thought at first, but I've since changed my mind. He loves you, Annie. He's sincere. Lovelle agrees."

"It just happened so fast."

Theenie patted her hand. "You can schedule dinner parties and luncheons and weddings, but you can't put love into a time frame." She suddenly frowned. "Where's your engagement ring?"

"Huh?" Annie glanced at her hand. "Holy

crap, it's gone!"

"Okay, everybody calm down," Destiny said an hour later, after all four of them had searched every nook and cranny for the ring.

"Calm down?" Annie cried. "What am I going to tell Wes?"

"It has to be here somewhere," Lovelle said. "It didn't just walk off."

"Annie, think," Theenie said. "When was the last time you noticed it?"

"I know I glanced down at it a number of times after I first put it on," she said, "but then I got busy. What if it slipped off and fell down the sink?"

"That has been known to happen," Destiny said. "Does Erdle know anything about plumbing?"

Annie nodded. "He makes most of the repairs around here. When he gets around to it," she added.

"His car is in the driveway," Lovelle said. "I'll go get him."

"Give me the box the ring came in," Destiny said. "I'll go into the living room where it's quiet so I can concentrate. Maybe something will come to me."

Annie grabbed the jeweler's box and handed it to her. "Good luck."

Erdle staggered in through the back door

a few minutes later, followed by Lovelle. "He's drunk, of course," she said.

Annie gave an enormous sigh of disgust. "What else is new?" She looked at him. His clothes were badly wrinkled; his hair stood in tufts. Lovelle had obviously awakened him. He held a plumber's wrench in one hand. His eyes widened at the trays of food sitting on the counter and kitchen table. "Wow!" He belched. "I've never seen so much food."

Annie had already cleared the cabinet beneath the kitchen sink. "Did Lovelle tell you my ring may have slid off my finger and gone down the drain?" she asked.

He scratched his head and blinked several times. "She might have mentioned it." He gazed back at the food. "What's all that?"

"Stuffed grape leaves, Roquefort grapes, wedding cookies, and . . ." She paused, wondering why she was bothering to answer. "I'm in a hurry."

"Why would anybody want to eat grape leaves?" he asked.

"Erdle, would you please —"

"Can I just have a couple of those cookies? I haven't eaten in a while."

Annie sighed. "Okay, but please hurry."

Erdle studied the tray of cookies carefully. "Eenie-meenie-miny-mo —"

"Oh, for Pete's sake!" Theenie said. "Just grab one and be done with it."

"Annie said I could have two."

Annie leaned against the counter and pressed her fingers to her temples. She could feel a headache coming on, but she was determined not to lose her temper.

Erdle selected a cookie from each tray and popped one of them in his mouth. "Hey, that's good."

The doorbell rang. "That's probably Jamie," Annie said. "She's dropping off her wedding dress."

"I'll get it," Theenie said, and hurried from the room.

Erdle made for the sink as he tossed the second cookie in his mouth and chomped down. "Ouch, damn!" he said, his hand flying to his jaw. "You must have put a rock in this one."

Annie frowned. "Huh?"

"I think I just broke a tooth on something hard." He pointed into his open mouth.

Annie sighed. Was there no end to all the craziness? She looked in Erdle's mouth. "Open wider," she said. He made an unintelligible sound and his mouth widened a smidgeon. Annie caught a flash of something gold. "My ring!" she cried, causing Lovelle to jump. Peaches sprang from the chair and hid behind a plant. "Don't swallow!"

Startled, Erdle immediately gulped, and the ring became lodged in his throat. He grabbed his neck with both hands. "Argh!" he said.

"Did you swallow it?" Annie shrieked, unaware that Theenie, Destiny, Jamie, and Vera were standing in the doorway with Fleas in tow. Peaches hissed and arched her back and then darted from behind the plant, claws bared. Fleas gave a yelp as Peaches raked one paw across his face. A howling Fleas turned and bounded from the kitchen with Peaches on his heels.

Erdle wheezed as he tried to suck in air.

"He's choking!" Lovelle said.

Annie grabbed him from the back and immediately began performing the Heimlich on him. Lovelle reached for a tumbler of orange juice on the counter and shoved it at him.

"Don't drink it!" Annie said.

Clearly panicked, Erdle ignored her, raising the glass to his lips and chugging. He swallowed and belched loudly.

"You swallowed it!" Annie yelled.

"Huh?" He blinked back dumbly.

She grabbed his shirt and shook him, almost causing him to drop the container of juice. "You swallowed my engagement ring!"

Theenie and Lovelle gasped.

"Spit it out!" Annie ordered, still shaking him.

"Miss Annie, stop!" he said.

"What's going on?" Jamie asked, trying to make herself heard over the commotion.

Theenie turned to her. "Wes gave Annie an engagement ring. She lost it. I think Erdle just swallowed it."

"Why would he do something stupid like that?" Vera said.

"It wasn't my fault," Erdle said, trying to catch his breath and pull free from Annie. "It was in the cookie."

"You and Wes are engaged?" Jamie asked Annie, clearly shocked.

Theenie and Lovelle managed to pull Erdle free of Annie's grasp. "Stop it, this instant!" Theenie told her. "You're supposed to be practicing anger management."

"He swallowed my ring!"

"It's not his fault," Theenie said. "The ring obviously slipped off your finger while you were making the cookies."

"Why didn't you tell me you and Wes had become engaged?" Jamie demanded.

Fleas tore through the kitchen and raced up the stairs, Peaches right behind him, snarling and hissing.

"It's not official," Annie said. "I'm still thinking about it." Something shattered upstairs, but it went ignored.

Erdle bolted toward the back door, but Annie was faster, throwing herself in front of him. "Oh no, you don't! I'm taking you to the emergency room to have your stomach pumped out."

The color drained from Erdle's face. He looked at Lovelle. "Do you have any vodka to go with the rest of this orange juice?"

Suddenly an earsplitting whistle pierced the air and everybody stopped in their tracks to see where it had come from. Vera pulled the whistle from her mouth. "Okay, I've listened to just about all I'm going to put up with," she said, "so I want everybody to shut up and do as I say." She pointed to Erdle. "Sit."

"Yes, ma'am." He pulled out the nearest chair and sat.

She looked at Jamie. "Go find those crazy animals and do something with them or I'm going to call the animal shelter and have them both picked up and you won't have a flower dog in your wedding."

Jamie nodded and raced up the stairs, calling out for Fleas.

"Now then," Vera said. "As I see it, there are only two ways to get to that ring, but having the poor man's stomach pumped out seems a bit extreme, so we'll have to take a different approach, if you get my drift."

Theenie nodded. "Why didn't I think of that? I have just the thing." She hurried up the stairs with the speed and agility of a woman half her age.

"Would somebody tell me what's goin' on?" Erdle asked.

"You'll find out soon enough," Vera told him.

Theenie returned, slightly out of breath, holding a large bottle. "This'll do the job," she said.

Annie stepped closer. "What is it?"

"Castor oil. My mother used to make us drink it when we got, um, *clogged up.* Once Erdle drinks this I guarantee you'll get your ring back, although it'll take a few hours at least. I want him to drink the whole bottle just to be sure."

"The *whole* bottle?" Annie asked.

"It won't hurt him," Theenie said. "Doctors used to have people drink this stuff all the time before certain tests."

"The *whole* bottle?" Annie repeated.

"Yep." Theenie uncapped the bottle.

"Oh no, you don't!" Erdle said, jumping from his chair. "You've lost your danged mind if you think I'm going to drink that nasty stuff."

Annie planted her hands on her hips. "You're going to drink it if I have to personally pour it down your throat."

"No way," he said, starting for the door.

"Let me take care of this," Vera said, pulling her Smith & Wesson .38 from her purse. She trained it on Erdle. "Maybe this will change your mind."

Everybody froze, including Erdle. "Lady, are you crazy? Put that thing down before you hurt somebody."

"Put that gun away, Vera," Jamie said from the bottom of the stairs. She held a hissing Peaches several feet in front of her, obviously trying to escape being clawed. "Have you forgotten all you had to go through after you shot the last person?"

Erdle swallowed and slid his gaze to Jamie. "You're saying this won't be her first homicide?" His voice squeaked.

"I haven't shot anybody in months," Vera said. "I only do it as a last resort."

Without taking his eyes off her, Erdle reclaimed his seat. Theenie handed him the bottle of castor oil. He took a sip and gagged. "Blah! That's the worst stuff I've ever tasted in my life! I can't go through with it."

Vera pulled the hammer back on the

pistol. Erdle quickly took another slug. He shuddered and made a face; then, taking a deep breath, he turned the bottle up and drained it. "Satisfied?" he asked Vera.

She nodded, put the hammer in place, and stuffed the gun in her purse.

Jamie looked at Annie. "May I put the cat outside? Fleas won't come out from under your bed."

"Of course," she said. "Oh, and I'll make sure Peaches is out when you arrive tomorrow."

Jamie looked relieved as she headed toward the back door with the cat.

"The forecast is calling for rain," Theenie said. "Peaches is scared of the rain."

"It's not going to rain on Jamie's wedding day," Destiny said.

Annie shrugged. "Well, if it does, I'll ask Doc to babysit. Peaches likes Doc. He used to feed her and change her litter box when I went out of town."

"Can I go now?" Erdle said wearily. "I feel sick."

Annie closed the distance between them. "Don't you *dare* throw up, Erdle Thorney!" she said in a threatening voice.

"My stomach doesn't feel so good," he whined.

"That's because you've introduced it to

375

something other than booze," she said.

"I'm gonna be sick," he wailed.

"Stop it!" Annie said, feeling as though her nerves would snap. "I swear, Erdle, if you throw up I'm going to take Vera's gun and shoot you myself."

"You're a crazy lady," he said, leaning dangerously to one side. "And mean as hell to boot. That's how come I know you killed your husband. And all this time I been protecting you. Even buried the body so nobody would find out. Crazy and mean is what you are."

Chapter Fifteen

Several gasps filled the room as Erdle's head fell back and he began to topple. Annie shrieked but caught him before he hit the floor. Jamie hurried over to help her. Very gently, they laid him on the floor, and then they looked at each other.

"He's out cold," Jamie told her.

"Did you hear what he said!" Annie cried. "He said he buried Charles."

"I heard," Theenie said. "I think we should call Lamar."

Jamie shook her head. "Not yet. We need to try and get more information out of him." She paused. "Let's get him to the sink and stick his head under cold water."

"Here we go again," Destiny said as she hurried over to help.

Theenie and Lovelle cleared the sink and counter as the three younger women dragged the man over. Annie pushed his head into the sink and Theenie turned on the cold water full force. Erdle came up coughing and sputtering. "You're trying to kill me!" he said to Annie. "So I don't tell what I know."

"Erdle, you idiot!" she shouted. "I didn't kill Charles. This is the last time I'm going to tell you." He didn't look convinced. "Do I *look* like a murderer?" she demanded.

"Do I look like a grave digger?" he replied, water streaming down his face. He blinked and rubbed his eyes. Lovelle hurried away and reappeared with a bathroom towel. Annie dried his hair while the others held him up. Vera pulled a chair across the room, and Annie and Jamie lowered him onto it as Destiny shoved a cup of black coffee in his face.

"Drink," Annie said.

Erdle blew into it and cautiously took a sip.

Once Annie was sure he could sit up on his own, she released him. "Start talking, Erdle, and don't stop until you've told us everything."

His gaze went to Vera. "Is she going to shoot me?"

Vera planted her hands on her hips. "No, but I'll pistol-whip you if you don't start moving your jaws."

He gave a sigh and looked at Annie, his

face beaded with sweat. "I saw him. Charles," he added. "He was laying at the foot of those stairs, deader'n all get-out."

"*When* did you see him?"

"Same day you left for your mama's. Act'ally, it was late that night."

"You told Lamar you were with your army buddy that weekend."

"I lost my keys and had to borrow his car so I could drive back and get my spare set. I keep them under the stairs to my place. My friend was passed out. He has a drinking problem, if you know what I mean."

"I think we can relate," Destiny said, giving an eye roll.

"Only reason I came in the house was 'cause the back door was standing wide open. Charles's car was in the driveway, so I figured I'd let him know in case somebody had broken in or something. I stepped inside the kitchen and turned on the lights and that's when I found him. He had a bad scratch on his face, so I thought —"

"You thought I'd scratched him and pushed him down the stairs," Annie finished for him.

His look was sheepish. "I reckon I wasn't thinking straight."

Annie wasn't interested in his apology at the moment. "Then what?"

"I dragged him out in the yard and buried him where I figured nobody would look. After I checked his pockets to see if he had anything important on him," he added. "Then I drove his car to the airport and hitched a ride back. When I arrived back at the motel some hours later, my friend was still passed out."

"What did you do with Charles's belongings?" Annie asked.

"I packed his bags and hid 'em. Raked leaves for two days once I came home. Burned his stuff with the leaves. Didn't find no money. Didn't know he'd hidden money in a hole in the closet."

"You're certain he was dead when you found him?" Jamie asked.

"Yep. Somebody smothered him. There was a pillow next to the body."

Annie closed her eyes and took a deep breath.

"That's all I know," Erdle said.

Jamie rubbed Annie's back, obviously trying to comfort her. "You didn't see anyone else on the property?" Jamie asked.

Erdle shook his head. "I told you everything. Can I have a sandwich? I don't want no more of those cookies."

"I'll make it," Jamie said. "Annie, you sit down before you fall down."

"Would you like a glass of brandy?" Lovelle asked.

Annie shook her head and took a seat at the kitchen table. "I don't drink anymore."

Once Jamie had served Erdle, she made room for him at the table so he could eat his sandwich. "Why don't we go into the living room and give Erdle a few minutes to himself?" she suggested.

Vera pointed a manicured finger at Erdle. "You move, you die."

He nodded.

"Come on, dear," Theenie said, helping Annie from the chair.

Annie did as she was told, following the women, her arms and legs feeling weighted.

"Don't you think we'd better go ahead and call the police now?" Theenie asked Jamie.

Jamie shook her head. "I don't think Annie is in any position to speak to them at the moment."

Annie was glad Jamie was there to take charge of the situation, because her brain had shut down on her.

Lovelle glanced over her shoulder as if to make sure they were alone. "Does anyone happen to know if it's against the law to bury somebody who is already dead?"

"Of course it is," Vera said. "You can't just

go around burying folks wherever it suits you. You probably have to buy some kind of permit."

Jamie looked thoughtful. "I hate to say it, but I think the murderer is still on the loose. I don't believe Donna Schaefer *or* Erdle put that pillow over Charles's face."

"That's what I'm thinking," Annie said.

"Annie, would you like for me to call Wes?" Theenie asked. "He always seems to know what to do."

She shook her head. "I don't want to have to explain about the ring what with all this other going on."

"I can solve that little problem," Destiny said. "Wal-Mart sells cubic zirconia rings that look like the real enchilada. I can probably find something similar to the ring Wes gave you. Trust me, he won't notice the difference."

Theenie nodded. "Good idea. We only have to fool Wes for six or eight hours. Until, well, you know."

"I won't be long," Destiny said, hurrying out.

"I'd like to discuss your, um, engagement when you're feeling better," Jamie told Annie.

"Don't worry; Wes is a good man," Theenie said. "I would have put up a fuss if

I didn't think so. I need to have a little talk with Erdle. He's going to have to stay here tonight. It'd be best if he slept on a cot in my room so that when the time comes I'll be there. Remember, I was a nurse's aide," she added, not for the first time. "May I get you something, hon?" she asked Annie.

Annie shook her head. "I'll help you break the news to Erdle in case he gives you any problems."

The women returned to the kitchen. Theenie told Erdle the plan.

"I'm not sleeping under the same roof with a bunch of crazy women," he said, his eyes darting at Vera as though he feared she would whip out her pistol again.

"You are *not* going to leave this house until I get my ring back," Annie said. "I expect you to stick to Theenie like glue until you, um, *deliver.*"

"I'll need a few items to ensure a successful and antiseptic retrieval," Theenie said.

"Say no more," Annie replied, hoping Theenie would not share. "Just take whatever you need."

"Why don't we start wrapping these trays of food and putting them away?" Lovelle suggested. "We can store the nonperishable items in the butler's pantry so we'll have room in the refrigerator."

"Vera and I will help," Jamie said, "but first I need to see if I can get Fleas out from under the bed." She hurried upstairs.

Annie was thankful she hadn't frosted Jamie's cake yet; she wanted it to be a surprise. With the help of the others the food was quickly put away. Annie heard Jamie grunting and groaning from the stairs and saw that she was doing her best to carry her dog down the stairs.

"You're going to throw out your back," Vera said, "and you won't be worth a flip on your honeymoon."

"I probably shouldn't be listening to stuff like that," Theenie said.

Jamie put Fleas down and held his collar. "I hate to be a pest, Annie, but do you have any peroxide?"

"I'll get some," Theenie said.

Annie suddenly noticed that Fleas had blood on one side of his nose and hurried over. "Did Peaches do that?"

"I don't think she likes bloodhounds," Jamie said, trying to make light of it so Annie wouldn't take on those worries as well.

"I'm so sorry," Annie said, rubbing the dog on his bony head. "Peaches is old and ornery like Doc."

Theenie returned with the peroxide and a handful of cotton balls. As Jamie and Annie held the dog still, she cleaned the wound. Fleas whined and moaned and scratched himself fiercely with one leg. "Peaches got him good," Theenie said. "Look how deep the scratch is. Good thing Doc isn't here; he'd insist on putting the poor thing down."

Lovelle nodded. "Yeah, Doc's a snarly old man, but he can't stand to see something suffer."

Jamie and Vera left once the kitchen was clean and Jamie had helped Annie carry a roll-away bed from the attic to Theenie's room so Erdle could stick close to the woman. They'd been gone less than ten minutes when a jubilant Destiny returned bearing a ring that strongly resembled Annie's engagement ring.

Annie held her hand out for all of them to see. "What do you think?"

Lovelle studied it closely. "I can tell the difference, but I'm with Destiny. I don't think Wes will notice." She yawned. "I'm exhausted. Why don't we call it a night?"

As tired as she was, Annie forced herself to take a shower before climbing into bed, but two hours later she was still staring at the ceiling, her mind racing. Every time she closed her eyes she saw Charles lying at the bottom of the stairs, a pillow pressed against his face. She drew comfort thinking perhaps he'd been unconscious at the time.

She picked at her tired brain, trying to find answers to the questions that plagued her until sheer exhaustion forced her eyes closed. She awoke once after a bad dream, but when she couldn't remember the details she turned over and went back to sleep.

In her next dream she was twelve years old, visiting her grandmother for the summer. They were standing on the back porch gazing down at the stray tomcat that showed up every morning for scraps of food.

"What's his name, Granny?" Annie asked the first time she saw the scrawny animal.

The woman chuckled. "I call him Lover Boy on account he spends his nights chasing females and getting into fights with the other male cats. Last time he got into a fight he showed up missing half his hair."

The old woman tossed a handful of chicken bones on the ground, and the cat pounced on them as though he hadn't eaten in days. After that, Annie made a point of collecting table scraps and only ate half her oatmeal in the morning so Lover Boy got enough to eat.

Then one morning Annie stepped out the door with her oatmeal bowl and found Lover Boy curled beside the bottom step. He looked up at her, his eyes glazed, his fur matted with dried blood. Her breath caught in her throat when she noted half of one ear had been torn away. She raced into the house for her grand-mother.

"Go get Doc," the old woman said after she'd checked the cat.

Doc took one look at the ailing feline and shook his head sadly. "He's bad off, Annie. Afraid I'm going to have to put him down."

Tears streamed down Annie's cheek as she watched Doc carry Lover Boy away.

Annie bolted upright in the bed. Her cheeks were wet from crying. She reached for the telephone and dialed Wes's cell phone number. No answer. She hung up and climbed from the bed, dressed quickly, and then made her way down the hall toward the kitchen stairs. At the back door she paused to unbolt it and slide the chain free. She winced as it creaked open, remind-ing her she needed to take an oil can to the hinges. She closed it behind her and started across the backyard where Annie's grand-mother had long ago pulled up her boxwood hedges so she could admire Doc's rose garden.

Wes opened his eyes when he heard his cell phone ring from the other side of the room, but it took several minutes for him to locate it. By the time he found it tucked in the pocket of his jeans it had stopped ringing. He switched on the lamp beside his bed and rubbed his eyes, trying to force himself awake. Finally, he punched a button on his phone and scrolled down, searching for the last number listed on his screen.

Despite the late hour, the downstairs lights burned brightly on the first floor of Doc's house. Having knocked several times as hard as she could, Annie gave up. She suspected Doc was watching TV in his den and couldn't hear her at the door. She lifted the flowerpot beside his door and reached for the key beneath it.

Inside, the TV blared from the den. Annie found Doc asleep in his recliner, an old quilt draped over him. She turned off the TV, and he jerked and opened his eyes. He frowned at the sight of her. "What's wrong?" he asked.

"We need to talk. It's important."

"What is so important that you have to barge into my house at two o'clock in the morning?" he said, his face red and mottled from sleep. He sounded out of sorts.

"It's about Charles," she said.

"Oh, good grief. Don't you watch the news or read the paper? They found the lady who did it."

"Donna Schaefer didn't kill him, Doc. Charles was alive when she left."

"How do you know?"

Annie sat on the nearby sofa. "Erdle came in later that night and found Charles dead, a pillow next to the body. He thought I'd killed him in one of my dumb temper fits, so he tried to cover it up by burying Charles in the backyard."

"Erdle buried him? Seems I remember he was gone at the time."

"He came back for something later that night. He took care of everything nice and neat."

"Why are you telling *me* this?" Doc said.

"You were pruning your rosebushes during that time, remember? From your garden you can see my backyard. And then you like to sit in your lawn chair with your cognac and look at them, sometimes for hours. You once said that's when you do your best thinking."

"Annie, would you get to the point? I'm an old man. I could pass on before you finish your story."

"You saw Donna Schaefer arrive at my house and then run out later. So you went over to investigate. Am I getting it right so far?"

Doc remained silent.

"You found Charles lying on the floor unconscious. You never liked Charles. You knew he had been cheating on me for some time, didn't you? Danny probably told you. You thought Charles was no better than an old tomcat. So there he was, lying there, helpless and unconscious. You went into the living room and got a pillow and —"

"No," Doc said, indignant. "What kind of person do you take me for? A coldhearted killer?" he asked. "Is that what you think?"

"Then tell me."

Doc pulled off his glasses, rubbed his eyes, and blinked several times. He stared straight ahead for a moment. "That's not the way it happened, Annie. Not at all." He sighed heavily.

"You're right about me sitting in my lawn chair. I sat in it until it was dark, then realized I was getting hungry. Before I could get up, I saw this woman pull up in her car and go into your house. The lights flashed on in your bedroom, and I could hear them arguing. The woman started yelling and carrying on something awful. Finally, I got enough of it and started for my back porch. Then I heard her scream, and she came tearing out of the house like the wrath of God was after her. I could hear her sobbing. She got into her car and left."

Once again Doc became quiet, as though he had slipped into another place. Annie sat quietly and waited. She heard a sound from the next room, saw a shadow. Saw Wes.

"I didn't go over right away," Doc finally said. "I thought of calling the police but decided against it. I came inside the house and cleaned up. Made myself a sandwich. When I went back out I noticed the back door was standing open, and I wondered why Charles had not closed it. So I walked on over.

"I found him lying at the bottom of the stairs. I knelt beside him, and he opened his eyes. I asked him if he was in pain. He said his neck was hurting him real bad, said he'd heard it snap and was afraid he'd broken it. I told him not to move." Doc paused and looked at Annie.

"See, I know about neck injuries and what they can do to a person. I had a friend who spent twenty years in a wheelchair begging to die. Twenty years is a long time to wait to die, Annie. I told Charles to rest, that I'd look after him. He closed his eyes, and I went into the next room for the pillow. I had no other choice but to put him down."

Wes stepped into the room and went to Annie. Doc didn't seem surprised; he didn't even look up. He just stared at the blank

TV screen, the wrinkles more prominent on his tired face.

Wes slipped his arms around Annie's waist. "You okay?"

She nodded. "How did you know to come here?"

"Stuff just started falling into place in my head today," he said. "When I saw your number come up on my phone, I knew you needed me."

She leaned against him. "Thank you."

Wes held her for a moment longer before releasing her. "You look exhausted, and tomorrow is the big day. Go home and get some sleep. I'll stay with Doc."

Annie nodded. She could not remember ever feeling so tired, and she knew whatever Wes decided to do, it would be the right thing. She stood.

Doc looked up. "I want you to know something, Annie. I *need* you to know. I would never have allowed you to go to prison for something I'd done."

She nodded. "I know." She touched his shoulder on her way out.

Annie and Jamie both held their breath and watched Fleas amble up the aisle in the large meeting room that had been decorated and turned into a wedding chapel of sorts, complete with a festooned arbor. Fleas wore a special collar that was adorned with white tea roses and baby's breath. As Annie had suspected would happen, some of the wedding guests raised an eyebrow as others chuckled or laughed out loud. Fleas paused halfway, turned, and looked at Jamie, who prodded him on with a single nod. He made his way toward the altar and sat, and Jamie grinned. Max looked proud. The minister simply gazed down at the dog as though he didn't know quite what to make of the whole thing. In the front row, Vera shook her head sadly.

Annie turned to Dee Dee, stunning in a kelly green sheath of raw silk. Diamonds and emeralds adorned her ears and throat and flashed each time she moved. Annie was almost certain the guests would not notice Dee Dee's ballerina-style bedroom slippers. "Okay, Dee Dee, you're up," she said.

Dee Dee put on a bright smile and took two graceful steps before she jerked to a halt and clutched her stomach. "Uh-oh!" She turned, her eyes wide in disbelief, her mouth forming a giant *O*.

Annie and Jamie gaped at Dee Dee's stained bedroom slippers, then at each other.

Nearby, Beenie covered his face with his

hands. "I knew she'd wait until the most inopportune moment."

Annie motioned for Lovelle, who grasped Dee Dee's hand. "Come with me, hon," she said.

"But who's going to be matron of honor?" Dee Dee asked.

Jamie looked at Annie. As if reading her mind, Annie shook her head. "I'm wearing a uniform." Her black skirt and starched white blouse matched the outfits her two assistants wore.

"You'll have to go," Dee Dee told Beenie, who wore a winter white tux.

"Me!" he cried. "I don't know anything about —"

Dee Dee shoved her bouquet at him and gave him a hard push through the double doors.

Beenie struck a pose and started up the aisle on his tiptoes, pausing and smiling at the guests as he literally floated toward the front like a swan.

Jamie did an eye roll. This could only happen at *her* wedding.

"I'm sorry," Dee Dee said to Jamie. "When you get a chance, please tell Frankie I need to go to the hospital." Lovelle quickly ushered her away.

"Time to go," Annie said, releasing her

hold on Jamie's elbow as the guests stood and waited for the bride. Annie had never seen a lovelier bride. Beenie had outdone himself on Jamie's hair and makeup, tucking tiny sprigs of baby's breath at her crown. "Don't forget to smile."

Jamie took a deep breath and started down the aisle. Suddenly she wasn't so nervous. She remembered to walk slowly as Annie had taught her and smiled at the guests, nodding here and there at those she recognized. Her gaze sought and found Vera's; the woman stood proudly on the front row, tears streaming down her face. Jamie blew her a kiss and mouthed a silent, *I love you.* Beside Vera, Billie, Christie, and Joel were all smiles. Jamie winked at them. As she neared the front, her gaze sought out Max, and the tender and loving look on his face almost stole her breath. She wondered what she had ever done to deserve him.

The crowd reclaimed their seats as Jamie took her place next to Beenie, who was doing his best to catch Frankie's attention and cutting his eyes toward the back of the chapel. The minister cocked his head to one side as though trying to figure out what Beenie was doing there.

Sitting in the middle of the second row,

Frankie arched his brows, and then, as though suddenly realizing something was amiss, the six-foot-six retired wrestler-turned-mayor stood and tried to make his way to the end of the row. "Excuse me," he said a little too loudly as one wedding guest after another was forced to stand in order to accommodate his exit. He stepped on a woman's foot, and she gave a yelp, even as he apologized profusely.

"Ohmigosh!" Beenie said, and nudged Jamie. "Dee Dee forgot to give me the ring." Before Jamie could respond, he stepped closer to the minister. "Could you hold off just a second? I'll be right back."

Jamie watched in amazement as Beenie hurried up the aisle, only a few feet behind Frankie.

Jamie could feel Max's eyes on her. She glanced his way and shook her head sadly as Frankie knocked loudly on the door to the bridal salon, right next to the crowded wedding chapel.

"Dee Dee, are you okay?" Frankie called out. "Open the door."

Jamie sighed and looked straight ahead.

The door opened. "My water broke, Frankie!" Dee Dee cried. "My dress is ruined, and it took the designer weeks to find the exact match for these earrings."

"I'm sure he wrote down the color, sweetheart," Frankie told her, "but I can always buy you different earrings."

"Beenie, what are *you* doing here?" Dee Dee demanded. "You're supposed to be up front with Jamie."

"You forgot to give me the ring!"

"Oh no!" she cried. "Here it is."

Dee Dee suddenly shrieked loudly. Inside the chapel, the guests craned their necks in order to see what was going on.

"I think I just had my first contraction," Dee Dee cried. "I don't like this, Frankie! I was told there would be no pain. I did *not* agree to pain."

"Hang on, sweetheart, I'll carry you out to the car."

Beenie raced up the aisle and took his place next to Jamie. "I have the ring," he whispered.

She nodded. "Yes, we heard the entire exchange," she said, giving him a tight smile. "Every last one of us," she added as chuckles and muffled laughter sounded from the crowd. She glanced at Max and Nick, who were staring straight ahead. She saw their shoulders move and knew they were doing their best to keep from bursting into hearty guffaws.

"Uh-oh," Beenie said, glancing down.

"This is not good."

Jamie followed his gaze. Fleas was half-sprawled on the floor beside her licking himself.

The minister cleared his voice, squared his shoulders, and gazed about the crowd. "What is marriage?" he asked. "To answer that question I'd like for us to ponder Scripture from the Book of Genesis."

Jamie and Max looked at each other and shrugged.

Ten minutes later, Jamie's eyes had glazed over, and her feet were killing her. Beside her, Beenie could not stop yawning, and Fleas had rolled onto his back and was snoring loudly.

"And so God saw that it was not right for Adam to be alone," Tuttle continued in a droning voice, "so He put Adam into a deep sleep —"

"This guy is putting me into a deep sleep," Beenie whispered to Annie, trying to stifle yet another yawn. "I wonder if Dee Dee's baby has started preschool yet?"

Fleas snorted and snored.

"And God took from Adam a rib and from that rib He created woman so that Adam could have a helpmate." Tuttle smiled. "And so I ask you again, what *is* marriage?"

Beenie's hand shot up. Jamie pulled it

down. "It's a rhetorical question," she whispered.

"Today, I have the honor of joining another man and another woman together, just as it was meant to be from the very beginning. But first, let us bow our heads and offer up a prayer for this very special couple."

Annie closed her eyes and prayed Tuttle would get on with it.

The minister closed the prayer and looked from Max to Jamie. Tuttle raised his book, adjusted his glasses, and began to read. "Dearly beloved . . ."

Suddenly Max's cell phone rang. Jamie and the minister looked incredulous.

"I'm sorry," Max whispered. "It's my emergency line."

Jamie blinked rapidly. "Do you have to answer it *now?*"

"Muffin is the only one who calls this line. And only if it's urgent." He pushed the button. "This better be good, Muffin," he said, and listened.

Jamie glanced over her shoulder and saw the dark frown on Vera's face as well as the surprised looks of those surrounding her.

Max hung up. "The hospital just called the cops on Frankie."

Jamie gasped; Nick frowned.

"Dee Dee arrived at the hospital scream-
ing like a banshee. Frankie immediately
spotted her doctor, wrestled him to the
floor, and put him in a headlock. Took a
half-dozen security men to pull him off,"
Max added. "He's in restraints and Dee
Dee has gone ballistic."

Jamie closed her eyes.

Max looked at Tuttle. "Could we get on
with it? Jamie and I are needed elsewhere."

"And I need to use the little boys' room,"
Beenie said.

From her place in the back row Annie
covered her face with both hands. She felt
ill. The wedding was not going well; in fact,
whatever could go wrong *had* gone wrong.
She glanced up as Wes took the chair next
to her.

"Sorry I'm late," he whispered so softly
that Annie had to lean closer in order to
hear. "I've been with Doc at the police station the entire time. Lamar wants to talk to
Erdle ASAP. I told him Theenie had ordered
Erdle to stay in bed because of a stomach
virus." He arched one brow. "What's wrong?
You look pale."

"The wedding is a bust."

His eyes softened. "I'm sorry, Red."

"I suppose I should look on the bright

400

side. Things can't possibly get any worse." Annie had barely gotten the words out of her mouth before she spotted Peaches heading down the aisle. Annie instantly froze. "Who let the cat in?" she hissed. Peaches sat down and looked around at the crowded room as though curious.

Tuttle spoke from the front. "Jamie, do you take Max to be your lawfully wedded husband? To love —"

"I do," Jamie interrupted, causing the minister to look up in surprise.

"Quick, let me out," Annie whispered to Wes, trying to think of a way to reach Peaches without drawing attention. If only she had food! She slipped from the row, bent her knees — no easy task in her tight black skirt — and duckwalked toward the cat. She was almost close enough to grab Peaches when all at once the animal's ears spiked and she arched her back. Annie reached for her, but the cat slipped through her fingers and made a mad dash toward the front.

"And, Max," Tuttle went on, "do you promise to love and cherish Jamie and place her above all others?"

"I do," Max said, smiling tenderly at Jamie.

Fleas looked up only a split second before

Peaches flew into him. The hound yelped loudly, startling those up front, who turned and stared in amazement. Fleas tried to escape, but Peaches was relentless. Flowers flew in every direction. Fleas howled and rose on his hind legs, trying to climb into Jamie's arms. His toenails sank into the delicate fabric of her dress, causing it to rip in several places. Jamie cried out when one of his nails scratched her.

"I knew that crazy dog would mess up everything!" Vera said loudly.

Fleas turned his head, obviously recognizing Vera's voice, and he bounded toward her. Vera shrieked as the hound jumped onto her lap.

Annie hurried toward the front. There was no use trying to be inconspicuous now. Peaches saw her coming and ran beneath a chair. Annie fell to her knees and crawled on all fours, even as Vera tried to push Fleas off her lap.

"I now pronounce you man and wife," Tuttle said quickly.

A burst of applause rose from the crowd as Max pulled Jamie into his arms for a long kiss, and when they turned around, the guests bolted to their feet and cheered loudly. Max hurried over to Vera, swept Fleas from her lap, and planted a kiss squarely on her mouth. Vera became flustered and began patting her hair in place.

Annie managed to grab Peaches and scramble up the aisle and out of the room, where she found Lovelle waiting. She thrust the cat into the woman's arms. "Torture her before you kill her."

Lovelle smiled sweetly. "I'll have her drawn and quartered, dear." She grunted as she lugged the cat away. "Why don't we grab a bite to eat, Peachums?" she said.

Jamie and Max joined Annie, and Jamie threw her arms around her. "I'm sorry we turned the wedding into a circus," she said, "but we played before a great crowd, don't you agree?"

Annie noted the guests spilling through the doorway, still cheering. "Is Fleas hurt?" She looked at the cowering dog, still in Max's arms.

Max grinned. "Only his pride." He winked and managed to pull an envelope from his pocket and hand it to her. "We have to go, Annie. Got to spring Frankie from the slammer."

Jamie kissed Annie on the cheek, and the two left through the front door.

Annie was relieved to see the rest of the guests leave. Somehow, despite all that had occurred, they had enjoyed themselves immensely, and although everything else had turned out crazy, dinner had been perfect. Jamie had since called. Max had convinced Dee Dee's doctor not to press charges against Frankie, but only after Frankie agreed not to sic Snakeman and his boa on the doctor as he'd threatened. Dee Dee was still in labor, but she was feeling no pain and having a grand time watching the Home Shopping Network on TV and placing orders as fast as she could.

Now, sitting in the swing on the piazza and enjoying the night air, Annie began to relax for the first time in weeks, even though she had concerns, some a result of what had occurred that day.

Erdle had still not delivered the ring.

Nunamaker, who had agreed to take Doc's case, was fairly certain the man would not spend time in prison, not only because of his advanced age, but also because Doc had acted out of mercy when he'd ended Charles's life.

Nunamaker had already discussed Erdle's part in the case, and the DA was considering probation, on the grounds that Erdle agreed to enter a six-month alcohol treatment facility, attend daily AA meetings, and submit to random drug and alcohol tests.

Danny had surprised Annie with a call shortly after the food had been served and had given her a temporary number where he could be reached, and they'd teased each other and laughed together like old times.

Annie was thankful their friendship had survived, and it made her even more determined to visit Eve Fortenberry in a few days and try to make peace.

The screen door opened and Wes stepped out bearing a plate with wedding cake. She had been too anxious during the wedding to notice the prick marks were already beginning to fade.

"You're missing all the goodies," he said, sitting down beside her.

Annie groaned. "After all the cooking I've done, I don't even want to look at food."

"This is the best cake I've ever tasted. Erdle must be feeling better, because he ate three huge pieces."

"He did?" Annie felt hopeful. Wes still didn't know about the missing ring, and those "in the know" had agreed there were some things that simply weren't worth sharing.

Wes finished his cake and set his empty plate on a nearby table. "So what do you think about serving this kind of cake at our wedding?"

"Assuming I'll marry you, of course."

"Assuming I won't change my mind by May."

"May?" She blinked. "Have you been talking to Destiny?"

He shook his head. "She left with that young senator. The one she said looked like Andy Garcia."

"What about your company in Columbia?" Annie asked.

Wes shrugged. "I can move my office to Hilton Head. There are a lot of rich people there. Couples with money like to cheat on each other, and they can afford the best hotels. I hate sitting in the parking lots of dumpy motels, you know?"

Annie hesitated. "We probably should discuss Theenie and Lovelle."

He grinned. "Hey, I love those two ladies. It wouldn't be the same if they moved out. It's bad enough Destiny chased off the ghost."

Annie leaned against him and gazed at the peach tree, surprised that it was already in full bloom. Either it had blossomed overnight or she'd been too busy to notice. The man beside her was a different story; he'd managed to insinuate himself into her life, her bed, and all her waking thoughts despite all that had happened. Not only that, he'd stuck by her. Despite the evidence against her, he'd been convinced all along of her innocence. Heck, he was even willing to marry her, knowing she had a temper.

It had to be love.

Sometimes you *did* know when it was right, she thought. Maybe she had known it the first time she'd laid eyes on those ridiculous boxer shorts.

"May works for me," Annie said.

"Great." Wes smiled. "It just so happens I know of this bed-and-breakfast that puts together awesome weddings. Only we're going to hire someone else to do the work." He pulled her close and kissed her.

"I can't think of a place I'd rather be married," she said, leaning against him, enjoying his arms around her waist. Annie spied Peaches skulking about in the yard, darting looks her way, obviously aware that her owner was still furious over the debacle with Fleas. Probably wondering if she was going to miss a meal over it, Annie thought.

The cat walked over to the peach tree and climbed to the lowest branch, which was no easy feat for a twenty-two-pounder. All at once, Peaches went limp and fell to the ground with a loud thud. She rolled over several times and came to a dead halt on her back, all four legs pointing skyward, head lolling to one side, tongue hanging out.

"I think I'll have a slice of that cake now," Annie said.

"I'll get it for you." Wes stood and went inside the house.

Annie sat there for a moment, enjoying the quiet. Suddenly she shivered as a gust of cool air swept over her, raising goose bumps along her arms and sending tingles along her backbone. Something moved just outside her peripheral vision, and she turned quickly. Nothing there. She felt her gaze drawn to one of the ballroom windows. The drapes parted, and Annie could feel someone watching her intently, a sense of knowing that she had experienced many times before.

Only nobody was there.

EPILOGUE

"Stop running, dammit!" Annie shouted the next morning as Erdle dashed down the back steps.

"He sure runs fast for a no-good drunk," Theenie said.

Erdle ducked behind one of the massive oaks. "You are *not* going to make me drink any more of that nasty stuff!" he yelled, pointing to the new bottle of castor oil in Theenie's hand. "I'm calling Lamar to come take me to jail."

Annie planted her hands on her hips. "You are *not* leaving this house with my ring in your, um, system. Don't make me get my rolling pin."

"You're a crazy lady, you know that?" he shouted. "Mean *and* crazy. And you wonder why I drink."

From the back door Destiny and Lovelle watched. "I can't believe Dee Dee was able to deliver a nine-pound baby boy and Erdle can't pass a one-karat ring," Destiny said. "Men can be such wimps."

"We'd better go out there and give the girls a hand," Lovelle said. The two started down the steps.

"Oh, good, we've got backup," Theenie said.

The four women circled Erdle, who clung to the tree as a drowning man would to a life raft. Theenie uncapped the bottle. "You three grab him, and I'll pour it down his gullet."

Suddenly Erdle's eyes widened. He winced and grabbed his stomach. "Argh." He doubled over and groaned.

Theenie put the cap on the bottle and patted his arm. "Follow me, dear," she said. Erdle nodded and staggered across the yard, sweat beading his brow. "And don't worry about a thing," Theenie said, "because I'll take good care of you. Did I tell you I was once a nurse's aide?"

Destiny turned to Annie. "Looks like it's just a matter of time."